Praise for *New York Times* bestselling author RaeAnne Thayne

"[Thayne] is a rising star in the romance world. Her books are wonderfully romantic, feel-good reads that end with me sighing over the last pages."
—#1 *New York Times* bestselling author Debbie Macomber

"Entertaining, heart-wrenching, and totally involving, this multithreaded story overflows with characters readers will adore."
—*Library Journal* on *Evergreen Springs* (starred review)

"RaeAnne Thayne is quickly becoming one of my favorite authors…. Once you start reading, you aren't going to be able to stop."
—*Fresh Fiction*

"Thayne's realistic characterization grounds the hope of falling in love with the trials and tribulations that so often come with it."
—*BookPage* on *Serenity Harbor*

"RaeAnne has a knack for capturing those emotions that come from the heart."
—*RT Book Reviews*

"Her engaging storytelling…will draw readers in from the very first page."
—*RT Book Reviews* on *Riverbend Road*

"Tiny Haven Point springs to vivid life in Thayne's capable hands as she spins another sweet, heartfelt story."
—*Library Journal* on *Redemption Bay*

Books by RaeAnne Thayne

HQN Books

The Cliff House

Haven Point

Snow Angel Cove
Redemption Bay
Evergreen Springs
Riverbend Road
Snowfall on Haven Point
Serenity Harbor
Sugar Pine Trail
The Cottages on Silver Beach
Season of Wonder
Coming Home for Christmas

Hope's Crossing

Blackberry Summer
Woodrose Mountain
Sweet Laurel Falls
Currant Creek Valley
Willowleaf Lane
Christmas in Snowflake Canyon
Wild Iris Ridge

For a complete list of books by RaeAnne Thayne,
please visit www.raeannethayne.com.

RaeAnne Thayne

Coming Home
for
Christmas

HQN™

HQN™

ISBN-13: 978-1-335-50499-9

Coming Home for Christmas

HQNBooks.com

To all the amazing readers who have contacted me
asking for Luke and Elizabeth's story.

Also, to all who have suffered traumatic brain injuries
and the family members and caregivers who love them.

Coming Home
for
Christmas

Chapter One

This was it.

Luke Hamilton waited outside the big, rambling Victorian house in a little coastal town in Oregon, hands shoved into the pockets of his coat against the wet slap of air and nerves churning through him.

Elizabeth was here. After all the years when he had been certain she was dead—that she had wandered into the mountains somewhere that cold day seven years earlier or she had somehow walked into the deep, unforgiving waters of Lake Haven—he was going to see her again.

Though he had been given months to wrap his head around the idea that his wife wasn't dead, that she was indeed living under another name in this town by the sea, it still didn't seem real.

How was he supposed to feel in this moment? He had no idea. He only knew he was filled with a crazy mix of anticipation, fear and the low fury that had been simmering inside him for months, since the moment FBI agent Elliot Bailey had produced a piece of paper with a name and an address.

Luke still couldn't quite believe she was in there, the wife he had not seen in seven years. The wife who had disappeared off the face of the earth, leaving plenty of people to speculate that he had somehow hurt her, even killed her.

For all those days and months and years, he had lived with the ghost of Elizabeth Sinclair and the love they had once shared.

He was never nervous, damn it. So why did his skin itch and his stomach seethe and his hands grip the cold metal of the porch railing as if his suddenly weak knees would give way and make him topple over if he let go?

A moment later, he sensed movement inside the foyer of the house. The woman he had spoken with when he had first pulled up to this address, the woman who had been hanging Christmas lights around the big, charming home and who had looked at him with such suspicion and had not invited him to wait inside, opened the door. One hand was thrust into her coat pocket around a questionable-looking bulge.

She was concealing either a handgun or a Taser or pepper spray. Since he had never met the woman before, Luke couldn't begin to guess which. Her features had lost none of that alert wariness that told him she would do whatever necessary to protect Elizabeth.

He wanted to tell her he would never hurt his wife, but it was a refrain he had grown tired of repeating. Over the years, he had become inured to people's opinions on the matter. Let them think what the hell they wanted. He knew the truth.

"Where is she?" he demanded.

There was a long pause, like some tension-filled moment just before the gunfight in Old West movies. He wouldn't have been surprised if tumbleweeds suddenly blew down the street.

Then, from behind the first woman, another figure stepped out onto the porch, slim and blonde and…shockingly familiar.

He stared, stunned to his bones. It was her. Not Elizabeth. *Her.* He had seen this woman around his small Idaho town of Haven Point several times over the last few years, fleeting glimpses only out of the corner of his gaze at a baseball game or a school program.

The mystery woman.

He assumed she had been there to watch one of the other children. Maybe an aunt from out of town, someone he didn't know.

Luke had noticed her…and had hated the tiny little glow of attraction that had sparked to life.

He hadn't wanted to be aware of any other woman. What was the point? For years, he thought his heart had died when Elizabeth walked away. He figured everything good and right inside him had shriveled up and he had nothing left to give another woman.

Despite his anger at himself for the unwilling attraction to a woman he could never have, he had come to look forward to those random glimpses of the beautiful mystery woman who wore sunglasses and floppy hats, whose hair was a similar color to his wife's but whose features were very different.

For the first time since he had pulled up to Brambleberry House, he began to wonder if he had been wrong. If *Elliot* had been wrong, if his investigation had somehow gone horribly off track.

What if this wasn't Elizabeth? What if it was all some terrible mistake?

He didn't know what to say, suddenly. Did he tell them

both he had erred, make some excuse and disappear? He was about to do just that when he saw her eyes, a clear, startling blue with a dark, almost black, ring around the irises.

He knew those eyes. It was her.

There was nervousness in them, yes, but no surprise, almost as if she had been expecting him.

"Elizabeth."

She flinched a little at the name. "No one has…called me that in a very long time."

Her voice was the second confirmation, the same husky alto that had haunted his dreams every single night for seven years.

The other woman stared at her. "Sonia. What is going on? Who is this man? Why is he calling you Elizabeth?"

"It is…a really long story, Rosa."

"He says he is your husband."

"He was. A long time ago."

The anger simmered hotter, flaring up like a controlled burn that was trying to jump the ditch. He did his best to tamp it down. He would not become his father, no matter the provocation.

"I'm still your husband. Nothing has changed. Until we divorce or you are declared dead, we are very much still married in the eyes of the law."

Her mouth opened again, eyes shocked as if she had never considered the possibility. Maybe as far as she was concerned, her act of walking away without a word had terminated their marriage.

It had in every way except the official one.

"I…guess that's probably true."

"That's why I'm here. I need you to come back to Haven Point so we can end this thing once and for all." He was unable to keep the bitterness out of his voice. "It shouldn't be that hard for you. You know the way. Apparently you've been back to town plenty of times. You just never bothered to stop and say hello to me or your two children."

Her skin, already pale in the weak December afternoon light, seemed to turn ashen, and Luke was immediately ashamed at his cruelty. He tried to be better than that, to take the higher ground in most situations. He was uncomfortably aware that this unwanted reunion with his long-missing wife would likely bring out the worst in him.

The other woman looked shocked. "You have children? I don't understand any of this, Sonia."

She winced. "It's so complicated, Rosa. I don't know...where to start. I... My name isn't Sonia, as you've obviously...figured out. He is right. It is Elizabeth Hamilton, and this...this is my husband, Lucas."

The other woman was slow to absorb the information, but after a shocked moment, her gaze narrowed and she moved imperceptibly in front of Elizabeth, as if her slight frame could protect her friend.

It was a familiar motion, one that intensified his shame. How many times had he done the same thing, throwing his body in front of his mother and then his stepmother? By the time he was big enough and tough enough to make a difference, his father was dead and no longer a threat.

"Are you afraid of this man?" Rosa demanded. "Has he hurt you? I can call Chief Townsend. He would be here in a moment."

Elizabeth put a hand on the other woman's arm. It was clear they were close friends. The wild pendulum of Luke's emotions right now swung back to anger. Somehow she had managed to form friendships with other people, to completely move on with her life, while he had been suffocating for seven years under the weight of rumor and suspicion.

"It is fine, Rosa. Thank you. Please don't worry about me. I…I need to speak with…with my husband. We have… much to discuss. Go on inside. I'll talk to you later and… and try to explain."

Rosa was clearly reluctant to leave. She hovered on the porch, sending him mistrustful looks. He wanted to tell her not to waste her energy. He'd spent years developing a thick skin when it came to people suspecting him of being a monster.

"I'm here," she said firmly. "I'll wait inside. You only have to call out. And Melissa is in her apartment as well. We won't let anything happen to you."

"Nothing is going to happen to me," Elizabeth assured her. "Luke won't hurt me."

"Don't be so sure of that," he muttered, though it was a lie. Some might think him a monster but he suspected Elizabeth knew he could never lay a hand on her.

First of all, it wasn't in his nature. Second, he had spent his entire life working toward self-mastery and iron control—doing whatever necessary to avoid becoming his father.

After another moment, Rosa turned around and slipped through the carved front door, reluctance apparent in every line of her body. On some level, Luke supposed he should be grateful Elizabeth had people willing to stand up and protect her.

"How did you…? How did you find me?"

He still didn't know everything Elliot had gone through to locate her. He knew the FBI agent had spent long hours tracking down leads after a truck driver came forward years later to say that on the night Elizabeth disappeared, the trucker thought she gave a woman resembling Elizabeth's description a ride to a truck stop in central Oregon.

Somehow from that slim piece of information, Elliot had undergone an impressive investigation on his own time and managed to put the pieces of the puzzle together. If not for Elliot, Luke wouldn't be here in front of this big oceanfront Victorian in Cannon Beach and this familiar but not familiar woman.

Thinking about Elliot Bailey always left him conflicted, too. He was grateful to the man but still found it weird to think of his former best friend with Megan, Luke's younger sister. After several months, he was almost used to the idea of them being together.

"I didn't." He jerked his attention back to the moment. "Elliot Bailey did. That's not really important, is it? The point is, now I know where you are. But then, I guess you were never really lost, were you? We only thought you were. You've certainly been back to Haven Point in your little disguise plenty of times over the years."

It burned him, knowing he hadn't recognized his own wife. When he looked closer now, knowing what he did, he could see more hints of the woman he had loved. The brows were the same, arched and delicate, and her lips were still full and lush. But her face was more narrow, her nose completely different and her cheekbones higher and more defined.

Why had she undergone so much plastic surgery? It was one more mystery amid dozens.

"What do you want, Luke?"

"I told you. I need you to come home. At this moment, the Lake Haven County district attorney's office is preparing to file charges against me related to your disappearance and apparent murder."

"My *what*?"

"Elliot has tried to convince the woman you're still very much alive. He hasn't had much luck, especially considering he's all but a member of the family and will be marrying my sister in a few months. The DA plans to move forward and arrest me in hopes of forcing me to tell them where I hid your body."

"Wait—what? Elliot and Megan are together? When did that happen?"

He barely refrained from grinding his teeth. "Not really the point, is it? This has gone on long enough. I'm going to be arrested, Elizabeth. Before the holidays, if my sources are right. The district attorney is determined to send a message that men in her jurisdiction can't get away with making their wives disappear. I'm going to go to jail, at least for a while. Our children have already spent enough Christmases without one parent. Do you want them to lose the other one?"

"Of course not."

He didn't know whether to believe her or not. How could he? He didn't even know this woman, despite the fact that she had once been closer to him than anyone else on earth.

"Then grab your things and let's go."

Her eyes looked huge in her face as she stared at him, making him more angry at himself for not recognizing her. He should have known her. Yes, she had worn sunglasses and hats, but he somehow still should have sensed Elizabeth looking back at him.

Once, those eyes had looked at him with passion, with hunger, with a love that made him ache. Now they were filled with fear and reluctance. "I... You want to leave right this minute?"

No. If he had any choice, he would keep her out of his life

and the lives of Cassie and Bridger forever. Circumstances and a zealous district attorney had made that impossible.

"Yeah. Yeah, I do."

"I can't just…just leave."

"Why? Seems to me you're really good at leaving."

She gripped her hands tightly together. "I have a life here in Cannon Beach. Responsibilities."

"What's the problem? You have a husband and two kids here that you don't want to walk away from?"

Though he told himself this wasn't the way to accomplish what he needed from her, he couldn't seem to stop his cruel words.

He was so damn angry. It didn't matter how many times he told himself he needed to stay in control. She had ripped apart the entire fabric of his life seven years ago, destroyed everything they had tried to create together.

He had thought she was dead. He had grieved, filled with raw guilt and wrenching pain that he hadn't been able to help her. For seven years, he had imagined the worst.

He had said earlier that she had never been lost, but both of them knew that wasn't strictly true. Seven years ago, the wife he had cherished with all his heart had been lost to him, trapped in a deep, dark place, a tangle of postpartum depression and grief over the accidental deaths of her parents.

He hadn't been able to reach her. Nor had any of the professionals he had taken her to or any of the therapies they had tried.

For seven years, until Elliot Bailey took up the search and found Sonia Davis, he thought his beloved Elizabeth had surrendered to that vast chasm of depression and taken her own life.

He had never imagined that she had simply moved away,

changed her appearance and her name and started a life without him and their children.

He let out a breath, pushing away the deep betrayal. "We have to go."

"I...I was planning to go to Haven Point next week. I have a plane ticket and everything."

"Not good enough. Sources tell me charges are being filed this week. The DA's office won't listen to reason, but I figure she'll have to listen when the supposed victim herself shows up. We have to get back to town before then. This storm is only going to intensify and I would like to beat it. Grab your things and let's go."

He wouldn't let her slip away this time. His children depended on it.

Luke was here.

After all these years, he was here, standing on the porch of Brambleberry House.

She couldn't quite believe this was really happening. Her day had started out so normally. She took her dozen different medications, meditated, went through the routine of exercises she used to keep her battered body from seizing up. She had gone to the greenhouse for a few hours. Her hands still smelled like the pine branches she had woven together for evergreen wreaths.

All in all, it had been a routine day. She never expected that before the day was out, she would be here talking to her husband, the man she had loved since she was eighteen years old.

She had imagined this day so many times, had dreamed of the chance to see him again, to explain the choices she had made and the terrible consequences that had resulted from those choices.

Now that he was here, she felt tongue-tied, constrained by all the years and miles and choices between them.

What could she say? No words would ever make up for what she had done.

Of course she couldn't go with him. She had a job here. She worked at the garden center and was busy this time of year selling Christmas trees and wreaths, working on floral arrangements, planning ahead for the growing season.

She was also responsible for the gardens here at Brambleberry House—though admittedly, that wasn't a very good excuse this time of year. She had already supervised the Christmas decorating in the garden and wouldn't have anything to do until spring began its slow return to this part of the Oregon Coast.

Returning to Haven Point didn't terrify her. As he pointed out, she had been back a dozen times over the last several years.

It was the idea of returning to Haven Point with Lucas Hamilton that made her blood run cold.

Her stomach twisted into knots. He wanted her to drive there with him. It was eight hours from here. Eight hours in a car with a man who had every reason to despise her. She couldn't possibly do it.

But what choice did she have? If she could believe him— and she had no reason to think he was lying, as he had always been honest with her—she had to return to Haven Point or he would be arrested. She couldn't let that happen. She had already put him and their children through so very much.

She owed him. This was the least she could do.

Accused of her murder! How was that even possible? Luke had never raised a hand to her, and she hated that there were apparently people in Lake Haven County who didn't know him well enough to understand that.

"Hurry up." Her husband's voice was resolute. "You can take your return flight once we're done with the legalities or you can rent a car in Boise and drive back."

She wished that were possible, but the simple act of driving a vehicle was one of the abilities she had lost.

Wild tendrils of panic made her palms sweat and her stomach roll. She wanted to go back to her second-floor apartment and curl up in her bed with the covers over her head.

"I...I need time to make arrangements." She tried one more time. "I can't just leave town without a word."

His raised eyebrow made her all too aware of the irony of what she just said. That was exactly what she had done seven years ago when she had walked away from him and their children and the life she had destroyed.

"One hour. You have one hour and then I'm coming to get you, wherever you are. You're going back to Haven Point, even if I have to tie you up and toss you into the bed of my pickup. Don't think I won't."

He was so cold, hard as tungsten. This version of Lucas Hamilton was very different from the one who had been all sweet tenderness during their dating years and the first glorious months of their marriage.

She had created this version. She had forced the joy out of him, not only because she left but during those troubled years in between.

It was time to make things right. She had to do her best to fix what she had destroyed.

"All right," she finally said, trying hard to keep the trembling out of her voice. "I can be ready in one hour. What will you do in that time? Do you...? Do you want to come in?"

She did not want him in her home, her sanctuary. Bramble-berry House had become her refuge over the past few years. She wouldn't say she had completely healed here, but this was at least where she had started the process.

"No. I'm fine."

"There are several nice…restaurants in town, if you need to grab a…bite to eat."

Did he notice the way she stammered now, the awkward pauses she hated? Of all the things she had lost, tangible and intangible, fluent speech was one of the gifts she missed the most. She hated scrambling around for words, having them right there on the tip of her tongue but not being able to find them.

"I have a sandwich in the truck. I'll eat there. To be honest, Elizabeth, I don't want to leave this spot. If I go anywhere, who knows if you would still be here when I come back?"

She nodded, hating his contempt but knowing that she deserved every bit of it. "I'll…try to be quick."

Her hands were shaking. *Everything* was shaking. She felt nauseous, and her head hurt. Oh, sweet heaven. She did not want to have a seizure today. They were mostly controlled these days but tended to sneak up on her when her reserves were low.

She slipped back into the house. As she had expected, Rosa was waiting inside the entryway, along with Melissa Fielding, the tenant of the first-floor apartment.

"What is going on?" the nurse asked, eyes filled with worry. "Rosa tells me that man says he is your husband and that your name is not Sonia Davis but Elizabeth something-or-other."

She sighed. "Rosa is right. Both of those things are…true. I'm…I'm sorry I didn't tell you. It is a very long and painful story. A past I…thought I had put behind me."

It was a lie. She hadn't put the past behind her. She lived with it every single day, haunting her every waking moment. Luke. Cassie. Bridger. They were etched on her heart.

The only bright spot about Luke bursting back into her life was the possibility that she might see her children beyond random glimpses from a distance. She might be able to talk to them. Hug them. Perhaps try to explain, if she could find the words.

"What does he want?" Melissa trailed after her up the stairs, Rosa behind her.

"He wants to...take me back to the place where I lived with...with him. Haven Point, Idaho."

"I hope you told him *no way in hell*," Melissa said. "You don't need to go anywhere with him. He might be your husband, but that doesn't make him your lord and master. He can't just show up out of the blue and drag you off like some caveman."

"Luke is not like that," she protested. "He is a good man. That is...that is why I have to go with him."

She paused outside her apartment door, desperate to be alone—to breathe, to think, to recover—but also well aware she needed to convince her friends not to call local law enforcement on her behalf. They were so concerned about her, she wouldn't put it past either of them.

"Look, I know you're...worried about me. I am grateful for that. More grateful than I can say."

She reached for their hands, these two women who had taken her into their generous hearts and befriended her. She had lied to them. She had deceived them about her identity, about her past, about everything.

It was yet one more thing to feel guilty about, though small compared to all she had done to her family.

"I'm sorry, but I don't have time to explain everything. I can tell you only that I made a…a terrible mistake once, many years ago. I thought I was doing the right thing at the time but…nothing turned out the way I planned. Now my… my husband needs me to go with him so that I can begin to try to make amends. I have to, for his sake and for our…for our children."

Rosa and Melissa gazed at her, wearing identical expressions of concern. "Are you certain this man, he means you no harm?" Rosa asked, her Spanish accent more pronounced than usual.

She was not certain of anything right now, except *that*. Despite his fury, Luke wouldn't hurt her. She knew that without one fiber of doubt.

"I will be fine. Thank you both for worrying about me. I should only be gone a…a few days. When I return, I can tell you…everything. All the things I should have said a long time ago. But now I really do have to go and pack a bag."

She could see the worry in their frowns. Rosa looked as if she wanted to argue more. She might be small, but she was fierce. Elizabeth had long sensed that Rosa herself had walked a dark and difficult road, though her friend never talked about it. Elizabeth had never pried. How could she, when she had so many secrets she couldn't share?

Melissa reached out and hugged her first. "If you're sure— and you seem as if you are—I don't know what else we can do but wish you luck."

"Thank you." Her throat was tight with a complex mix of emotions as she returned the hug.

Rosa hugged her next. "Be careful, my dear."

"Of course."

"You have our numbers," Rosa said. "If you are at all worried about anything, you call us. Right away. No matter what, one of us will come to get you."

Those emotions threatened to spill over. "I will. Thank you. Thank you both."

"Now. What can we do to help you pack?" Rosa asked.

Everyone deserved friends like these, people to count on during life's inevitable storms. She had once had similar friends back in Haven Point and had turned her back on everyone who tried to help her.

She would not make that mistake again.

"I have a suitcase in my room, already...half filled. Can you find that while I...grab my medicine?"

"You got it."

She deliberately focused her attention on the tasks required to pack, not on the panic that made her feel light-headed.

After all this time, she was going back to Haven Point. As herself, this time, not as the woman she had become seven years ago when she walked away.

Chapter Two

She didn't take an hour to pack. She already had most of her travel things ready, preparing for the trip she had planned to take in a few days to Haven Point.

By now, she had a routine whenever she returned to the area. She stayed in the nearby community of Shelter Springs at the same hotel every time, an inexpensive, impersonal chain affair just off the highway to Boise.

The hotel was on the bus route to Haven Point, which made it easier for her to get to the neighboring town. She ate the continental breakfast offered by the hotel early enough to avoid most business travelers and either made her own lunch in her hotel room with cold cuts or cups of soup or chose the same busy fast-food restaurants where no one would pay any attention to her.

When her visit was done, she loaded up her bag, caught the shuttle back to the airport and flew home.

Alone, as always.

The system was elaborate and clunky, designed specifically so that she did not run the risk of bumping into someone who might have known her back then.

She probably stressed unnecessarily. Who would recognize her? She wasn't the same person. She did not look the same and certainly did not feel the same. All that she had survived had changed her in fundamental ways.

She carefully packed her medicine and the collapsible cane she hated but sometimes needed, then grabbed chargers for her electronic devices, the things she always tended to leave behind.

After one last check of the packing list she kept on her phone for her frequent trips, she zipped the suitcase, then sat on the edge of the bed.

While she had something to do, her attention focused on preparing to leave, she could shove down the wild turmoil of her emotions at seeing her husband again. Now that her bag was packed, she felt them pressing in on her again, a mixture of apprehension and fear blended with an undeniable relief.

He couldn't possibly believe her but she had planned to tell him her identity when she returned to Haven Point next week. It was time to come forward. Beyond time. She could no longer hide from the past.

She sat for several moments longer, breathing in and breathing out, trying to find whatever small measure of peace she could in this creaky, quirky old house. Finally, she released one more heavy breath, then rose unsteadily from the bed, extended the handle on her rolling suitcase and walked out the door of her apartment, locking it behind her.

She wasn't at all surprised to find Rosa and Melissa waiting for her in the small furnished landing outside of her apartment. Melissa's daughter, Skye, and Rosa's dog, Fiona, a beautiful Irish setter, waited, too. Her own little makeshift family.

"Are you sure about this?" Melissa asked, her tone as worried as her expression. "I have to tell you, I don't think you should just take off with some man we've never seen before—someone who just shows up out of the blue and expects you to drop everything and leave town with him."

She wasn't surprised at their objections. For some reason, Melissa and Rosa thought it was their job to take care of her, whether that was helping her with her laundry, giving her rides to the grocery store or taking her to doctor appointments.

She had found no small degree of comfort from their concern, but she needed to stand on her own.

"I have to. Please don't worry. I'll be fine."

"Will you be back for Christmas?" Skye asked, worry knitting lines across the girl's forehead.

Her heart ached but she managed to muster a smile for the girl. "I should only be gone a few days. Maybe a week."

"You promised you would help me put out carrots for the reindeer on Christmas Eve."

"I won't forget, sweetheart."

She had done her best to steel her emotions against Skye, to protect herself from the hurt of seeing this girl growing up happy and strong under her mother's loving care.

Her own daughter was only a few years older than Skye. For the past seven years, Cassie and her brother had been without their mother. Elizabeth knew she couldn't make it right, all the hurt she had caused by her disastrous decisions, but she could at least give Luke and their children a little closure.

"I'll be back before you know it," she told them all.

"Are you very sure?" Rosa asked one last time.

When she nodded, her friend sighed but took the handle of the suitcase and headed for the stairs to the ground floor.

When they all reached the entryway, Elizabeth felt tongue-tied with all she wanted to say. She didn't have time for any explanations. Luke would be waiting.

She hugged her friends and saved her biggest hug for Skye. "You watch over my garden for me, will you?"

"You bet," Skye said. "And Fiona will help."

"I know. She's a great dog."

She petted the dog's head, filled with intense longing for slow summer evenings when she could sit on a bench in the garden with Fiona curled up at her feet while the ocean murmured its endless song.

Finally, she couldn't put it off any longer. It was time to face her husband.

She straightened, gripped the handle of her suitcase and walked out to the wide wraparound porch.

He was waiting for her. No surprise there. Her husband was a man of his word. When Luke said he would be somewhere in an hour, he meant an hour.

She thought she saw that flare of awareness in his eyes again, but he quickly blinked it away before she could be sure. His mouth tightened. "I was hoping I wouldn't have to come in and drag you out."

She didn't bother with a response. For all his hard talk, she knew he wouldn't go that far. Or, she corrected, at least the man she had left seven years ago would never behave like a caveman. She wasn't entirely sure about this version of Luke Hamilton, with the unsmiling mouth and the hard light in his eyes that hadn't been there before, even during the worst days of their marriage.

"I'm ready," she said.

"Let's go, then. We've got a long drive."

Without waiting for her to respond, he grabbed her suitcase and marched toward his vehicle through the lightly falling snow. He threw it into the back of the pickup, which at least had a covered bed to keep out the elements.

Her bones ached as she walked down the steps and limped toward the pickup truck. She did her best to ignore the pain, as she usually did. The low pressure system from storms always seemed to make the pain worse. She had already taken the maximum dosage of over-the-counter pain medicine but it wasn't quite taking the edge off. She didn't trust herself with anything stronger.

At the door of the vehicle, she hovered uncertainly, struck with the humiliating realization that she was stuck. She couldn't step up into the vehicle. It simply was too high. She couldn't move her bad leg that far and didn't have the upper body strength to pull herself up.

"We've got to move," he growled. "Storm's going to get stronger."

How could she possibly tell him she needed help? She closed her eyes, shame as cold as the wind blowing off the water.

She could do this. Somehow. Over the last years, she had discovered stores of strength she never would have guessed she had inside her. She gripped the metal bar beside the door—the sissy handle, her dad used to call it—and tried to step up at the same time, but her foot slipped off the running board.

Luke made a sound from the other side of the truck but came around quickly.

"You should have said something," he said gruffly.

Like what? *Sorry, but I have the muscle tone of a baby bird?*

Without a word, he put his hands at her waist and lifted her into the pickup as if she weighed nothing, less than a feather from that baby bird.

It was the first time he'd touched her in seven years. The first time any man had touched her, except medical professionals.

The contact, fleeting and awkward, still was enough to fill her with an intense ache.

She had craved his touch once, had lived for those moments they could be together. She had loved everything about his big, rangy body, from the curve of his shoulders to the hardness of his chest to the line of dark hair that dipped to points lower.

The memories seemed to roll across her mind, faster and faster. His mouth on hers, his hands in her hair, falling asleep with his warm skin against her.

Until this moment, she hadn't realized how very much she missed a man's touch. Not just any man. *This* man.

She gave a shaky breath as he closed the vehicle door. Then she settled into her seat and pulled her seat belt across with hands that trembled.

She couldn't do this. Eight hours alone in a vehicle with Luke Hamilton. How could she survive it?

He climbed in and fastened his seat belt, then pulled away from Brambleberry House. As she watched her refuge disappear in the rearview window, she told herself it was only a drive. She could endure it.

She had lived through much worse over the past seven years.

Luke drove at a steady pace through the falling snow, heading east on the winding road toward Portland. On summer

Sunday evenings, Elizabeth knew, this road would be packed with tired, sunburned beachgoers heading back to Portland for the week ahead. Now, on a Sunday evening in December, they encountered very little traffic going in either direction.

He said nothing, the silence in the vehicle oppressive and heavy. With each mile marker they passed, she felt as if the weight of the past pressed down harder.

"How did Elliot find me?" she finally had to ask again.

He sent her a sideways look before jerking his gaze back to the road. "You will have to ask him. I don't know all the details."

"I'm still having a hard time believing he and…Megan are together. Last I knew, she was still grieving Wyatt Bailey. Now…you tell me she's marrying his brother."

"She grieved for Wyatt for a long time. But I guess people tend to move on eventually."

He said the words in an even tone but guilt still burned through her. She had earned his fury through her choices.

"What is Megan up to? Is she…still running the inn?"

He didn't answer her for a full moment, focused on driving through a tight series of curves. Finally, he glanced over. "Don't expect that we're going to chat the entire drive to Haven Point." His jaw was firm, his hands tight on the steering wheel. "I don't want to talk to you. I don't want anything to do with you. In fact, I'm going to pretend you're not here, which isn't that hard since you haven't been for seven years."

She folded her hands in her lap, telling herself she couldn't let his words wound her. "You don't want to know…what happened or why I left?"

"I especially don't want to hear that. I don't give a damn, Elizabeth. After all these years, I can honestly say that. You can spill all your secrets, spin all your explanations, to the district attorney."

She wanted to argue but knew it would be pointless. Her words would tangle and she wouldn't be able to get them out anyway. "Fine. But I'm not going to…sit here in silence."

She turned on the radio, which was set to the classic rock she knew he enjoyed. She was half tempted to turn the dial to something she knew would annoy him—Christmas music, maybe—but she didn't want to push.

After several more moments of tense silence, the leaden weight of everything still unsaid between them, she settled into the corner and closed her eyes. She intended only to escape the awkwardness for a moment, but the day's events and the adrenaline crash after the shock of seeing him again seemed to catch up with her.

She would never have expected it, but somehow she slept.

Elizabeth.

Here.

Sleeping next to him. Or at least pretending to—he couldn't be sure. Her eyes were closed, her breathing even and measured, but he couldn't tell if she was genuinely asleep or simply avoiding conversation. He couldn't really blame her for that, since he'd shut her down hard when she tried to talk to him.

She was close enough he could touch her if he wanted—which he absolutely didn't.

His hands tightened again on the steering wheel. At this rate, his fingers would stiffen into claws by the time they reached home.

Since the moment Elliot had handed him that piece of paper with a single name and an address, he had imagined this moment, when he would see her again.

His whole world had been rocked by the revelation that she wasn't dead. Months later he still hadn't recovered. He had done his best to put it aside, figuring if she wanted him to know where she was, she would have told him herself.

After finding out about the district attorney's plans the day before, that choice had been taken out of his hands.

He had to retrieve her and take her back to Idaho so he could clear his name. He had been so focused on the task at hand, though, that he hadn't given the rest of it much thought.

The grim reality was sinking in now. He would have to spend several hours trapped in a vehicle with the wife who had walked out on him and their children without a backward look.

Or had she looked back? He had to wonder. If she hadn't looked back, why would she continue returning to Haven Point to check up on her children?

He thought of her the last time he had seen the mystery woman, at a play Cassie's school had performed for Halloween. Cassie and a couple of her friends had played a trio of witches trying to prove they weren't as bad as everyone thought. He remembered seeing the intriguing stranger—how again hadn't he guessed she was Elizabeth in disguise?—sitting in the back row, clapping enthusiastically.

That jarring information seemed again to twist everything he thought he knew about her.

He cringed, remembering he'd actually had the wild idea at the play that the next time he saw her, he should strike up a conversation to at least ask her name and what child she was there to support.

What if he'd done it, walked up to her and tried to talk to her without knowing she was his own freaking wife?

He felt like a fool.

He released a breath, fighting down the resurgence of anger.

How was he supposed to endure several more hours of this proximity with her?

He could handle it. For the sake of his children, he had no choice. He had to clear his name. A cloud of suspicion followed him everywhere he went in Haven Point and it was long past time he shed it.

He knew Cassie and Bridger heard the whispers. While he had his undeniable supporters, with his sister and her friends chief among them, plenty of people in Haven Point still believed he had murdered his wife and dropped her body down an abandoned mine shaft or carried it up into the mountains where it had never been found.

Hell, the new Lake Haven district attorney was so convinced Luke had done just that, she was willing to press charges above the protests of nearly everyone in local law enforcement.

He had to move on. He had known where Elizabeth was for months. He could have hauled her back to town long ago and this whole thing would have been done, but he hadn't been able to bring himself to face her.

He hadn't been ready, he supposed, and had needed time to absorb the new reality that she hadn't taken her own life—she had only chosen to walk away from the one they had created together.

The winds began to blow harder as he left Portland, swirling sleet and snow against the windshield. It was taking most of his concentration to keep the vehicle on the road, yet Elizabeth slept on soundly, face tucked against the leather seat as if she didn't have a care in the world.

Once, she had been the best thing in his life, the one who made him laugh and see the joy and beauty around him.

Sometimes he felt as if he had loved her forever, but it hadn't been until the summer after her junior year of college that he'd really known her as anything more than one of his younger sister's friends.

They had been at a party, some Fourth of July thing at the lake. He hadn't wanted to go, too busy working construction and studying for the tests he needed for his general contractor license to take the time, but a friend had dragged him along.

She had worn a light blue swimming suit with stars on it, he remembered, and her smile had been brighter than the hot summer sun glinting off the lake.

He had fallen hard, right then and there.

He had dated plenty of women. He'd been twenty-five, not an innocent, but none of them had been as funny or as smart or as openhearted as Elizabeth Sinclair. Somehow that night while fireworks exploded over the lake, he had tumbled in love with her. To his everlasting astonishment, she had fallen right back.

They had married a year later, after she graduated, and he still remembered the magic of their first months of wedded bliss. They thought they could do anything, could conquer the whole world. She was working as a secretary/receptionist at an insurance office in Shelter Springs while he had continued working construction. Before they married, they had saved up for a down payment on a house and made an offer on the little house on Riverbend Road in need of serious repairs.

Together, they had started fixing up the place, and everything had been exciting and wonderful. For the first time in his life, he felt as if fate had dealt him a pretty good hand. They had even started working toward having a family. Neither of them wanted to wait.

Then her parents had been killed in a tragic boating accident on Lake Haven, her mother falling out of a fishing boat and her father drowning while he tried to rescue her.

Everything had changed.

Elizabeth had gone from happy and loving and generous to lost and grieving and withdrawn in a blink.

She had been dealing with hard things. He understood that. The deaths of her parents had hit her hard, knocking the legs out from under her. The Sinclairs had adored their only daughter and she had loved them back. They had been a warm and loving family, one of the first things that had drawn him to her.

He had tried to support her, to say all the things he thought she needed to hear, to simply hold her when she needed it. None of it had been enough. Instead of turning toward him, she had turned away.

A month after her parents died, she found out she was two months pregnant with Cassie. She had burst into tears when she told him, not happy tears but grief-stricken that she could no longer share the joyous news with her parents, two people she loved so dearly.

Though he knew she tried to be happy about the pregnancy, to compartmentalize her pain over losing her parents and focus instead on the impending birth, he sensed she was only going through the motions. Her smiles had been too bright, her enthusiasm not quite genuine.

He thought the birth of their daughter would jolt her out of the sadness she couldn't shake. Instead, what he understood now was postpartum depression had hit her hard.

Treatment and therapy had helped, but Elizabeth never quite returned to the woman she'd been the first year of their marriage.

Time would heal, the therapists said, and he held on to

that, praying they could find each other again once things returned to normal.

When she told him she wanted to have another baby, he resisted hard, but eventually she had worn him down and convinced him things would be different this time, that it would be the best thing for their marriage.

It hadn't been. The next two years were hell. This time the postpartum hit with harsh ferocity. After Bridger was born, she had days when she couldn't get out of bed. She lost weight and lost interest in all the things she usually enjoyed.

They went to round after round of specialists, but none of their therapies seemed to make a difference. By the time she disappeared, when Cassie was almost three and Bridger less than a year, he couldn't leave her alone with the children. He hired someone to stay with them through the day and took care of them all night.

He had lost his wife long before she actually disappeared.

Anger and misery were a twisted coil in his chest as he drove east through the increasing snow along the Columbia River.

He wanted those early days back, that heady flush of love they had shared, with an ache that bordered on desperation. Right now they didn't even seem real, like a home movie he had watched of somebody else's life.

He couldn't have them back. All he could do now was move forward: clear his name, get the divorce and let her walk away for good this time.

It was what he wanted and what his children needed.

For their sake and his own, he couldn't let this unexpected attraction he felt for Elizabeth 2.0 get in the way.

Chapter Three

S leep had become her sanctuary over the past seven years. Here, in dreams, Elizabeth could escape into the life she ached to recapture. She was free of the pain that had become her constant silent companion, the grinding headaches that could hit out of the blue, the muscle spasms that left her in tears. Especially the terrifying seizures that she had to fight off with every ounce of her strength.

She could be with her family again. Cassie, Bridger. Luke. While she was sleeping, she could become the best version of herself, the mother she had *wanted* to be. She sat on the floor and played with her children; she held them in her lap and rocked them to sleep; she could read to them for hours on end.

Though she did have the occasional nightmare, for the most part, sleep was just about the best thing in the world, and she loved sliding into her bed in her room by the big windows at Brambleberry House, pulling the soft blankets up around her shoulders and escaping into the heavenly fantasy.

Alas, morning always came. While she might have liked to hibernate, nestled under the covers for months where her mind could live in that joyful fantasy world, her body had pesky physical needs, like food and drink and medication. Plus, she unfortunately had to go outside of the house and work at a job that could provide enough income to pay for those necessities.

The transition was never easy. Her subconscious fought the return to reality, trying to squeeze out as much REM as possible. She always awoke slowly, reluctantly. This time, the journey to consciousness seemed harder than usual.

Her eyes fluttered open. For a few seconds, she couldn't remember where she was or why she had this vague sense of dread surrounding her. She sensed movement but didn't know where she was going. It was dark. She was a passenger in a moving vehicle. Outside the darkened windows, she saw the gleam of snow in headlights.

Panic, thick and hard, hit her then, and she suddenly couldn't breathe. Another night. Another storm. Searing, devastating pain.

Sometimes the idyllic refuge of her dreams could shift to a nightmare in an instant.

A cry escaped her and the sound of her own voice dragged her further to the other side of sleep.

"Easy. It's okay."

Odd. What was Luke's voice doing in her nightmare? It was a discordant, jarring note in the otherwise familiar setting. He hadn't been there that night. She had left him and their children.

Reality hit her like a fist punching through the windshield. She opened her eyes the rest of the way, turned in her seat and found him through the darkness, hard and unforgiving as he drove through the storm.

"Luke."

He shifted his eyes briefly from the road. "Were you expecting someone else when you woke up? Hoping you could open your eyes and find out I was just a bad dream?"

He was a good dream. Always the best dream.

"No. Sorry." She sat up, trying to ignore a wicked cramp in her leg.

"Where are we?"

"About a hundred or so miles past Portland. You slept a few hours. I need to pull off at the next town for gas."

He was driving slowly through the storm, she could tell by the trees inching past the window. She could see few other cars on the road.

"Something's wrong," she said, panic surging again. "There's no...traffic coming from the other direction."

"I know." He kept his gaze focused on the road. Now she noticed his knuckles were white on the steering wheel. Was that from her presence or from the storm? Or both?

"Maybe...maybe it's an accident or something else has closed the freeway."

"Maybe."

"You don't think so."

"Don't know. I've been trying to get news on the radio but can't find any local stations."

He pointed to a sign on the shoulder indicating an exit two miles ahead with services. "Maybe we can find out more when we fill up."

A lifetime crawled by in the time it took him to cover those few miles. He drove silently, the only sounds in the vehicle the hum of the heater and the beat of the wipers. By the time he took the exit, she felt wrung dry from the tension. The gas station was part of a cluster of rural houses, maybe six or seven. She was struck by the Christmas lights gleaming a welcome through the snow. Elizabeth had almost forgotten Christmas was only a week away.

Luke drove up to a gas pump, then finally shifted toward her. "Do you need to go in?"

Mostly, she wanted a minute away from him and this tension. If nothing else, moving might help ease the muscle cramp in her leg.

"Yes. I'll only be...a moment."

Blowing snow hit her as she opened the vehicle door. She shivered but gripped the door frame and lowered herself out gingerly. For one horrifying moment, she was afraid her leg would not support her weight, but she willed all the strength she had into it and was able to make her painstaking way inside the convenience store.

"Hello," the clerk greeted her.

Elizabeth forced a smile and made her way straight to the restroom. There, she looked at herself in the mirror, struck as she always was when she looked at her reflection by the woman there who was her but wasn't her.

When she emerged from the restroom, she found Luke walking through the empty snack aisle with a basket over his arm. He had a deli sandwich, a bag of chips, a couple of protein bars and a banana that looked a few days past its prime.

"Would you like anything?" he asked.

She shook her head. "I'm good."

"You need to eat. Grab something. This is dinner."

She wanted to argue that she wasn't hungry and wasn't sure she could eat as long as she was with him, but that would simply be foolish. She had to eat to maintain her strength, something she was quite certain she would need over the next few days.

She grabbed a bag of nuts and some dried apple slices. Luke gave her a look and deliberately picked up a second premade sandwich and added it to his collection.

The cashier set down her magazine when they approached the checkout. She was in her sixties, her skin weathered, and she sported red hair in a shade that couldn't possibly be natural. "Where you folks heading?"

"A town east of Boise. Haven Point."

She squinted at them. "Haven't you been listening to the weather report? It's nasty out there. This storm is hitting hard. They're telling people to stay off the freeway tonight."

"It's never as bad as they say it will be," Luke said.

"Usually I'd agree with you but this one is a doozy. About an hour east of here, you're going to be fighting black ice and blizzard conditions. There was a big pileup that's closed all traffic coming this direction."

"That's why we didn't see anyone," Elizabeth exclaimed, her stomach muscles clenching.

"We'll be fine. I'm in a big truck with four-wheel drive."

"It's always the guys with four-wheel drive who think they can get through anything and end up off the road," the cashier said. "That won't do you diddly if it's icy. Four-wheel-drive vehicles slide off just as easy as front-wheel."

"Thanks for the reminder," Luke said. "But we've got to keep going. Family emergency."

"Well, good luck to you, then," she said, shaking her head in a pitying sort of way.

Luke paid for their supplies and the gas, and they walked back outside. Just in the short time they'd been inside, the wind had picked up. Now those snowflakes felt like tiny ice-cold missiles, and visibility had dropped to only a few hundred feet.

Elizabeth tried to fight down her panic, remembering another night, another storm.

She did not want to be out in this. She wanted to be safe at home next to her fireplace at Brambleberry House with a mug of hot cocoa and a mystery novel.

Luke was a good driver, she reminded herself as he helped her inside the truck again and she fastened her seat belt. He always had been.

He would keep her safe.

She repeated that mantra for the next half hour, with Luke driving no more than twenty miles per hour. Neither of them said anything, focused only on the increasing fury of the storm.

After what seemed a lifetime, he released a frustrated sigh.

"We're not going to make it any farther tonight. Might as well catch a few hours of sleep while the storm blows over and then take off again in the morning when the roads are clear. Look online and see if you can find us a couple of rooms in the next town."

This sparsely populated and remote part of Oregon wasn't exactly overflowing with towns that boasted four-star hotels. Add in the storm that was basically crippling transportation and she wasn't optimistic about their chances. Still, she was grateful she still had cell service and something to do to take her mind off the weather conditions and the fear that hovered just on the edge of her mind.

Sure enough, she searched on her phone for hotels in the next town and found only two. When she called, neither had vacancies. Not so much as a broom closet.

She had more luck with the town after that, about ten more miles along the interstate.

"Looks like there's one room with two beds in a motel in the next town," she said, looking at the hotel app she used to book her trips to Haven Point.

"Call them and book it. I'm afraid it might take us a half an hour or more to get there and I would hate for it to be sold out when we show up. You can take a credit card out of my wallet."

He lifted a hip to pull it out, then handed it over, still warm from being in his pocket.

She took it quickly so he could return both hands to the wheel. Using the light from her phone, she opened it and started to search for a credit card. Before she could find one, she stopped on a snapshot inside the wallet, in a little pocket with a clear cover.

Their children.

Cassie and Bridger were hugging each other, faces turned to the camera with matching smiles.

Next to them was another picture. Older. This one was of a much younger Luke with his arm around a woman with blond hair and blue eyes. They looked at each other with a love that was as plain as if hearts and flowers suddenly floated off the image.

She felt as if all the oxygen had been sucked out of the vehicle, as if her lungs couldn't expand enough to take in the necessary air.

She missed them, this couple who had been so in love. She missed the evenings they would spend snuggled together, sharing secrets and dreams; she missed the pure contentment she felt in his arms; she missed the serenity of knowing someone loved her completely.

She missed that woman, too.

It had been seven years since she'd seen a picture of herself the way she used to be.

She had forgotten. The angle of her nose and the little bump where she had broken it in second grade trying to ice-skate down the slide at the playground. The mouth that looked like the mother she had never forgotten, even during the time she considered the blank years.

Luke looked so young. Not at all like the hard, forbidding man who sat beside her. He had been closed off when they married, his spirit bruised by a cruel, abusive father, yet there had been a softness to him then. A sweetness. She had always attributed that to Megan's mother, Sharon, his stepmother from the age of about six, who had loved and nurtured the lost little boy he had been.

She fought the urge now to rub her finger on that familiar, beloved face, as if she could absorb him through her skin and somehow resurrect some of that sweetness and joy.

"Well? Did you find a credit card?"

She jerked her gaze from the picture to the man beside her. "Sorry. Just a minute." She dug out a card and flashed it to him. "Will this work?"

"That's fine."

With great reluctance, she closed the wallet on that picture and dialed the number to the hotel, then pushed the required sequence of numbers to connect with an operator.

The line rang at least ten times before a woman answered, sounding flustered.

"Riverside Inn."

"Hi. I was...wondering about booking a room tonight. We are...traveling and stranded by the storm."

She hated her hesitant, faltering voice and hated most of

all that Luke heard it. So far she had been able to conceal the way her mind tangled sometimes over the right words. At other times, the right ones slipped away completely.

"You and everyone else, honey."

"Your...your website said you had availability."

"I've got one room left. How long will it take you to make it here?"

"I...don't know. But I was...hoping I could reserve it with a credit card."

"That works. Good thing you called. That's probably the last available room in a hundred miles. Let me open up a reservation."

After they went through the particulars of booking the room on Luke's card, Elizabeth thanked the woman.

"I hear it's ugly out there. Be safe, Mrs. Hamilton."

No one had called her that in so many years. "I... Thank you."

She disconnected the call and carefully slid Luke's credit card back into the pocket of his wallet, fighting the urge to flip through the pictures again and stare at all of them. He probably had more of the children, maybe when they were younger.

"All set?"

She nodded and carefully closed the wallet again. "It was the last room. You were right about booking it over the phone. Here's your wallet."

"I can't put it back in my pocket while I'm driving. Just set it on the console," he said before turning his attention back to the road and the snow blowing across.

Now that she had nothing to do but focus on the storm, her anxiety increased. Even closing her eyes didn't keep it at bay because she could still hear the wipers on high and the tires churning through the snowy conditions.

"I don't know how to get to the motel," he said as the next exit loomed ahead of them. "Can you find directions?"

Did he sense she could cope better when she had a task? "Of course," she answered, and punched in the coordinates of the inn to her phone, then recited the turn-by-turn instructions to him. It seemed like forever but was probably only a few more moments before he found the building with the neon sign out front that read Riverside Inn.

He pulled into a parking space, one of the few remaining. "Took a while but we made it. You okay?"

Sure. She was going to be spending the night in a little hotel room with the only man she'd ever loved—a man who happened to hate her with every fiber of his being. Why wouldn't she be okay?

"Fine," she answered, quite certain he knew it was a lie.

The hotel's website hadn't exaggerated its charm, as websites often did. It was actually quite lovely. Red and green Christmas lights ran along the eaves and a brightly lit Christmas tree twinkled a cheery welcome through the blowing snow.

"You need help getting out?" he asked.

"No. Grab the bags," she answered.

He nodded and went to the bed of the pickup truck to collect their luggage.

She opened her door and slid down into ankle-deep snow. Sometimes she could be so stupid and stubborn. She should have accepted his help. She could have used her cane but it was back with her suitcase. Stupid her.

The prospect of walking the twenty feet from the pickup truck to the front door of the inn through the snow was as daunting as climbing Mount Hood. Her balance wasn't the greatest under the best of circumstances. Throw in icy conditions and she seemed predestined for a fall.

Still, she started out after him and had only made it a few faltering steps when he returned without the luggage.

He thrust out his arm. "Here. Grab hold. I should have thought to help you first before taking the bags."

His words weren't quite an apology but close to it. She was torn between embarrassment that she needed his help and gratitude that he saw the need and stepped forward so that she didn't have to ask.

"Sorry. I'm not very...stable on ice."

In her fleeting glance at his features, she saw questions in his eyes, but his mouth tightened and he remained silent. She turned her attention back to the sidewalk. He had to wonder about her physical condition and the obvious speech issues that were new since she had left him, but he didn't ask.

Luke dropped her arm as soon as they walked through the outside door into the welcome warmth of the inn's lobby. She told herself she had no right to be hurt by his obvious unwillingness to touch her, but it still stung.

A half dozen people stood in line, either looking for rooms or waiting to check in.

"I'm sorry but we don't have anything left," the flustered clerk was saying to a desperate-looking couple. "I understand an emergency shelter has been set up for stranded travelers at the elementary school, which is two blocks to the east."

Oh dear. The situation was worse than she'd thought. She wasn't looking forward to spending the night in a hotel room with Luke, but at least they had a room with beds and wouldn't have to sleep on a cot in a classroom somewhere.

"Take a seat and I'll check us in," Luke said, gesturing

to the only open spot in the lobby, next to a very pregnant woman who was trying to entertain a toddler on her lap with her cell phone.

Elizabeth made her way to the seating area, surrounding a river rock fireplace where a gas blaze cheerfully burned.

The woman with the toddler smiled at Elizabeth. "This is crazy, isn't it? I thought we were taking a simple trip to visit my folks in Boise before the holidays. It's my dad's seventy-fifth birthday tomorrow. This blizzard came out of nowhere. When we checked the weather, they said it would only be a few inches, so we thought we were fine."

Poor thing. Traveling with little ones had to be tough enough without road emergencies. "Do you have a room?" she asked, with some vague, crazy idea of giving her theirs. Elizabeth wouldn't want to sleep at the elementary school, but it would be better than having to live with the guilt at knowing she sent this pregnant woman and darling little girl back out into that storm.

"We do. We called ahead and were fortunate enough to book one of the last two rooms in town."

"I think we got the other one."

The woman smiled at her. "Yay us." She nodded to the line at the reception desk. "Is that your husband in line behind mine?"

She wanted to say Luke wasn't her husband, but it seemed foolish to protest. He was, anyway. She just hadn't been any sort of wife to him for the last seven years.

Instead, she simply nodded.

"Lucky you," the woman said with a grin. "I'm Lindsey Lowell, and this is my little girl, Aubrey."

"Hi, Aubrey. Hi, Lindsey. I'm...Sonia Davis."

She caught a little on the name that had been given to her

seven years ago. Even after a few hours, she was already back to being Elizabeth in her head.

"Hi," Aubrey said. "I'm this many."

She held up two fingers and Elizabeth smiled. "That's big. What are you playing?"

"Balloons. I share." The girl held out the phone for Elizabeth.

"Um. Thanks." She wasn't quite sure what to say or do.

"I show you." Without waiting for permission, Aubrey climbed from her mother's lap to Elizabeth's, demonstrating how to pop the balloons on the phone app.

"Aubrey. Honey. Come back."

"No. It's fine," Elizabeth said. She didn't have the chance to interact with an adorable little girl very often. If nothing else, it would give the pregnant mom a break for a moment.

A few moments later, she was engrossed in the girl, who delighted in showing her how to blow the balloons up bigger and make them float across the screen, then how to pop them rather violently with a finger.

It was actually calming in a zen sort of way, a little like playing with Bubble Wrap.

"Pretty," Aubrey exclaimed, clapping her hands when Elizabeth inflated a purple balloon until it filled the whole screen. The girl pointed her chubby little index finger at the phone and popped it with a relish that made Elizabeth smile.

She was so busy playing with the girl, she didn't notice Luke return until she suddenly sensed his presence. She looked up in time to see something dark flash across his expression.

She had rarely played with their own children like this. She had wanted to, had ached to be the mother they needed, but the dark emptiness had been overwhelming.

We would all be better off without you.

The memory of those words coming from his mouth was as crystal clear as if he had said them moments earlier.

How funny that she still had many gaps in her memory but that one was so distinct. She could see the pain in his eyes, hear the frustration in his voice as he said them.

She had goaded him into it during one of her terrible days, had begged him over and over again to admit it.

He hadn't wanted to but she had finally worn him down. *Fine. You want me to say it? Right now it's true. We would all be better off without you.*

She hadn't been able to be the wife he needed during those four years or a mother for their children.

There had been good days during that time; she was certain of it. Before she got pregnant with Bridger, she had tried so hard to be a good mother to Cassie, but she knew the bad times had far outnumbered the good.

"Our room is ready," he said gruffly.

She didn't want to go with him. She wanted to stay here in this lobby, surrounded by noise and chaos and children.

"Goodbye, Lindsey. It was…nice to meet you. Safe travels to you and…good luck with your little one."

"Thank you. Goodbye, Sonia."

Luke's mouth tightened at the name. He looked at the woman and the bags surrounding her. "Do you need help carrying your things to your room?"

"No. We didn't bring much and my husband can carry what we have. Thank you, though."

Elizabeth rose and followed Luke across the lobby to an elevator in an alcove next to the fireplace.

"You're back to Sonia again?" he asked after pushing the button for their floor.

She didn't like feeling defensive. She hadn't chosen to use

a different name. Circumstances had been thrust upon her without her knowledge or consent. "It's been my name for seven years. Elizabeth... She seems like a different person."

He didn't say anything more as he led the way to the third floor and down the hall to their room.

He unlocked the door and held it open for her. It was a comfortable space, far more so than she had feared they would end up sharing. The furniture looked new, two queen beds made out of honey-colored pine and covered in lodge-look comforters. There was even space for a small sitting area with a sofa and easy chair.

As far as hotel rooms went, this one was fairly large. Still, unless it was the size of a ballroom, any place would still be too small for her to be comfortable spending several hours alone with Luke in it.

He set their luggage down. "Do you need something to eat or will the sandwiches we bought earlier do? The front desk clerk said they have vending machines and there's a restaurant still open next door."

"I'm not hungry," she answered. "But if I need something, a sandwich is fine."

He stood for a moment, big and rangy and obviously as unenthusiastic as she was about being trapped in this hotel room together.

"I left my phone in the truck. I'm going to grab it and maybe make a few calls down in the lobby. I'll try to stay out of your way."

Before she could answer, he turned around and headed out of the hotel room, leaving her alone once more.

Chapter Four

He closed the door outside the hotel room, aware he had just blatantly lied to his wife. His phone wasn't in the truck; it was in his pocket. He had used the phone only as an excuse so he wouldn't have to sit in that hotel room with Elizabeth either in silence or in stilted, awkward conversation.

He wanted to spend as little time as possible with her. It was bad enough that he had been trapped with her for the last four hours. He needed a little distance to get his head back on straight.

He headed down to the lobby, which was still chaotic but not quite as frenzied as it had been when they arrived. While he was tempted to go to the restaurant next door and see if they had a bar attached, he knew that wouldn't solve anything.

He didn't drink much, his answer to growing up with an abusive alcoholic for a father. Sometimes he longed for the oblivion, but he feared what would happen once he started down that road.

Instead, he managed to find a relatively quiet corner and sat for a minute checking his email and messages. Nothing was urgent, only a few scheduling conflicts with subcontractors on a couple of the houses he was building in Shelter Springs. He could deal with them after he returned to town.

That done, he finally checked the time and saw it was 8:00 p.m., not too late to talk to the kids.

His sister had called him three times that day and he had sent each to voice mail, not up to the battle he knew would ensue, but she needed to know he wouldn't be back that night.

Megan answered on the second ring. "Luke. It is about time you called. I've been worried sick! What is going on? Where are you?"

"Stuck in central Oregon. We ran into a storm and won't be back until morning."

"We?"

He sighed. "Elizabeth. I told you I was coming to get her."

"Wrong. You told me nothing. Less than nothing. I've had just about enough of men and their cryptic explanations today."

That must mean Elliot Bailey was still busy with his latest undercover investigation for the FBI. He'd been gone three weeks and Megan wasn't happy about the situation, especially when they were supposed to marry in less than a month.

"You can't just drop the kids off and announce you're going after Elizabeth, then walk out the door before I can ask any questions," she said.

He hadn't been fair to his sister. He had known that as soon as he drove away. His only excuse had been that he'd reacted out of anger and frustration after Cade Emmett called him early that morning, what seemed a lifetime and hundreds of miles ago. The Haven Point police chief called to warn him the new county district attorney, a temporary appointment until the next election, was preparing to file charges against him in the disappearance and presumed murder of his wife.

The wife he had known for months was alive and well and living on the Oregon Coast.

His reaction had been visceral, with not much thought behind it, though he'd had plenty of time to think on the eight-hour drive from Boise to the coast.

"The morning was crazy," he answered. "I'm sorry. I wasn't thinking after Cade called. Thanks for taking the kids, by the way."

"Of course. You know they're always welcome here. I guess you won't be back tonight, then."

"No. A big storm has traffic at a standstill. I'm hoping we can get an early start first thing in the morning."

"The kids are fine. Since Elliot still isn't back, I might just take them back to your place so they can sleep in their own beds."

"No problem. Thanks. I owe you."

He knew this was only one tiny drop of debt in the vast ocean he owed his sister.

"So. You have Elizabeth with you?"

"Not at this particular moment in time. She's up in the room. But yes. She's coming back with me to clear things up once and for all."

"That will be a relief," Megan said. "Are you...okay?"

He squirmed at the concern in his sister's voice. He knew what she was asking. How was he handling seeing her again?

He didn't know how to answer. He was stuck in a hotel room with a woman he had once loved with all his heart, had grieved for deeply when he thought she was dead and had come to despise now that he knew she had chosen to walk away from the life they were building.

Yeah, he'd had better days.

"I'm fine." He gave his second lie of the evening. "I just wish I could be home with the kids. How are they doing? Did you have a good day?"

"Yes. I took them to church," she answered.

Luke didn't miss the hesitancy in her voice. He knew his sister well enough to sense she wasn't telling him something. "What happened? What's going on?"

"Nothing you need to worry about. You have enough on your plate right now. We can talk when you get home."

"Megan. What happened."

She sighed. "I guess I need to tell you. Bridger got in a fight after Sunday school."

"No, he didn't!"

"Do you think I would lie about something like that?"

Bridger was not that kind of kid. He was sweet and good-natured, always willing to focus on the good in other people. "I'm sure there was some kind of misunderstanding."

"Maybe. One of the other parents saw the whole thing and intervened before it could get too ugly. Apparently another kid said something mean to Bridger and he punched him."

"Who was it?"

"Jedediah Sparks. That kid is a pistol. The apple doesn't fall far from the tree, you know?"

He did know. Jed's father, Billy, and his mother, Arlene, were some of Luke's most vocal critics, making sly comments about wife killers and criminals going free whenever they happened to inhabit the same space. The boy probably heard all kinds of nasty gossip from his parents.

"Did Bridger say why he lost his temper?"

"He's not talking. He only said it was a difference of opinion and he wanted to make the other kid shut up. He feels awful."

"He *should* feel awful."

"He's upset about punching someone in church and thinks God is going to be mad at him. More than that, he's afraid *you're* going to be mad at him. Or at least disappointed. He said you always told him the most important lesson a man has to learn is how to control his temper."

Megan didn't say more, but Luke knew what she was thinking. They had both shared the same son of a bitch for a father. Paul Hamilton had never given a single damn about controlling his temper. He had been harsh, demanding, cruel. Both Luke and his sister had barely survived their childhood.

"Is he already in bed? I'd like to talk to him."

"He is. They were pretty tired after helping me shovel snow earlier at the inn."

"Are you okay staying overnight with them? I'm sorry to do that to you. I can find someone else if you have things to do. I'm hoping we can get an early start, but I don't know how long this weather will hold out."

"We will be great. Tomorrow is a slow day for me. I'm just working on photos and my schedule is totally flexible. I can get the kids off to school and work after that."

"Thank you. I owe you." Again, the words seemed wholly inadequate. "I'll keep you posted about the weather here."

"Is that all you have to say? You don't want to tell me your impressions about Elizabeth?"

He shifted, telling himself the sudden warmth seeping through him came from the gas fireplace in the lobby. "Nothing to tell. She's a stranger now."

"You must have had a million questions. What kind of

explanation did she give? Why did she run off? Why did she change her name? Where has she been all these years while you have been raising your children, living under a cloud of suspicion?"

He gazed into the dancing flames, thinking of the woman probably asleep in the room upstairs. "I don't know any more than I did this morning. She's still a mystery. I told her I didn't want to know anything. I don't care. She can tell her story to the district attorney tomorrow."

Okay, that had been a stupid, stubborn thing to say, his knee-jerk reaction. He was afraid that the more he knew, the angrier he would become.

The most important lesson a man has to learn is how to control his temper.

It was the advice he'd given his son and also the advice he most needed to follow himself. He found it tough enough to keep his temper contained around Elizabeth. He feared the task would become impossible once he knew the full story about her reasons for leaving him.

"Seriously?" Megan pressed. "You don't know anything?"

He knew Elizabeth was still lovely, though very different from the woman he had married. He knew he was still attracted to her. He knew he missed the wife he had loved with a deep, yearning ache.

"Not much. She doesn't look the same. You wouldn't know her if you bumped into her on the street, but I do know she's been back to Haven Point at least a few times over the years. I recognized her and realized I've...seen her around town before."

Megan's outrage seemed to pop and sizzle over the phone line. "*What?* And she never stopped to see the kids? Every time I think I can't despise the woman more, I discover I'm wrong."

For one crazy moment, Luke was almost tempted to defend Elizabeth. She seemed so fragile, so vulnerable, the sort of wounded creature he had always tried to nurture back to health.

What the hell was wrong with him?

She had left him. Worse, she had left the kids. That was unforgivable, as far as he was concerned.

"How's the wedding planning?" he asked, a blatant ploy to distract her.

To his relief, the diversion worked. "It's good. But next time I decide to plan a winter wedding, remind me not to."

"I hope you don't plan another wedding ever," he replied.

"So do I."

"What do you hear from Elliot?"

Megan sighed. "Nothing. I know it's the job and one of the things I'm going to have to learn to live with, but I hate having him out of contact. I need him here, you know?"

He didn't like thinking about Megan and Elliot together, especially considering recent history between them. While it would take a long time to repair the damage of the past seven years when the FBI agent had suspected him of harming his wife, Luke still respected him. Elliot had always focused on doing the right thing. He had been the one to locate Elizabeth, through tireless investigation that he'd undertaken for Megan's sake, not for Luke's.

The man came close to being good enough for Megan, though nobody could ever really hit that bar.

"Oh, that's Cyrus. I need to take him out."

He pictured her funny-looking little dog and almost smiled. "Okay. I'll let you go. Thanks again for taking care of the kids. I can't tell you exactly what time I'll be back but I'll be in touch."

"Be careful," she said. Luke had a feeling she wasn't just talking about the roads.

"Yeah. Thanks. Give them both a hug for me in the morning and tell Bridger to stay away from Jedediah."

"I will. Maybe I can get him to tell me a few more details about what set him off."

After he said goodbye to his sister and ended the call, Luke sat for a long moment in the lobby. He had a feeling the desk clerk wouldn't be happy if he just stretched out in this comfy chair and went to sleep down here, but he really didn't want to go back to that hotel room to face Elizabeth yet.

Outside, the storm was either on momentary hiatus or had slowed a little. The intensity seemed to have decreased. Instead of blowing horizontally, the snow seemed to be falling in the usual manner.

He was so tired from hours of driving but knew he would be too restless to sleep. On impulse, he headed for the front desk, where the same clerk who had checked them in earlier still worked.

His family had run an inn for most of his life. Megan still oversaw the Haven Point Inn. He knew exactly how many little details went into giving guests an enjoyable experience and how hard it could be to accomplish everything necessary.

"Hi. I've been sitting behind the wheel all day and need to burn off some energy. Do you mind if I take a shovel and clear off the front walk?"

The woman's face brightened. "Mind? Are you kidding? Our maintenance guy is up to his eyeballs trying to fix a problem with the swimming pool. We've got twenty kids who want to swim and the situation is getting desperate. You would be a lifesaver."

Luke grabbed the shovel from the closet she pointed to and headed out into the storm, grateful he'd still been wearing his coat when he walked down to use the phone.

In the end, he shoveled the walks all around the small inn. The physical exertion helped calm his brain, almost a form of meditation. By the time he finished, his muscles burned, but he felt much more able to rest.

"Thank you," the clerk said when he came inside again. "That was so kind of you. The least I can do is give you a coupon for a meal at the restaurant next door. We offer a free breakfast of muffins and fruit, but they have a more elaborate spread."

"Thanks, but I'm hoping we'll be making an early start and won't have time for a sit-down breakfast. There was a nice young couple just ahead of us when we checked in. A couple with a little girl. You could give it to them."

"I'll do that. That's very nice of you. Thank you."

"Good night."

He couldn't put it off any longer. He had to go to the room. Cheeks still cold from the elements, Luke made his way up to the elevator, bracing himself the whole way to deal with her again.

When he opened the door to the hotel room, he found it mostly dark, illuminated only by the bathroom light. It took his eyes a few moments to adjust to the dim conditions. When they did, he saw she had picked the bed closest to the window and was under the covers, unmoving. Was she asleep? He couldn't say. Her breathing seemed regular and steady but she might have been faking.

He grabbed his duffel and headed into the bathroom to get

ready for bed. He hadn't been planning to stay the night but also hadn't known what he would face in Oregon. He was glad some sixth sense had prompted him to be prepared for a night on the road. He at least had a T-shirt and gym shorts he could sleep in.

When he came out of the bathroom, he couldn't see that she had moved.

Odd. She had always been a restless sleeper. He couldn't count the number of nights he had awakened with her sprawled across him, warm and soft, the comforter somewhere at their feet or on the floor. He used to love wrapping his arms around her and holding her, cherishing the pure perfection of the moment while he counted the moments until he could legitimately awaken her with a kiss.

He pushed away the ache and slipped into his own bed, wishing it were a little farther away so he didn't have to listen to her breathing.

He had become the restless sleeper now. Since she left, he rarely slept all the way through the night, as if something in his subconscious continued to wake up, looking for her. It made him furious and empty at the same time.

He stared up at the ceiling in the room, tinted red and green from the snow-covered Christmas lights filtering in through a gap in the curtains.

Finally, exhausted from hours of driving and from the emotional tumult of the day, he slept.

He awoke to whimpering coming from the other bed. For a moment when he first awoke, he couldn't remember where he was. Was that Cassie or Bridger having a bad dream?

He saw red and green lights filtering through the curtains and remembered then. He was in a hotel somewhere in Oregon. That wasn't one of his kids. It was the wife he hadn't seen in years.

He rolled onto his side, facing her. He could just make out her features in the dim light, twisted with either pain or fear. As he listened, trying to decide whether to wake her, the sound turned into more than whimpering. She cried out, the emotion in her voice tortured and raw. "No. Please. My babies. I need my babies."

He frowned, sitting up and scrubbing his face to push away the remaining tendrils of sleep.

"I'm not Sonia. I'm Elizabeth. Why won't you believe me? Please. Please! Don't leave me trapped here."

She said a few more things, her words garbled and unintelligible but the distress coming through with grim clarity.

Finally he couldn't take it anymore. He flipped on the light on the table between the two beds. "Lizzie? Wake up. You're dreaming."

"Luke. Oh, Luke." She said his name on a sob, her eyes still closed. He was fairly sure she wasn't awake but he couldn't be sure. He *did* know he hated her tears.

"Hey, now. Don't cry."

Though he knew it was probably one of the more stupid things he could do, he couldn't resist sliding out of bed and sitting on the edge of hers. She was trembling. He could feel the bed vibrating with her small movements.

"Don't cry," he repeated. "You're dreaming."

Except this didn't seem like a dream. She wasn't here. She was…somewhere else.

He reached a hand out to calm her. That was all he really intended but the next moment she was somehow in his arms.

In an instant, seven years melted away. She was here and she was his.

He had forgotten how perfectly she fit in his arms, how her head nestled against his chest at precisely the right angle and her arms wrapped around his waist. She smelled the same, that mix of citrus and vanilla that always made his mouth water.

He wanted to bury his face in her hair and inhale, to burn that scent into his memory again.

He knew the instant she started to awaken. Her whimpering slowed and then stopped altogether. She sighed, and for perhaps sixty seconds, she relaxed in his arms, her body going boneless and calm before he could feel her muscles tighten and she started to fight against his hold.

"Don't hurt me. Please don't hurt me. Take what you want but don't hurt me."

He hated those words. He had *never* hurt her. He even hated raising his voice. How many times had he walked away when she would explode at him, lashing out in her pain that he should leave her, that he was better off without her?

"Easy. Easy. It's me. It's Luke."

She scrambled to the other side of the bed, those familiar-unfamiliar features twisting with confusion. In the low light, she looked...haunted.

"Luke. What are you...?" Her blue eyes widened and he watched memory click back. "Oh."

"You had a bad dream. You were crying in your sleep."

"Was I?" She blinked, obviously trying to make sense of the last few moments. She pulled the blanket to her shoulders like a shield, becoming guarded once more. "What... what did I say?"

"You begged me not to hurt you. And you also said you were Elizabeth. Not Sonia."

"I would say...I'm a little of both now."

"You also said something about being trapped. It sounded pretty frightening. What did you mean?"

She looked away, focusing on the banal artwork in the room. "Nothing. I was rambling in my sleep, I suppose. You know how...dreams can be." She swallowed. "What time is it? Has the weather cleared?"

His jaw worked, aware she was trying to avoid the questions. She didn't want to talk about the nightmare or about what her subconscious may have revealed.

Since he wasn't entirely sure he was ready to hear her answers, he decided to let her change the subject. "A little after four. The snow had eased a little when I went to sleep around midnight. I'll take a look."

Though the room was carpeted, the floor was still cold on his bare feet as he slid out of bed and walked to the window. Dawn was still a few hours away. The storm had dropped several more inches since midnight but it looked as if the winds had died down. With luck, crews had been hard at work in the early hours clearing the freeway and they could get on their way at first light.

Good. He wasn't sure he could take another night, trapped in a hotel room with her.

"It's still too early to take off again. We should try to catch a few more hours, then get an early start."

"All right. I'm...sorry I woke you."

He thought about telling her she'd been giving him sleepless nights for seven years but didn't want to admit that to her.

"Good night," he answered, then climbed back into bed, rolled to face the wall and tried to do the impossible—put her out of his mind long enough to slip back into sleep.

Chapter Five

Had he fallen back asleep? When she looked under her lashes at the form in the bed next to her, Elizabeth couldn't really tell. Luke gave every indication that he was sleeping. He didn't move a muscle and his breathing was even and steady.

She couldn't return to sleep, maybe because she had dozed so much the afternoon before and then had gone to bed earlier than usual after Luke left, simply because she didn't know what else to do.

Now, in the aftermath of what she knew was probably a small seizure, the fragments of the nightmare stayed with her, stark and terrifying. Not a nightmare. More memories that she had managed to shove down.

Driving through the storm the day before had brought back a plethora of things she had avoided facing. Her helplessness, regret, fear. And the long hard journey she had traveled since leaving Haven Point.

She shifted on the bed, watching the play of red and green on the wall from the Christmas lights hanging on the exterior of the hotel.

She knew nothing good came from hashing and rehashing the past. She had learned grim lessons from that journey. Right now, she had to focus on how she was going to make it through the next few days.

At least she would be able to see her children. Maybe even hug them. If the price for that glorious gift was time spent with a man who hated her, she was more than willing to pay for it.

"Yes, the interstate is open now. But I would still stay put if I were you."

The highway patrol officer at the checkpoint before the freeway entrance looked cold and exhausted, with rosy cheeks, bleary eyes and heavy lines pulling down the corners of his mouth as he spoke. "This is the safest place for you, at least for a few hours. The roads might be open but they're still slick and snow-packed."

"Even on the interstate?" Luke asked.

"After the storm came a nasty fog that's socked in everything from here to Boise. It will be at least noon before we can advise travel again for anything except emergencies. I know it's an inconvenience, but it's only a handful of hours."

Luke's hands tightened on the steering wheel. He didn't look at her but awareness still seethed between them.

He didn't want to wait another few hours to be rid of her.

He didn't have to say the words for her to know what was going through his mind. She knew she had earned every ounce of his scorn, though that did not make it any easier to bear.

"I appreciate the advice, sir, but I'm sure we'll be fine. We have four-wheel drive and I put the chains on this morning. We'll go slow."

The patrolman shook his head. "I can't stop you since the roads are open. I tried to warn you. Just remember that."

After that ominous warning, Luke nodded, waved at the man, then pulled slowly away from the checkpoint and onto the freeway.

They proceeded much as the officer had warned, at a slow pace, though it seemed conditions were better than she had feared. While there were certainly pockets of fog, they lifted for long stretches of time, revealing a pristine white landscape that made her grateful for her sunglasses.

She tried to make conversation at random intervals, but Luke shut her off every time with terse, monosyllabic answers. Eventually she tired of fighting the silent treatment and reached into her bag for a novel.

She had never been much of a reader, always too busy playing with friends or helping her dad out in the garden. Months of forced inactivity and the long tedium of a recovery with little else to do had introduced her to the sheer joy of losing herself in a story, reading about someone else's troubles and triumphs instead of dwelling on her own all the time.

This book was fascinating and well written, and she was able to immerse herself in the story, grateful for the diversion from the tension, until Luke stopped for gas again near the Idaho border.

She got out to stretch her tight, aching leg and limped into the convenience store to use the facilities, then bought another protein bar and an apple.

She wasn't inside long, but when she returned, Luke was already sitting behind the wheel, ready to go. The man could be a machine sometimes. He didn't even seem to need so much as a cup of coffee to keep him going.

"We made...better time than I expected," she said when they were on the road again.

"Still too slow," he said. "But I'm glad we didn't hang around at the inn."

He didn't seem inclined to say more and Elizabeth sighed. She tried to return to her book but increasingly felt her attention wandering.

She had so many questions she wanted to ask him. About the children, about his construction business, about the community she had once loved. He didn't want questions from her. He didn't want anything.

A lump rose in her throat at the sobering realization, but she swallowed it down along with a bite of her protein bar.

While she didn't feel particularly tired, the tedium and her restless night—added to the extra medication she had taken to make sure she didn't have another seizure—eventually caught up with her.

After she found her attention wandering away from the story and realized she couldn't remember what she was reading, she moved her bookmark back to the previous chapter heading, closed her book and created a makeshift pillow out of her coat. She didn't expect to sleep—Haven Point was only a few hours away, after all. Yet one moment she was watching the lines go by outside the windshield, the next she had escaped into her dreams.

She wasn't sure how long she was out of it. When she awoke, the trees and mountains on either side of the road began to seem familiar. She knew this landscape, had seen it from the time she and her parents moved here when she was ten.

They were close to Haven Point. Her heart started to pound and her hands felt sweaty. Oh Lord. She couldn't do this.

Luke seemed to become more grim and foreboding the closer they traveled to their hometown. His jaw looked hard enough now to slice through granite.

"I'm...sorry I fell asleep."

He glanced over, his eyes as hard as the rest of him. "It was fine. The fog lifted right after you fell asleep. It hasn't been a bad drive since then."

She turned her attention out the window, catching glimpses of the pure blue of the lake through the trees as they neared it.

She loved that lake as much as she hated it. Yes, it had brought her joy through her childhood. She had wonderful memories of picnics by the shore, swimming at the beach near downtown, kayaking with her girlfriends in high school.

But it had taken so much from her.

Every mile seemed to contain more memories, not only of Luke but of her parents. Her childhood had been filled with joy, with parents who adored each other and her from the moment she was born, in stark contrast to what Luke endured.

Whenever she thought about the few things he had revealed about his childhood, she wanted to cry. Those memories had come back to her slowly, probably because they were so painful. She remembered he hadn't wanted to tell her anything, preferring to focus on the present and about the future they wanted to build rather than his heartbreaking past.

His sister had revealed more. Megan had been the one to tell Elizabeth about their brute of a father, his drunken rages, his abuse and how he had singled out Luke for the worst of it.

Her husband would not have been happy with his sister

for telling her that. He had only told her that his relationship with his father had not been a good one.

Like so many other things, Luke had shoved down his deepest emotions. He tried so hard not to show anger but sometimes that had translated into burying everything so deep, it was hard to bring anything out. Joy, happiness, love. She knew he felt those things, but during their marriage, he had struggled to show them.

She and her parents had provided a sanctuary for him, a place where he had been loved and accepted from the moment they started dating. She could remember her father taking Luke on fishing trips into the mountains and her mother showing him something she was growing in their beautiful gardens. Luke had lapped up their attention.

When her parents had died so unexpectedly, she had withdrawn into herself and her pain, leaving him with nothing.

She fought the urge to rub her hand against the ache in her chest. Unlike her parents, she had made the *choice* to leave him alone and she couldn't blame him if he could never forgive her for that.

As Luke drove around the lake toward home through a beautiful wintry scene, blue skies contrasting with the new snow that coated everything, her heart began to pound. Whenever she returned to Haven Point to see the children's plays or ball games—always sitting in the back, always trying to stay anonymous—she felt the same sense of peace, as if this was the one place in the world she belonged.

Sometimes before heading back to Boise to the airport, she would have the car service she hired drive past their house, the one on Riverbend Road. If she were extraordinarily lucky, she might see the children playing outside in the yard with their dog or Luke doing something around the house.

Those moments were rare and precious and she cherished them, yet they were like a beautiful, perfect rose that came with plenty of thorns. Seeing the children at home, growing bigger each time she saw them, also made her feel terribly lonely as she rode out of town. She would often cry silent tears the entire way to the airport.

This time would be different. This time she would actually be able to see them. Talk to them. No matter how difficult it was to see Luke again, she could hold on to that joyful thought.

What would they think of her? The reality of the situation started to seep through. Would they be as angry and closed off as Luke? Or would they maybe be a little bit happy to see her again?

As he turned onto their road, panic welled up, cold and relentless, and she had to force herself to breathe slowly and evenly. She could handle this. Couldn't she?

When he pulled into the driveway, she thought the house looked cold and rather forlorn. She could see no sign of life.

Luke turned off the engine. "I tried to find a room for you at the inn when we stopped for gas, but Megan says they're full. Some holiday event going on at Caine Tech and they've booked the whole place."

No room at the inn. How appropriate for this time of year.

"I don't mind. This will be fine," she answered. Did he really think she would rather stay at a hotel instead of with their children?

"There's not much here," he said, an odd sort of warning in his voice. He unlocked the door and walked inside. As soon as she followed, she knew exactly what he meant.

The place was empty.

No pictures on the walls, no knickknacks, no furniture except an old sofa.

The house where she and Luke had started their marriage with so many high hopes was now a hollow shell.

"I don't...I don't understand. Where are...Cassie and Bridger?"

He set her suitcase down with a thump beside the front door. "In school until I pick them up. Then they'll be at home. My home."

"Oh. I thought..." Her words trailed off as she only now realized how stupid and shortsighted she had been.

"You thought I would let you see them? Talk to them? Hell no, Elizabeth."

Of course he wouldn't let her see the children. She should never have been foolish enough to expect otherwise. Disappointment rolled over her like a snowplow, with sharp, fierce intensity.

"You...won't?"

"You lost any rights where Bridger and Cassie are concerned when you walked away from us. I won't let you break their hearts again."

She could feel herself sway, her legs unsteady. For one horrible moment she was afraid she would fall to her knees. She reached behind her for the wall, hoping he didn't notice the gesture.

"I would never hurt them," she said, her voice small.

"What do you think you have been doing for the past seven years?"

She had hated his silence during the drive but this bitterness was far worse. Elizabeth closed her eyes, the pain and loss and loneliness almost more than she could bear.

He would never agree, but everything she had done had

been in her misguided effort to protect her children. They were the entire reason she had left in the first place.

"I...see."

"You created this situation, Elizabeth. Because of you, I have been their sole caregiver. I'm the only one who gets to decide what's right for them. You gave me that responsibility when you left—before then, actually, when you checked out emotionally after Bridger came along."

She drew in an unsteady breath, hating his reminder of what a terrible state she had been in, lost and depressed and overwhelmed.

She had suffered severe postpartum depression made worse by the clinical depression. She hadn't asked for it, had she? Hadn't wanted it. He made it sound as if she had chosen to be depressed instead of fighting it with everything she had. She had tried prescription medicine, therapy, everything the doctors recommended. The next step would have been an inpatient program, which in retrospect had probably been exactly what she had needed.

That was the past. Hadn't she paid the price all these years?

She found it hideously ironic that the only good thing to come out of the severe brain injury she suffered in the accident had been that the cloud of soul-stealing depression had lifted.

She had traded one problem for about two dozen more.

Luke stood beside the door, unyielding and rigid as one of the oak trees growing outside. She wanted to yell at him, to fight and argue and pound her fist against his chest until he let her see her children. She couldn't. The harsh truth was, he was exactly right. She had lost any right to even call herself a mother.

"What...what am I supposed to do in the meantime in a... house with no furniture?"

"There's furniture. The kitchen table is still here and one of the bedrooms is furnished. You can use the sofa there that the kids and I decided not to move to the new house. It's only one night. In the morning, we can meet with the attorney and clear everything up. Then I'll pay for your flight back to Oregon."

He wanted her gone. That was clear enough. Their reunion was less than twenty-four hours old and he couldn't bear to have her around.

Once, he had loved her with all his heart. He used to whisper that she was everything he'd ever wanted, like his birthday and Christmas and the Fourth of July all wrapped into one person.

That was a long time ago. So much water had traveled under their bridge.

"All right." What else could she say?

"There should be food in the refrigerator. Megan said she dropped a few things off for you so you don't starve."

"That's...decent of her."

She wasn't sure where the sarcasm came from. Maybe it was her alternative to breaking into sobs.

Luke gave her a sharp look. "It is. Believe me. Meg doesn't want you here. None of us do. If it were up to me, you would have stayed gone. I've known where you were for months but didn't come after you. That option to leave you alone is gone now. I need to clear my name. That is the one and only reason you're here, not for some joyful reunion with the kids, where you get to act like nothing has happened."

His words were a sobering reminder of everything he'd been through. Her husband and children had suffered because of her. She had a chance to make it right, at least when it came to keeping him out of jail over the holidays. He was right. That was the only reason she was here.

She had been in limbo since her memory started to return, living for those times when she was able to come back and watch her family from a distance. The visits weren't healthy. She knew that. Maybe it was time for her to make a complete break. Though the idea of never seeing any of them again made her feel as if the house were falling down around her, perhaps it would be better for all of them if she helped Luke clear his name and then walked away for the last time.

"Fair enough. I…guess I'll see you in the morning, then. What time will you be here?"

"The earlier the better. Around eight."

She wanted to tell him to hug the children extra tightly for their mother but caught the words before they could escape.

After he left, she wanted to sink down into the middle of the floor and cry.

The house seemed so forlorn and empty without Luke and their children in it. She remembered the day they left the escrow company after they closed on the house, before they were even married.

The world had seemed joyous and bright and full of possibilities.

When they heard this little house beside the river had gone on the market, they had been so thrilled. It had been in a sorry state, a historic three-bedroom starter home built of logs and rock from the river without much charm or style. The best part had been the location, with spectacular views across the river to the Redemption Mountains.

She had lived here alone before their wedding, and she, Luke and her parents had worked together to fix it up. With his contractor skills, he had added the front porch, the shutters, the little glassed-in sunroom on the back where she had loved to sit in the afternoons.

They had worked together, laughed together, dreamed together here in this little house.

She walked through the house, stopping to look in Cassie's room. They had painted it together after Elizabeth's parents died, a pale lavender with white trim. It had been so very difficult to ready a nursery when her world had been rocked by losing her parents only months earlier, but she had thought having her daughter would help bring joy and light into her world again amid the darkness of her grief.

Instead, she seemed to slip further into the morass, feeling wholly inadequate as a mother and longing more than anything that her own mother could be there to help her.

She had started to climb out of it by the time Cassie was about three or four months old. Things had been better, she knew they had.

She had even started to feel…happy again. That was the reason she had wanted another child. If one child increased her happiness, two might even help her feel normal again.

Instead, the postpartum depression that hit her after Bridger had been debilitating. She remembered being so jealous of other women she knew at church or in the community who seemed to handle all the challenges of motherhood with ease. She hadn't been one of them. She had lived in a constant state of exhaustion and inadequacy.

Her face felt cold and it took a moment to realize she was crying, tears dripping down her cheeks.

She wiped at them with her sleeve, upset at herself.

She couldn't go back. That way was blocked by pain and suffering and regret. That was the one overriding lesson she had learned over the past seven years.

The only option available for her was to put one shaky foot in front of the other and do her best to make it through another day.

Chapter Six

He was a coldhearted bastard, just like his father had been. Luke drove away from the home on Riverbend Road with an ugly taste in his mouth and the grim awareness that he had been an ass.

You lost any rights where Bridger and Cassie are concerned when you walked away from us. I won't let you break their hearts again.

She had looked stunned and devastated at his declaration but what choice did he have? He had to protect the kids. They were his priority. They didn't need the emotional tumult of having her wander in and out of their lives when she felt like it. She had abandoned them and she didn't deserve another chance.

It was harder than he might have expected to tamp down his anger, now that he had spent hours in her company.

In contrast to their old house, the log home he had spent the last year building glowed with warmth from every window. Megan must be there.

He walked inside, his shoulders tight from the drive and a headache brewing at his temples, and was immediately greeted by the kids' dog, Finn, a sweet-natured, curly-haired mutt from the shelter he suspected was a mix of yellow Lab and miniature poodle.

Something delicious was cooking on the stove—vegetable soup, if he had to guess—and Megan sat at the kitchen table with her laptop open.

She looked up with a smile. "Hi. You made it. I was worried about you."

"The roads weren't as bad, once we hit the state line. Thanks for pinch-hitting for me with the kids. I know I didn't give you much choice."

"I didn't mind. I don't see them as often as I would like anyway during the school year. They were a welcome distraction, I promise."

He knew she had a lot on her plate, with an absent fiancé and a wedding to plan.

"Are you hungry?" Megan asked. "I made minestrone soup in the slow cooker. It's ready whenever, if you want it."

His stomach grumbled, reminding him breakfast had been hours ago at the Riverside Inn. "Soup sounds good. Thanks." He ladled some into a bowl, then sat down at the table. "Did you find out anything more about Bridger and his fight?"

She raised an eyebrow. "Your son is stubborn. I have no idea where he gets that. He's still not talking, at least to me. You might have better luck wriggling it out of him."

"I'll do my best."

Luke took a spoonful of soup, feeling immediately comforted by the rich tomato-and-vegetable concoction that reminded him of the meals his stepmother used to make.

"Go ahead and keep working. I'm sorry I interrupted."

"I was just finishing when you came in. I used the few minutes of quiet here to catch up on my email. For the first time in weeks, I think my inbox is under control. For today, anyway."

"Any word from our favorite FBI agent?"

He regretted the question when he saw her mouth tighten. "No. Nothing. I'm discovering I'm not very good at the waiting game."

Elliot, an FBI agent now in the Boise office, had been working undercover for the last month, unreachable. That state of affairs was hard on Megan but had implications for Luke as well. If Elliot were around, he might have been able to talk some sense into the new district attorney and clear up the entire thing. Elliot was one of the few who knew the truth.

"He was supposed to be done last week but I have to assume there's been some delay with the arrests. I'm keeping my fingers crossed he will be here for Christmas."

Maybe it was time for Elliot to leave the FBI business and focus exclusively on the true crime books he penned in his off hours. His latest book was still on bestseller lists, months after its release.

"What else has been going on while I've been gone?" He had only been away from Haven Point for thirty-six hours yet it felt like a lifetime.

"Oh no. That's not going to work. You're as bad as your son at avoiding questions. You can try to distract me all you want but you won't be able to get out of telling me everything. So, Elizabeth. What is she like now? What does she have to say for herself?"

Luke swallowed another spoonful of soup before he answered. He didn't want to talk about his soon-to-be ex-wife at all but didn't know how to avoid it. If anyone deserved information, it was Megan. Without her and Elliot's efforts over the summer to locate his wife and clear his name, he would still fear Elizabeth was dead.

"What explanation did she give?" Megan pressed. "Obviously nothing would excuse her actions, but I keep hoping she had some good reason to stay away. Witness protection or something. Or maybe she was abducted by aliens."

Luke shifted, unwilling to tell his sister he still had no idea why Elizabeth had left him or why she had stayed away for so long. They had exchanged very few words for the entire journey, none of them meaningful. "Like I told her, I don't want to know. She can tell the district attorney tomorrow."

"Seriously? You didn't ask?"

"Her reasons don't really matter, do they? The result is what's important. She left. That's all I need to know. She didn't want to be married to me anymore. She didn't want to be a mother to two of the most amazing kids on the planet. Nothing she could tell me would change that."

Megan shook her head in disbelief. "I do not understand you."

Big surprise there. Luke didn't understand himself. He didn't want to think he was a coward, but he had a feeling there was no other explanation for his reluctance to at least *ask* her during their long hours of driving together.

He wasn't sure he wanted to know all the ways he had failed Elizabeth during their marriage. It was far easier to blame her than take some of that responsibility onto himself.

His reluctance was probably also the reason he hadn't gone after her the moment Elliot had provided him with her name and address months ago at Megan's first art show opening for her brilliant photography.

He would know soon enough. He could no longer avoid the truth, once it was out there.

He set down his spoon, his appetite suddenly gone. "That was delicious. Thanks."

"You're welcome. I made it earlier today, after you asked me to take something over to the Riverbend Road house."

"I appreciate that, especially because I know you would probably rather give her dead slugs and poison apples."

Megan laughed. "I thought about it. Believe me. But we're trying to get you cleared of killing your wife. It wouldn't help our cause if I actually tried to follow through on what people have accused you of doing for years."

Those accusations had hurt, especially at first. He remembered how horrible it had been the first time he'd been questioned by the police in her disappearance. John Bailey, Elliot's father and the police chief at the time, seemed to have done a thorough job of investigating. He'd even turned his investigation over to the county sheriff's office for their scrutiny. Nobody had ever found proof that Luke had done anything to his wife, but that, of course, hadn't stopped the rumor mill from churning.

"By this time tomorrow, this will all be over. We can put the past behind us and start moving forward."

Worry creased Megan's forehead. "I hope so. I'm afraid clearing your name won't be a slam dunk. In some people's eyes, you've been the villain in this play for seven years."

"I don't care how people view me. I just don't want them to drag the kids into it."

He knew it was too late for that. He was fairly certain Bridger's fight had something to do with him and the persistent belief in some people around town that he had killed his wife.

Before Megan could answer, the front door burst open and Cassie and Bridger came running in, shedding coats and backpacks along the way.

"Dad! You're home!" Cassie exclaimed. She rushed to him and threw her arms around him as if he'd been stuck on a mountaintop somewhere for weeks.

At nearly ten, she was becoming a young woman. She had her mother's blond hair and mouth but Luke's green eyes. In another few years, he would be fighting off the boys. For now, she was still his little girl.

"I missed you," Bridger said. "Where did you go?"

He hugged his son. "Hey, bud. I missed you, too. I had some business to take care of out of town. Sorry I didn't give you a little more advance notice."

On the rare times he traveled out of town for business, he tried to give the children fair warning about the details of his trips. He wanted to think neither of them suffered abandonment issues after their mother left but knew that was probably naive of him.

At the advice of one of her teachers, Cassie had undergone a few months of counseling some years earlier when she was having trouble making friends. They learned she didn't trust people easily. As she grew older, that seemed to have resolved, for the most part. He did his best to provide them with a loving, warm home life but knew it probably wasn't enough to erase the scars from not having their mother.

He had never wanted to tell them his suspicions that she had killed herself. They didn't ask about Elizabeth often, but when they did, he had only told them she had been sick, that she went away to get help and he wasn't sure what happened to her after that.

It seemed a wholly inadequate explanation, one more fumbling effort in his parenting repertoire, but was the best he could come up with.

"It's okay," Cassie said now. "We had fun with Aunt Megan."

"We went to church and then we made snickerdoodles," Bridger said.

"Did you have one?" Cassie asked.

"No. I haven't seen any cookies." He narrowed his gaze at his sister. "Why didn't I know we had cookies? Have you been holding out on me?"

"Maybe I wanted them all to myself," his sister teased. "I know how you are with cookies."

She removed a container out of the cupboard and pulled back the lid to reveal snickerdoodles dusted with cinnamon sugar.

"Ooh. My favorite."

"That's why we made them," Megan said. "I wanted to make sugar cookies but your children insisted you would enjoy snickerdoodles more."

"That's why I have the most amazing kids in the world," he said, smiling at both of them before taking one of the cookies out and biting into it.

Cassie and Bridger were amazing—smart and funny and kind. Both were growing up to become decent people and it was up to him as their father to protect them, even if the person who posed the biggest threat to their emotional well-being right now was their mother.

After throwing off the groove with his unexpected trip to Oregon, Luke decided not to ask Bridger about the altercation he had had until after homework was done, they had eaten dinner and cleaned the kitchen and were settling down for bed. Some discussions were better one-on-one anyway.

They had a few routines by now. The kids showered and then they would settle in the great room of their house to read one of the books out of their Christmas collection or a chapter in the middle-grade novel they were all enjoying together.

Luke had to fight his own exhaustion from his long two days but managed to make it through the story and send Cassie on to bed. After making sure Bridger had brushed his teeth and settled into bed, Luke straightened the covers and sat on the chair next to him.

"So. Aunt Megan tells me you got into an argument yesterday after Sunday school."

Bridger released a big sigh, as if he had been waiting for this moment since Luke arrived home.

"She told you," he said, sounding betrayed.

"Yeah. Of course she told me. Did you think I wouldn't want to know that my son has been fighting in church?"

"I only hit Jedediah once. Okay, twice."

"That was two times too many, son, unless he was hurting someone else and you had to stop him."

"I know." Bridger looked guilty and ashamed.

"What happened?" Luke asked.

Bridger hugged his pillow. "Do I have to tell you?"

"You do. Nothing you tell me will make it right, but I would like to know."

His son sighed. "I don't want to say."

"Was it about someone else?" Luke guessed. "Someone in this family?"

Bridger gave a small nod. "Yes. He wouldn't stop saying bad things. I told him he was lying and he would be in trouble if he didn't stop. He didn't. He kept saying it again and again. He was calling you a name."

Just as he'd suspected. He might not have jumped there

with any other kid, but he knew Jedediah, knew his dad was a bully who had hated Luke since they were in school together.

"I kept telling him over and over to be quiet, that you're not a murderer, but he just laughed and said I was probably gonna grow up and be a murderer, too. I'm not, Dad. I'm *not*."

Luke's throat ached with emotion. Damn it. He had suspected that. He hated so much that his son was exposed to this kind of ugliness from other children. "I know, Bridge. I'm sorry that happened."

"I just wanted him to be quiet and stop saying mean things. But I shouldn't have punched him. I know it was wrong and I told him sorry right after, but then he punched me harder, so I punched *him* harder, and then Mrs. Palmer came in and made us say we were sorry and sit apart from each other."

Luke's heart seemed to squeeze. "You don't need to defend me, Bridger. I appreciate you trying to protect me, but it's not necessary. We know the truth. It doesn't matter what other people think, right?"

His words rang hollow. To kids, it mattered very much what people thought of them and their family. He remembered word getting around school after his father had been arrested for something or other and how ashamed he had been.

"Why do people call you that?"

He ran a hand over his son's hair. "It doesn't matter. It's not true. The people who care about our family know it's not true. Their opinion is all that should matter. Next time Jedediah says anything, just ignore him. Once he figures out he can't get a reaction out of you, he'll stop."

"I'm sorry I got in a fight, Dad."

"I know you were defending me and I appreciate it. You know that's still not a good excuse for losing your temper and hurting someone else, right? If that had happened at school, you would have been suspended."

"I know. I won't do it again, I promise."

After he hugged his son good-night, Luke turned off the light and closed the door.

He hated that his children had to bear the burden of their mother's choices. That was the reason he had gone to Oregon, had forced himself to face her again.

He had to keep that in mind over the next few days. His discomfort was nothing when compared to making life better and easier for his kids.

"What do you mean, she's going to be out of the office all day? We had an appointment."

"I am aware of your appointment and the reason for it." The voice of the district attorney's assistant was brisk and cool. "I'm afraid we have to postpone. That's why I'm calling. Ms. Torres had an unexpected family emergency and was called out of town over the weekend and then her return plans were delayed because of weather. She won't be back until late this evening."

Luke felt as if all his carefully laid plans were crumbling into dust. He did not want Elizabeth in town one more night. He wanted this done so she could be on her way and he could focus on enjoying Christmas with his children.

"I can put you on her calendar first thing in the morning. Will that work?"

What choice did he have? If the woman wasn't there, she wasn't there. He didn't know what he could do about it. He'd filled his quota of dragging women back to town.

"First thing. Like, crack of dawn."

"Her first available appointment is at 8:00 a.m."

"Fine. Put us down for that."

"Yes, sir."

He hung up, knowing there was nothing he could do to fix the situation.

He had hoped he would be able to clear the whole matter up and send Elizabeth packing by noon. Instead, now he was going to have to go tell her she would have to stick around Haven Point for another day.

Elizabeth studied the mantel, then reached to adjust the pine boughs she had brought inside, along with some winter berries and cuttings from the red-twigged dogwood she and Luke had planted together when they first moved here.

The sharp, sweet scent from the pine seeped through the room, making the stark, empty living room a little more homey. The house had only needed a few easy touches to bring it back to life.

Even in her solitary apartment in Brambleberry House, she had tried hard to celebrate the holidays, however she could. It had been the link to both her children and her own childhood, a time when she had been unreservedly happy.

At least the house didn't seem so sterile now. It looked more lived in. Luke was an experienced contractor and had to know he would have an easier time selling something that was staged better.

The little house was showing the inevitable wear and tear of the last few years. Everything needed sprucing up.

If it were her house still, she would put a new backsplash in the kitchen, the easy stick-down kind. She would paint a couple of the rooms that looked dingy and tired, and she would even consider replacing some of the carpeting.

It wasn't her house. Not anymore. She had given up any right to it when she had run away that last desperate night.

She pushed away the memories, thinking she should probably eat something. Luke said he would pick her up early. She had been up since long before dawn but hadn't been able to bring herself to eat any of the yogurt or cereal she found in the kitchen. The bowl of soup she had enjoyed the evening before seemed a long time ago, but she was too nervous to eat.

Today, she would have to tell Luke the truth.

All of it. Every ugly detail. He would be there when she confessed all her sins and mistakes to the district attorney.

She didn't want to do this. She wanted to stay here, tucked into the uncomfortable twin bed where she had spent the night, in the lavender room she and Luke had painted for Cassie.

She knew it was the right thing to do. But right was very different from easy.

She had to eat, especially because she needed to take her seizure medication, which didn't sit well on an empty stomach, so she forced herself to eat some yogurt. She was toasting a slice of the homemade whole wheat bread she found in the cupboard when she heard a key in the door.

Luke.

Her stomach jumped with a strange mix of anxiety and undeniable anticipation at seeing her husband again.

She had dreamed about him the night before, of those first glorious months they had spent in this house when she had felt safe and warm and loved completely.

That was the reason she had awakened so early, not the uncomfortable bed or the sterile surroundings that no amount of greenery could really fix.

She ached for her husband and was filled with sadness and regret, remembering the love they had once shared.

"I'm in the...kitchen," she called out.

A moment later, Luke walked inside. He looked big, tough, dangerous.

Wonderful.

She hadn't forgotten him. She had carried the memory of his face and the children's even when everything else had been a blank; it had only taken her a long time to figure out how they fit into her world.

"Morning. I...I think I'm ready. I need to finish...my toast."

She felt tongue-tied, awkward, the words jumping around in her head like a tangle of paper clips, and she couldn't seem to find the ones she needed. She had been doing so well in recent years with the dysphasia that had afflicted her after her brain injury. Seeing Luke again seemed to have jumbled everything up in her head again and the right words seemed as slippery as baby alligators.

"You can take all the time you want now. All day. You don't have to rush. The district attorney canceled our appointment this morning."

Luke did not look happy about that turn of events. Not at all. His eyes were the deep, tumultuous color of a stormy afternoon on the lake.

"Oh no."

"She apparently had a family emergency out of town and ran into the same storm that hit us. But we are on her schedule first thing in the morning."

She could tell the idea didn't make him any happier than it did her. She wanted this cleared up.

"What...am I supposed to do all day here, then? Yesterday was…long here by myself." She had finished her book a few hours after he dropped her off. She had more on her electronic reader but her eyes couldn't focus on it for long stretches at a time.

"I guess you can do more decorating. What's all this?"

She flushed, feeling stupid. What had seemed a good idea the evening before when she had been dying of boredom now appeared silly. Childish, even.

"The house needed…a little freshening up. It seems…sad. Empty. I thought you would have an easier time selling if it were staged…a little better."

His brows rose in surprise and he looked around at the few holiday decorations she had made out of things she found outside.

"I appreciate that but I shouldn't have a hard time selling it. Property in this area goes at a premium these days, especially now that Caine Tech has moved into the old Kilpatrick Boatworks. With values up, it made sense for me to build another house on the land I had and put this one on the market."

It might make economic sense but she wondered whether the kids had struggled with leaving the only home they had ever known. She had no say in his decision, though. As he pointed out so bluntly the day before, she had in effect made him the custodial parent when she left. While legally she still had rights, morally it was a different situation.

She turned away to hide the emotion she was afraid he might see in her eyes. "I saw some paint cans…in one of the bedrooms. Were you planning to repaint before the house goes on the market?"

"That's the plan, anyway, when I get around to it. I don't know when that might be. This is a hectic time of year and I didn't expect to be driving to Oregon and back before the holidays. On the other hand, I guess it beats being in jail over Christmas."

She flushed, feeling guilty all over again at everything she had set into motion that fateful night. "I can paint for you, if you'd like."

He frowned, showing those new lines in his forehead that made him look ruggedly distinguished. "No need. I'll get to it eventually."

"Why wait? I don't mind painting. I...enjoy it, actually."

"You enjoy painting?"

It was much like gardening, taking a fresh canvas and re-invigorating it, bringing life and beauty to something tired.

"There's something...satisfying about giving something a fresh coat of paint, hiding the inevitable dings and scrapes on the wall and helping it...look new again."

He gave her a careful look and she knew she was blushing again, hoping he didn't try to suss out any hidden meaning in her words. Painting was simply painting. It wasn't a meta-phor for anything else.

After a moment, he shrugged. "Knock yourself out. You can find paint supplies in the shed, where we always used to keep them."

"I checked there earlier but it was locked."

"Oh. Right. Um, the code is the same. I never changed it. Your birthday, my birthday and our anniversary."

He had kept her birthday as part of the security code to the shed? Did he think about her each time he punched it in?

She had thrown away the life they could have had. Being back in Haven Point was one painful reminder after another.

Though she sensed it was a futile effort, she decided to press him one more time about letting her see the children while she was here. "Since I will be here an extra day, I would love the chance to see the…children."

His features turned hard. "Did you think my answer would change overnight? No. Still no."

"I only want to see them. You don't even have to tell them who I am. I doubt they remember the person I used to be and I…I don't look the same."

He hadn't said anything about all the plastic surgery she had undergone. She had to wonder what he thought about it. Did he think she had done everything purely for cosmetic reasons?

"They will have no idea I'm their mother. You can introduce me as…a friend."

It was a pitifully weak suggestion, but she was desperate.

"Doesn't matter what *they* know. It's what I know that matters. You're not meeting them. You've done enough to hurt them for the rest of their lives. Abandoning them when they were still babies is going to leave scars on their psyche they will never recover from. I'm not letting you back into their lives to hurt them all over again."

"I only want to see them," she pressed. "What's the harm? Just for a moment."

"No."

Suddenly, she was angry. More furious than she had been in a very long time. She was angry at the circumstances, angry at herself certainly, but also angry at Luke for shutting her out.

"You're not being fair."

She should never have said the words. They were born out of a place of fear and sadness, but she knew as soon as she said them how wrong they were.

His dark expression confirmed it. "Fair?" he said, his voice low and intense. "Let's talk about fair."

"Luke—"

"No. I would like to know what the word means to you. Was it *fair* that you left me to think you were dead for seven years, that you left me to mourn you all this time?"

"No," she said, her voice small.

"Was it fair that you left me to raise the kids by myself? To be the only one there for the first day of kindergarten, the first lost tooth, Bridger's first steps?"

She shook her head. What else could she do?

"I'll tell you what's not fair. For seven years, I've grieved for you, thinking the woman I loved had chosen to end her life. Now, suddenly, I have to accept the idea that that woman didn't die. She just chose to leave and start a new life without us."

The vast pain in the voice of this man who was always so contained with his emotions shocked her, left her reeling.

She had caused so much hurt. Even these past few years, when she had finally begun to heal, she should have come forward and told him everything. She had shown courage in other aspects of her life. She knew she had. So why had she been so very afraid to face Luke with the truth?

She had absolutely no right to be angry with him for not letting her see the children. *No* right. This was a situation she had created herself.

"What's not *fair* is the miserable position you put me in," he went on, his voice fierce. "For seven years I've been sentenced to a hellish limbo, with half the people in town believing I killed you and disposed of you in some hideous way. I couldn't call myself a widower because I didn't know if you were really dead. God knows, I couldn't move on and date someone else, even if any other woman in Lake Haven County would ever twice look at a man like me, who might or might not have murdered his wife."

Her throat closed with emotions, regret and sorrow and guilt. She had to clear them away to speak. "Why...why didn't you try to have me legally declared dead?"

"Because I didn't want to." The raw emotion in his voice seared through her.

"Luke."

His name. That was all she could manage through the tangle of emotions.

He gazed down at her, his expression almost...tortured.

One moment he was skewering her with his furious expression; the next he threw his arms around her, yanked her toward him and lowered his mouth to hers.

Shock held her motionless for only a moment. Then the sheer delicious glory of being in his arms again overwhelmed her. She wrapped her arms around him and returned his kiss with all the pent-up longing she had held inside her these long years of being alone.

The heat that had always been between them flared, wild and unrestrained. His mouth was hard on hers, fierce, demanding. Delicious. There was no trace of tenderness, only anger and loss, betrayal and sorrow and desire, all twisted together.

When he finally yanked his mouth away and released her as if she had scorched him, she stumbled backward, her knees drained of all strength. Her soul felt drained, too.

"Does that answer your question?" he asked, his voice raspy and low. "I never stopped hoping you would come back. Even when I was ninety-nine percent certain you were dead, that tiny one percent of hope wanted desperately to be wrong."

He released a heavy breath and she watched in fascination as he tucked away any trace of emotion, becoming self-contained and expressionless once more.

"Do what you want to the house. Paint or don't paint. I don't care. This place means nothing to me anymore. The kids and I have moved on and are happy in our new house. I just want this one sold and out of my life."

Like her. She meant nothing to him either, that wild, heated kiss notwithstanding. She did her best to blink back tears but was afraid he still saw them.

"I don't know how much I can do in only one day but I'll...I'll try."

He looked as if he wanted to argue but finally gave her one more long look and headed out the door.

After he left, Elizabeth touched her lips, the long-familiar taste lingering there. Oh, how she had missed him.

She still loved him.

Had never stopped.

She collapsed onto the sagging sofa, unable to contain all the emotions raging through her. She loved Luke and wanted what was best for him. That could never be her. Not then and especially not now, with all her baggage.

She might not be able to be part of his life or their children's lives, but she could do one small thing for them. She could freshen up this house a little bit, make it more attractive to prospective buyers.

It was a small gift, but one she wanted desperately to give them.

Chapter Seven

She worked until around noon, until her stomach's grumbling reminded her that a solitary, half-eaten piece of toast was not enough to sustain her through several hours of hard work. She was going to have to find something else to eat.

She had finished prepping the children's bedrooms—taping windows and trim, filling in holes in the walls, covering the wood floors with plastic.

While she welcomed having something to do, the process also left her melancholy. She hadn't been here when Bridger drew on the wall of his bedroom with markers that she could still glimpse traces of. She hadn't seen what artwork Cassie cared about enough to hang in her bedroom.

She was a stranger to her own children. She had tried to stay connected to them in her own pitiful way, coming for secret visits three or four times a year. She couldn't really know them, though. Not from those brief glimpses, on the outside looking in.

By the time she took a break for lunch, her muscles ached and her bad leg was tight. She needed a good hard walk to exercise it.

Out the window, the snow had stopped. Everything was white and beautiful. Suddenly, the small house seemed claustrophobic. She wanted to be out in that magical winter wonderland.

Even as she thought it, fear held her back. What if she fell? The results would be disastrous.

She would use her cane, she decided. As none of the food in the kitchen looked appetizing and she needed some fresh air anyway and to work out the cramp in her leg, she would use her cane to carefully make her way to Haven Point's small downtown area for something to eat.

She thought of some of the restaurants where she used to eat here in Haven Point. Her favorite was Serrano's. Maybe she would just swing over there and grab a bite. No one would recognize her. She looked nothing like Elizabeth Sinclair Hamilton anymore. For the past seven years, she had been Sonia Petrovich Davis, the wounded, damaged widow of a kind man who had reached out to help her on another snowy day.

With a pang, she thought of John Davis, the stranger she had only known a few hours but who had completely changed the course of her life.

Poor man. She whispered a prayer for him, as she always did when he crossed her mind.

They had been two lost souls that night, both grieving for all they had lost. How could she have guessed that his act of kindness in giving her a ride would have such disastrous consequences for them both?

Thinking of John reminded her of his sister, Alice, who

had become one of her biggest supporters and dearest friends. Elizabeth hadn't spoken with her in a few weeks, but they had plans to meet for lunch during the holidays.

Alice, a therapist in Portland, had been pushing her for months to come back to Idaho. Elizabeth could picture her, small, bespectacled, looking at least a decade younger than her sixty years.

She could almost hear her voice in her head.

You'll never be able to move on until you face and embrace your past.

Alice knew everything. She was the only one, besides Elizabeth. When Elizabeth's memory started to come back, when she first started to realize she wasn't Sonia Petrovich Davis after all, John's Russian-born wife of only a few months, she had been so afraid to tell Alice, who had stood by her for years and become her dearest friend. She was an impostor. Not by choice but the strangest of chances.

Alice had been understandably shocked, of course, then unfailingly supportive. In therapy sessions and in their personal interactions, she had been urging Elizabeth to come back to town and face her husband, her children, the life she had left behind.

What would Alice think if she knew Elizabeth was here, that she had returned to Haven Point and was currently standing in the house she had shared with Luke?

She would probably tell her she wasn't done yet. That she had to tell her husband everything, all her ugly secrets.

Elizabeth's stomach grumbled and she sighed. She could sit here in this warm kitchen eating food she didn't want, ashamed and meek. Or she could step out into the world she had left.

She knew what Alice would tell her.

She was tired. She had spent seven years hiding away, lost in her guilt and her fear and her shame. She was tired of being a passive observer in her own life. Hadn't she already made the decision to change the status quo before Luke showed up on her doorstep? She had known it was past time to tell him the truth, to own her mistakes.

She didn't have to be held hostage to her circumstances. Nor did she need to be a hostage in this house. She wanted to be out in that lovely winter afternoon and she needed something to eat. The only one keeping her here, cowering in her fear, was herself.

She squared her shoulders and went looking for her coat and gloves, then picked up her cane with some reluctance, knowing she would need it for stability on the snowy roads.

Outside the little house she and Luke had bought together, she took a deep breath and closed the door behind her. She did indeed feel as if she had walked out of prison.

The December day was beautiful, crisp, the air heavy with the mingled wintry scents of snow and pine and the river, so familiar to her from her childhood.

It snowed occasionally on the Oregon Coast but nothing substantial that stuck for long. They did have winter storms in Cannon Beach, with cold wind blowing off the Pacific and icy rain that soaked through everything.

The previous year, they'd had a terrible storm that had caused extensive flooding and wind damage. She hated those storms. If at all possible, she would hide away in her second-floor apartment of Brambleberry House, tucked under her blankets with a cup of tea and a book and possibly her friend Rosa's dog, Fiona, for extra support.

The changes to Haven Point were obvious as she made her way downtown. When she left, the little hamlet beside the lake had been struggling financially, especially after Ben Kilpatrick closed his family's boatworks. Many of the downtown businesses had been shuttered and empty for years, their facades in dire need of paint and the planter boxes and flower baskets filled with weeds.

Now the town looked prosperous, bustling, with new construction going in and most of the existing storefronts showing signs of recent remodeling. Everything was fresh and new. Charming.

During the past few years of covert visits to town, she had learned what was behind the town's revitalization. She knew Aidan Caine, the famous tech genius, had purchased half the town from Ben Kilpatrick years ago. After relocating a division of Caine Tech to the community, Aidan and his wife, Eliza, were now working on rehabbing the storefronts and bringing in a mix of residential and business development to the area.

How many of those projects had Luke worked on in his capacity as a contractor? He appeared to have been keeping busy with work over the years. She was glad. He was an excellent contractor. Scrupulously honest, hardworking, creative.

It seemed odd to be walking down the street in plain view of everyone, especially after the complicated routines she usually went through to keep her identity secret whenever she visited.

The truth was, nobody was really paying attention to her anyway. People were going about their business shopping or heading into restaurants. She had probably worried for nothing.

Still, she gripped her cane more tightly as she walked into Serrano's, the town's favorite gathering spot.

The restaurant had undergone remodeling as well. The

interior seemed brighter, more welcoming than she remembered. The young hostess gave her a polite smile that held no trace of recognition.

"Hi. Welcome to Serrano's. How many in your party?"

Ah. The dreaded question. "One," she answered. She should be used to answering that by now.

"Great. Follow me." The woman led her to a booth in the front window, where she would be on display to everyone in town. She almost told the hostess to move her somewhere quiet in the corner but decided against it. The whole point of being back in town was to tell people she was alive and clear Luke's name. It made no sense for her to hide away.

"Here you go," the hostess said, handing her a menu.

Not everything had changed. The menu was still similar and she recognized her favorite soup. She ordered a bowl as well as a half sandwich, then proceeded to people-watch out the window while she ate.

She used to hate eating alone, but the past seven years had changed her perspective. She had learned to take advantage of the time to catch up on her reading, write in her journal, or observe the world around her for patterns and connections.

Now, for instance, she watched a steady stream of women heading into the darling store on the corner, Point Made Flowers and Gifts.

What were they all doing?

She knew the shop was owned by McKenzie Shaw, who had been a friend of hers in high school. For years, she'd been dying to go in whenever she returned to town but had feared McKenzie might recognize her. She had no excuse now.

After finishing her meal and paying the tab, she walked outside. With the typical fickle weather on Lake Haven, the charming afternoon had turned cold and blustery.

Funny, how the mood of Lake Haven could shift so abruptly. Warm and serene one moment, turning angry the next.

She was glad of her cane and her coat as she made her way across the street to the gift shop, unable to resist her curiosity any longer.

With heart pounding, she pushed open the door and was met by the smell of cinnamon and clove and pine, as if Christmas had been bottled into a scent. She was also greeted by a large red poodle that instantly made her miss Fiona.

"Hello there," she murmured to the dog, who wagged her puff of a tail and planted her haunches next to Elizabeth.

"Be with you in a minute," a voice she recognized as belonging to McKenzie called out.

"No hurry," she answered. From the back room, she heard women's voices in conversation. Again, she had to wonder what everyone was doing here, but she turned her attention to enjoying the store.

This was her favorite kind of place, filled with flowers and crafts and all the things she loved. At the home and garden center where she worked in Cannon Beach, she had tried to bring this same kind of flair but wasn't entirely sure she had managed to pull it off.

Hearing women's laughter made her immediately miss Melissa and Rosa. Rosa, especially, would probably spend hours browsing the handmade unique items that filled the shelves. Rosa ran a gift store in Cannon Beach, one she had taken over from her aunt Anna. Elizabeth knew she loved visiting other stores to see what merchants did to display their wares.

McKenzie was particularly creative, using old milk crates and antique suitcases stacked onto each other. Elizabeth found treasures around every corner.

The adorable dog followed close behind her, making Elizabeth wish she could sit down on the floor and pet that curly reddish-brown fur.

A few moments later, McKenzie Shaw emerged from the back room. Not Shaw anymore, Elizabeth remembered. She had overheard gossip during visits here that her old friend had married Ben Kilpatrick. It was McKenzie, mayor of Haven Point, who had been largely responsible for Caine Tech moving to town, and she had been heavily involved in the dramatic revitalization.

"Hi there. Welcome to Point Made."

"Thank you," she said quietly, doing her best to keep the nerves out of her voice. "You have a...lovely store."

McKenzie smiled. "All of our items are crafted by local artisans and make the perfect gift for everyone on your shopping list."

"I can see that. I especially...love your...floral arrangements. Where did you find the...globe amaranth?"

McKenzie's attention seemed to sharpen and she gave her a closer look. "I have a supplier in town who grows them and dries them for me. They're spectacular, aren't they?"

"Yes. I've never seen that particular color."

She had always loved gardening, working with her hands in the dirt, but had never realized what a knack she had for growing things and for floral arranging until she left town. Discovering that particular skill had been an unexpected gift, one she had come to cherish.

"You know your flowers. Are you a florist?"

"I work in a...nursery on the Oregon Coast," she said.

"Oh, that's a beautiful area with spectacular flowers. I'm always jealous of your growing season."

She had come to cherish that, too, the wild Pacific coastline with its deep, mysterious forests, steep cliffs, gorgeous lighthouses.

Since leaving the rehab center in Portland, she had come to call Cannon Beach home. She had friends there, people who cared about her, yet she had never truly felt she belonged anywhere but here.

"You might like to see this, then."

McKenzie gestured toward a corner of the store that Elizabeth hadn't yet explored. There, growing in pride of place, was a large blue Phalaenopsis orchid.

"Oh my," she breathed, struck by the luxurious blossoms and the deep, rich color. "It's stunning."

"Thanks. I've been growing it for years. People who don't know flowers do not appreciate how much work goes into orchids."

"It's beautiful. Thank you…for sharing it with me."

McKenzie's smile was genuine. "You're welcome. Any fellow flower lover is an instant friend."

They were old friends, not instant friends. Elizabeth wanted to say something about the slumber parties they used to have together and the prank they had played on some football players their senior year. She still wasn't sure how to handle this whole reveal, so she opted to remain silent for now while she figured it out.

"I'm McKenzie Kilpatrick. This is my store and I see you've met my best friend, Paprika."

She waited, obviously expecting Elizabeth to offer her name in return.

"Hello," she said, not sure how else to answer.

"Are you staying in town or just passing through?"

Elizabeth had no idea how to answer that. "I'm in town… for only a few days."

"You picked a gorgeous time to be here. Lake Haven is especially beautiful at Christmastime. Too bad you weren't here last weekend when we had our Lights on the Lake Festival."

She remembered those festivals, when boat owners would decorate their watercraft with lights and holiday scenes and float between Haven Point and Shelter Springs. It used to be one of the highlights of the year for her.

"I'm sure it was...lovely."

"It's always a good time, but to be honest, I'm always kind of glad when it's over and we can focus on the holidays."

"Hey, Kenz. We're running out of wire. Do you have more?" a woman called from the back room.

McKenzie rolled her eyes at Elizabeth. "Sorry about that. We've got a project going on in the other room. We're making wreaths to auction off to benefit a good cause."

"Oh. What a...nice thing to do."

McKenzie had always reached out to help those in need. It was part of her nature, one of the things that drew people to her. She was always thinking about others.

"They've actually turned out really well. Would you like to come see?"

Elizabeth hesitated, not certain if she ought to barge into what seemed a private party. All her instincts were telling her she should make her way back to the little house on Riverbend Road.

McKenzie was hard to resist, though. She smiled, gesturing toward the back room, and after a moment, Elizabeth followed.

The luscious aroma of evergreen cuttings came from the large pile on the table in front of a dozen women who were talking and laughing and sharing stories.

Elizabeth recognized several of the women. McKenzie's

sister Devin was sitting in a corner talking to a couple of older women, sisters and best friends Eppie and Hazel Brewer.

She saw Wynona Bailey, who had been another friend of hers in school and who was also Elliot Bailey's younger sister. Wyn, and her younger sister, Katrina, along with Kat's friend Samantha Fremont, appeared to be struggling to twist the evergreen around the frames.

Elizabeth wanted to wave and slip back out the door but couldn't resist offering a little advice. "If you…use one continuous wire, you don't have to make as many wire cuts. The greenery will…hide it."

McKenzie looked impressed. "You are so right. That would be much easier. Everybody, listen to our new expert. I'm sorry. I didn't catch your name."

What would these women say if she calmly announced she was Elizabeth Sinclair Hamilton, back from the dead? She tried to imagine their shocked reaction and couldn't quite wrap her head around it. Yes, she needed to go public with her identity but wasn't quite sure this was the proper venue.

"My friends call me…Sonia," she murmured.

"Sonia, I don't suppose you might have a few minutes to help us out, do you? The wreaths are being auctioned at a party this weekend."

What was waiting for her at that empty little house? Memories, sadness and paint cans.

"Sure," she said on impulse. "I…would be happy to…help."

She would only stay awhile, she told herself, then would return to the house.

A woman she didn't know moved her chair to make room for Elizabeth, offering a bright smile as she did. Another handed her some gloves and an empty wreath form and she went to work.

This was her comfort zone, where she felt most at ease. She quickly covered the form with wired evergreens, then added picks from the selection in the middle of the table.

The women were chatting about their booth's success during the Lights on the Lake Festival and things they wanted to do differently the next year. They were obviously good friends. Elizabeth was content to listen to the gossip, unobtrusively trying to put names with faces for some that she only recognized vaguely.

"Do you have family around here? You seem really familiar to me."

It took Elizabeth a few moments to realize McKenzie's question was directed at her. Again, she had no idea how to answer. She had a family here. A husband, children. Of course, she couldn't say so without going into the entire complicated story.

"Not anymore. What did you say the...wreaths were for again?" she asked, to head off any more questions.

As she had hoped, her diversion worked.

"We belong to a group called the Haven Point Helping Hands. Wherever we see a need in our community, we try to step up and fill it. Sometimes it's the library. Sometimes it's the food bank. Sometimes it's a struggling family in town. This year, we're trying to build an adaptive playground for children with disabilities. We've raised most of the money and hope to break ground in the spring."

"We love to help," Eliza Caine said. "But most of the time, we're really only looking for any excuse to get together."

Elizabeth settled back into the work, grateful for the chance to sit and listen to the murmur of women's voices. There was something soothing about it. Restful, even.

She had missed her friends. Even before she left, she had

shut out those close friendships she had here. Perhaps if she had reached out during her darkest days or hadn't been so very worried about people thinking less of her because of her inability to cope with the stress of her life, she might have handled things better.

"Don't you think, Sonia?"

It took her a moment to shift gears in her brain. Changes of topic were always difficult for her to keep up with since the accident. "I'm sorry. I was thinking of something else. Could you repeat the question?"

Devin, McKenzie's older sister, gave her a reassuring smile. "We can be a bit overwhelming as a group, I'm afraid," she said.

"It's not that. I'm sorry. I think what you're doing here is…wonderful."

"Maybe you can start a similar group where you come from," McKenzie suggested.

"Where is that?" Eliza asked.

"I'm from…all over, but for the last few years I've been living on the…Oregon Coast."

"I love that area," Hazel offered. "It's gorgeous. Plus, you sometimes can run into really sexy surfers, am I right?"

Elizabeth blinked. The woman had to be at least eighty by now. "I…suppose."

Others were sharing their favorite areas on the Oregon Coast when a newcomer entered the workroom, pulling off a scarf and hat as she came in.

Elizabeth's stomach dropped and she suddenly wanted to disappear.

"Megan. There you are. I was afraid you weren't going to be able to make it," McKenzie exclaimed.

"Sorry I'm late. We were doing all the checkouts for the

conference that's been at the hotel and there were some problems with the billing. I'm here now, though. What did I miss?"

Megan gave a general smile to the group. Then Elizabeth felt her gaze stop on her. The other woman frowned.

Megan couldn't possibly recognize her, could she? The reconstructive plastic surgery had done a thorough job of erasing most traces of the woman she had been.

Somehow she sensed that Megan saw past it anyway and knew exactly who she was.

"Megan. This is Sonia," McKenzie said. "I'm afraid I forgot your last name. In the spirit of the season, she kindly offered to help us with the wreaths. She works at a garden center in Oregon and is obviously an expert. She can make three wreaths to every one that the rest of us finish. Isn't it nice of her to help us?"

"Lovely." Megan's tone conveyed exactly the opposite of her words.

"If you want to eat first, there's some soup in the slow cookers on the counter."

"I'm suddenly not very hungry," Megan said.

"What do you hear from our stubborn older brother?" Wyn asked her.

It was obvious from the sudden tension rippling through the room that everyone was worried about the FBI agent.

"Nothing. But I'm sure he's fine. He'll get in touch when he can."

Next to her, Katrina squeezed her arm. "He's tough. Don't worry. He'll be home driving us all crazy before you know it."

The conversation moved to Katrina's children—children Elizabeth had no idea she even had. She put her head down working hard to finish her wreath. When she was done, she pushed her chair away from the table, driven by a fierce urge to escape before Megan announced her real identity to everyone.

She had to come clean to these women, the real movers and shakers of Haven Point, but she wasn't ready to do that yet.

"Thank you for…letting me help you, but I'm afraid I have to…go," she answered.

"Oh, too bad," McKenzie said, still looking closely at her as if trying to figure out why she seemed familiar. "You were so much help. Thank you!"

"Good…good luck with your fund-raiser."

She grabbed her coat and the despised cane, offered a stiff smile to the room in general, then hurried back to the main area of the store. She was almost to the door when she realized someone had followed her.

Megan.

Dread washed over her and she turned, gripping her cane tightly.

She found Megan glaring at her, features tight with anger and her eyes blazing. "I know who you are. You're Elizabeth."

"Yes." What else could she say?

"I can't believe you have the nerve to walk into town as if nothing has happened, as if you're just some kindly stranger passing by and offering to help out."

She had not offered. She had been enlisted by McKenzie. And if she'd had the slightest idea that Megan would be there, she never would have walked back into that workroom.

"Why did you tell them your name is Sonia? The least you can do is start telling everyone the truth so you can get Luke off the hook."

"Don't…you think Luke deserves that truth before…everyone else?"

"I think Luke deserved the truth seven years ago. You have no idea what he and your children have been through since you walked away, do you?" Megan demanded, each word sharp and vicious.

Elizabeth gripped her cane, fully aware her sister-in-law didn't want her to answer.

"Everywhere they go, whispers follow. For seven years, he has lived under a cloud of suspicion. It's been horrible. A nightmare. All because one selfish woman walked away without a backward look."

Oh, that was so very untrue. She had done nothing but look back over those years.

"I'm...sorry," she said, the words wholly inadequate.

"If you were sorry, you would have come back a long time ago," Megan snapped. "If you were truly sorry, you wouldn't have left in the first place."

She had no way to defend herself against the truth. "I know."

"They're better off without you now. All three of them. The kids barely remember you and Luke needs to move on. My brother has had enough sorrow and grief in his life. He deserves to find a good, honorable woman who is willing to truly be a partner to him. Something you've never been, even before you left."

The fury coming out of Megan hurt more than she'd expected. She and her sister-in-law had once been dear friends. She had considered Megan the sister she never had. Now it was clear the woman despised her as much as Luke did.

"I don't know what your game is, coming back in and out of town. When Luke told me that, I was so angry. Now I recognize you. I've seen you at the kids' games and plays and things. You can't keep doing that. I need to say this now, while I have the chance. As I see it, you only have one option. Clear Luke's name, sign the divorce papers and walk away. That's what you have to do. Nothing else."

Elizabeth released a breath, realizing her legs were trembling. She would have fallen if not for the cane.

"Finish up here with the legal system and then leave for good. That's the best thing you can do now for your children and for Luke."

Without another word, Megan turned around and returned to the workroom, leaving Elizabeth shattered, shaky, sick.

She felt as if she had just been shivved.

She knew Megan had been acting out of protectiveness for the children and Luke. She was grateful the woman cared so much for their well-being, but her stark words still burned.

Megan was absolutely correct. Elizabeth's only role in town was to clear Luke's name and free him once and for all so he could finally go on with his life.

She was fooling herself if she thought she had the right to anything else.

Chapter Eight

"Hurry up, kids. You've got ten minutes."

"Why do we have to go so early? School doesn't start for an hour," Bridger complained.

Of late, Luke's son had picked up a bit of a bad attitude in the mornings. He liked to dawdle through his breakfast, stop to tease his sister, take forever finding his shoes and socks. Luke had finally resorted to having Bridger set out everything he would need the night before so their mornings weren't so hectic. He had even printed a checklist for Bridger to go through, which usually did a pretty good job of helping the boy stay on task.

"I told you last night, remember? I have an appointment this morning. I'm taking you to the inn and Aunt Megan will take you to school."

"You never told us what kind of appointment you have," Cassie said with a suspicious look. She had been giving him a lot of those looks lately. He had a feeling his daughter suspected something was up, starting with his trip to Oregon.

"Business. That's all. Come on. Grab your backpack."

"Do you remember that we have rehearsals for the Christmas show every day after school the rest of the week except today? We won't be able to take the bus those days. You'll have to pick us up at school at five."

Shoot. He'd forgotten to tell his housekeeper, who filled in with childcare after school. "I'll let Jan know. Don't worry. I'll figure it out."

Childcare was by far the toughest hurdle he had to overcome as a single father with a demanding job as a contractor. Sometimes he could be flexible with his schedule, taking the kids along with him to job sites or planning his work around their after-school activities.

Sometimes, like now, he had a million irons in the fire. Jan Mulvaney was wonderful to help him out with errands and light housekeeping and running the kids to practices and things. She had a busy life with a dozen grandkids of her own and sometimes he had to turn to Megan for help. Once Megan and Elliot married, his sister wouldn't be as available. Eventually they would want to start their own family, which would leave her even less time to help him out.

He selfishly hoped that didn't happen for a year or two, until Cassie was old enough to take on more responsibilities for herself and her brother if Luke had job commitments.

Whatever happened, he would figure it out. He always did.

Yeah, it would be better for everyone if Luke didn't have to juggle everything on his own, but that wasn't the way his life had turned out. He had long ago given up the temptation to dwell on self-pity.

"You'll take the bus today, though, right?"

She nodded. "We don't start practicing until tomorrow."

"I can pick you up after rehearsals the rest of the week. I'll plan on five, but if that changes, call me." He hated that his ten-year-old daughter had a phone, but that was the reality of their world.

He checked his watch. He was picking up Elizabeth in less than half an hour. "I really do need to go. Are you guys about done?"

Bridger pushed away from the table and checked his list. "I have to brush my teeth and put on my shoes. That's all."

"Can you help me with my hair?" Cassie asked.

Oh, the dreaded question. Above all the single-dad issues he faced, hair was his Rubicon. He would rather have a long talk with her about menstruation than have to wield a curling iron.

"I can do braids. You know that's about it."

"I don't want braids today. I was hoping for maybe a messy bun."

"I'm afraid you'll have to ask your aunt if you want anything but a ponytail or a braid. You know hair isn't my specialty."

"You won't even try," she groused, hitting a nerve since he knew she was right. "My hair always looks so dumb. I look like I'm five."

"I think you always look very nice."

"You're supposed to say that. You're my dad. Which is the whole problem."

"That I'm your dad?"

"Yes." She stomped away to pick up her backpack with the rapid-fire mood shifts that had become more common lately. "You never even try to do anything but braids or ponytails. I bet Mom would have been able to help me with my hair."

Bridger sent her a shocked look, probably because Cassie rarely referred to their mother.

"Maybe," Luke replied evenly. "But she's not here, is she? I am and I'm doing the best I can, kid."

Cassie had the grace to look a little ashamed. "I know." She fidgeted with her backpack strap. "I just get so tired of boring ponytails."

He sighed. Why was this parenting gig so hard? It seemed like there was always some area where he was failing. Homework patrol, proper nutrition planning, extracurricular activities. Now hair. He couldn't do everything.

"Maybe we could try getting up a half hour earlier and experiment a little," he offered.

Her chin wobbled a little and he was horribly afraid she was going to cry. What had he said now? The last six months or so as she approached ten, he felt like he had to watch every word or he might set her off.

"Thanks. I'm sorry. You're the best dad in the whole world."

She threw her arms around his waist and he gave her a hug in return. Her words were ridiculously far from the truth, but he'd take them this morning as he prepared to meet with Elizabeth and an attorney who wanted to put him in prison.

"And you're the best daughter."

"What about me?" Bridger asked, making Cassie roll her eyes.

"You're the biggest pest," she said, but she hugged her brother, too.

Somehow, they made it out the door without more drama, other than Bridger suddenly reminding Luke as they loaded up into his pickup that he was supposed to take two dozen cookies to school the next day.

Since the school had a strictly store-bought treat policy, Luke figured he could swing into the bakery on his way home and pick up a couple dozen sugar cookies.

Until she and Elliot married and moved into a house he was buying along the lakeshore, Megan was living in a small cottage on the property of the inn she had inherited from her grandmother, his stepmother's mother. Though she was no longer actively involved in the day-to-day running of the property, only in an advisory capacity, she still liked to stay close and help out where needed.

When they arrived at her place, Megan was standing outside on her porch, photographing the early morning light coming up over the mountains above the lake.

"Gorgeous day, isn't it?" she asked.

"Sure," Luke said. He was too nervous about the upcoming meeting to pay much attention, though now that she pointed it out, he noted the amber and violet streaks coming up over the mountain.

"Good morning, darling children," Megan said. Though she smiled, Luke noted circles under her eyes. He had a feeling she wasn't sleeping well, too worried about Elliot and his assignment.

"Can we go grab some breakfast?" Bridger asked after stowing his backpack in her small living room.

"You just had cereal," Luke reminded him.

"But they have scrambled eggs at the inn breakfast. You're always saying I need more protein in the mornings so I can focus better," Bridger said.

He really hated when his own words came back to haunt him.

Megan grinned. "It's fine with me. We're only at half capacity today. There should be plenty of food."

"But I wanted you to help me with my hair, like I texted you," Cassie said.

"How about this? We work on your hair for fifteen minutes or so then head up to the inn to grab eggs before I take you to school. Does that work, Bridger?"

"Works for me," he said cheerfully, plopping onto her easy chair and pulling out his book.

Whew. Problem solved. "All right," Luke said. "I've got to go. Have a great day at school, both of you. Thanks, sis."

"Bye, Dad," his kids said in unison. Cassie gave him an extra-long hug, as if to apologize for her outburst earlier, but Bridger only waved him off, already engrossed in the book.

"Today's the day," Megan said after she walked out onto the porch with him into the cold morning. "You get to clear your name and sign the divorce papers in one fell swoop."

"Yes." He should be in the mood to celebrate, shouldn't he? So why did he have this ache in his gut, this sense that he was heading toward deep waters he didn't know if he had the skills to navigate?

He should never have kissed Elizabeth the day before. The memory of that embrace had haunted him all night long, reminding him of how very much he had missed holding her, kissing her, making love to her.

He had been alone too damn long. As he'd told her, he didn't feel like he could date anyone else when there was that small chance that she wasn't dead. What did he have to offer another woman? A couple of kids and a broken heart.

He hadn't kissed a woman in years. He'd forgotten how delicious it was to sink into her mouth, to taste her arousal, to feel her tremble at his touch.

He didn't need to remember this right now, as he was about

to pick her up to go clear his name and then sign divorce papers, damn it. He pushed the memory away.

"I saw her yesterday," Megan was saying. "She wandered into Point Made Flowers and Gifts, right in the middle of a Haven Point Helping Hands gathering. When I showed up late, I found her sitting in the middle of the crowd and making wreaths like she belonged there."

He frowned. "Really?"

Why would Elizabeth go to McKenzie Kilpatrick's florist shop? She and McKenzie had been friends long ago but he wouldn't have expected her to show up in public like that.

"Did she tell everyone who she was?"

"No. If she had, everyone would have been hounding me with questions after she left, but nobody said a word. She introduced herself as Sonia."

Sonia. Why had she changed everything, even her name?

"She doesn't look at all the same. She's like a totally different person. I never would have recognized her, if you hadn't mentioned that she has been coming to town in disguise. What is that about? The plastic surgery, the assumed name. Is she a spy or something?"

A spy. He hadn't considered that option. There was another one to add to his list. He supposed anything was possible, but somehow espionage didn't seem very likely. Elliot would know more about that than Luke.

Whatever the reason, he would find out in a few hours.

"How did you know it was her?"

Megan shrugged. "I can't explain it, but the moment I walked in, I just knew. I remembered you saying she's been coming back to town and the woman I saw at McKenzie's store looked familiar. Not Elizabeth-familiar but still like someone I knew I had seen before. Then I remembered seeing her around town a few times, sitting in the back at base-ball games or whatever, wearing sunglasses and scarves like some kind of movie star in hiding. I always thought she was someone's aunt from out of town or something. I can't be-lieve I never once suspected it was Elizabeth."

He still couldn't quite believe that part of this puzzle him-self. Why had she never come forward? Why the big mystery?

Nerves twisted through him. He would know everything in a few hours, whether he wanted to or not.

"I can't wait for you to have your life back," Megan said.

"Yeah. Won't that be great," he said, though some part of him couldn't help wondering what it would be like to have his *wife* back instead.

His stomach was in knots as he pulled up to the little house on Riverbend Road.

A snowman smiled from the fenced front yard—a snow-man that definitely had not been there the day before.

Elizabeth must have built it herself sometime the previous day. He tried to picture her out here alone in the snow, roll-ing a snowball around and around until it was big enough, then another and another.

The image left him with a strange lump in his throat that he quickly swallowed away. He wouldn't feel sorry for her. She had made her choices.

He marched up to the door and rang the doorbell, though it felt strange to do so at his own damn house. She answered a few seconds later, as if she had been waiting for him.

"Hi. Sorry. I'm almost ready. I just need to finish my hair."

Apparently his whole day was centered around females and their hair. "We still have time. The appointment isn't for another forty-five minutes and it's only a fifteen-minute drive to Shelter Springs."

He was perpetually early, figuring it was better to be too early than too late.

"I shouldn't be long."

She hurried away, leaving him standing in the living room she had decorated for the holidays. He really needed to get the kids' tree up. It had been on the agenda for the weekend, but that phone call warning him about his impending arrest had kind of pushed holiday decorating down on his priority list.

A few moments later, she came out wearing a coat and wrapping what looked to be a new scarf around her neck.

"Okay. I guess I'm ready."

Her hands were trembling, the only sign she gave that she might be nervous. It annoyed him more than it should. She had no right to be nervous. He was the one whose future was at stake here.

As they walked back outside, they passed that snowman again. "Aren't you a little old to build snowmen?"

She looked embarrassed. "I haven't lived where there's this much...snow in a long time and couldn't resist. I...didn't sleep well last night and finally...decided to go for a walk in the snow early this morning. Building a snowman was a...a whim."

He again felt that wave of sympathy, thinking of her out there by herself in the snow, but he pushed it away.

If she was alone, it was by choice. She had a family who had loved her once and she had walked away from them all.

He drove in silence down the familiar road around Lake Haven toward Shelter Springs, his mind on the appointment ahead.

"It's so beautiful," Elizabeth said when they were about halfway between the two towns. "I had forgotten."

"Beautiful."

"Look at how the sun…gleams on the snow. How the trees seem to be…wearing fringy coats. The contrast of blue and white on the lake. All I remembered was…was how dark and cold the winters could be here. Not how…magical life can look after a storm."

His hands tightened on the steering wheel. Yeah, it could look magical. Or it could look icy and frozen. It all depended on perspective.

How was he going to get past the next hour in her company? He hated being attracted to her all over again or the warm, tender feelings trying to take root inside him like the first brave daffodils poking through the snow in the spring.

Damn her for making him feel again. He didn't want to. He had turned everything off after she left. She had *made* him become as cold and sterile as that landscape.

He pulled into the courthouse parking lot a moment later and turned off the engine.

"Here we are. Let's get this done so you can sign the divorce papers and go back to Oregon on the earliest flight."

She opened her mouth as if to say something. Instead, she closed it again, reached for her door handle and slid out of the vehicle, leaving him feeling as if he'd just crushed the first daffodil of the year and ground it to dust beneath his boot.

Chapter Nine

Divorce.

She didn't even like to think about the word. It was ugly and hard and so very final. She had known it was coming. What other possibility was there for them, under the circumstances?

It still hurt.

Her stomach ached, probably because she hadn't been able to swallow anything that morning. She felt shaky, light-headed, and her heart was pounding so hard she was surprised he didn't say something about it.

She did some circle breathing in a futile effort to steady her nerves. She had nothing to be nervous about, she reminded herself. She was only here to tell him exactly what had happened seven years ago.

She could only hope her words didn't fail her or, heaven forbid, that she didn't have a seizure right in the middle of this appointment with the district attorney.

No. She could handle this. She only had to keep her thoughts collected, stick to the truth. Everything she said could be verified. She could bring in plenty of people who had been part of her strange, twisted journey. Doctors, rehab specialists, therapists. John's sister, Alice.

She rubbed her suddenly clammy palms on her trousers.

She could do this. No big deal. All she had to do for this appointment was pretend she was there again in Alice's safe office with the zero gravity chair and the saltwater aquarium and the ferns in wicker plant stands.

The panic receded a little but didn't completely leave her. She knew it wouldn't until she was done with this.

Once the truth was out there, then what?

She had no idea, which was probably a major reason for her nerves. Would Luke hate her for the choices she had made and her decision to stay away?

She almost laughed, though she knew there was a touch of hysteria to it. He already hated her. How much more could he despise her?

The historic courthouse in Shelter Springs, the neighboring town that served as the county seat in the Lake Haven area, was brightly decorated for the holidays. A huge Christmas tree with giant blue and silver ornaments greeted them when they walked inside and garlands had been draped up the steps with more of the huge orbs.

Her knee felt shaky as she walked beside him. She probably should have brought her cane along, knowing this would be stressful emotionally and physically for her. A little additional support never hurt, wherever she could find it.

She could do this. She had managed plenty of hard things before.

He marched purposefully up the staircase, barely looking to make sure she was still coming with him.

She was almost tempted to turn around and flee through the massive front doors. She had done that once, though, and just look how well that turned out for her.

She thought about taking the elevator but decided against it. She lived on the second floor of Brambleberry House, despite Rosa's and Melissa's repeated efforts to persuade her to move down to Melissa's apartment on the first floor. Elizabeth needed that climb. It represented far more than the daily effort it took to grip the railing and move one step at a time.

Just as she made that walk every day, she could do this one. She was only to the landing when Luke must have realized she was not beside him. He came back down and held out an arm, without saying anything.

She refused it. "I'm fine. I don't need help."

Still, he stayed by her side as she made her slow way up the stairs. He was as tense as she was, she suddenly realized. She had been so wrapped up in her own nerves, she hadn't really noticed, but now she saw his shoulders were tight, his jaw set.

On the second floor of the building, he paused outside a door with a brass sign that read Christina Torres, Lake Haven District Attorney.

"This is it." His voice was raspy.

"Yes."

"Are you okay? Need some water or something?"

"No. I'm fine."

For the first time since he had shown up on her doorstep in Cannon Beach, she saw something like regret on his face. "I'm sorry I had to drag you here. I know you didn't want to come back and face all the questions. But I have to clear my name."

"I know. It doesn't matter. It's fine. I was going to…to tell you everything anyway. I know you don't believe me, but it's the truth. I'm only sorry it took me so long to feel… strong enough."

He looked as if he wanted to say something else but must have decided against it. Instead, he pushed the door and walked inside.

"Hi, Louise."

"Oh. Hi, Mr. Hamilton. You're here." The middle-aged receptionist looked suddenly nervous, as any normal woman would be when confronted with a tough, dangerous-looking man who radiated tension.

"Yeah. Is she back?"

"Yes. She came in on the red-eye. She's had a long night. Are you sure you don't want to reschedule?"

"No. I want to get this over with."

"All right. Ms. Torres is on another call right now but should be ready for you in a moment. Go ahead and take a seat."

She forced a smile at them both, stealing furtive looks at Elizabeth. Her nameplate read Louise Reeder and she seemed familiar in one of those *I swear I know you somehow* ways, but she couldn't quite place her. She thought perhaps Louise had worked at the hospital where Elizabeth had given birth to Cassie and Bridger.

Luke chose to stand but Elizabeth was afraid her knees wouldn't support her much longer. She sank onto the sofa, feeling self-conscious. Those furtive looks were becoming more obvious. No doubt the receptionist was curious about her identity, wondering if she really was the elusive Elizabeth Sinclair Hamilton.

How shortsighted she had been. Why had it never occurred

to her that people might not believe her when she said she was Elizabeth?

What if all this was for nothing and Luke ended up being arrested and going on trial anyway?

Her stomach ached again and she pressed a hand to the nerves fluttering there. Oh, how she wished Melissa or Rosa could be here with her. She wasn't sure she had the strength to get through this on her own.

She focused again on her breathing. By the time the receptionist's phone buzzed fifteen minutes later, Elizabeth hadn't quite achieved a level of zen but most of her nausea had subsided.

Luke, on the other hand, looked more and more grim with every passing moment.

"She's ready for you now," the receptionist said stiffly.

"Thanks, Louise," Luke said. He headed for the attorney's door. Again, Elizabeth fought the urge to rush out the office and down the stairs, but she took one last deep breath and followed him.

"Good luck," she thought she heard Louise mutter, which struck her as more ominous than encouraging.

The district attorney's office had that sort of pretentious, over-fancy look of some bureaucratic spaces. Designed to either impress or intimidate, it was dark-paneled and oppressive, with heavy lamps and built-in bookshelves that displayed precisely ordered law books.

Behind the massive desk was an incongruously diminutive woman several inches shorter than Elizabeth, slight with elegant salt-and-pepper hair cut in a pageboy. A plate on her desk read Christina Torres, District Attorney. She seemed young for such a weighty job.

She didn't rise to greet them but gestured to two chairs in

front of her desk. "Mr. Hamilton. It's highly irregular for me to talk to you without your attorney present."

"I don't need or want my attorney. I told you that before and I'll say it again. That's also exactly what I told him."

"You should know I will be recording this discussion. I am an officer of the court and you should know that anything you say can and will be used against you."

"Since you took over as acting DA, you've made it clear you are hell-bent on charging me in the disappearance of my wife, any way you can. Evidence or not. You won't listen to your own law enforcement officers when they assure you my wife isn't dead."

"You mean Sheriff Bailey, the brother of FBI Special Agent Elliot Bailey, who will be marrying your sister in a few months? I wonder why I have chosen to take his counsel with a grain of salt."

He frowned. "Because you're an obstinate lawyer who came into office with a preconceived grudge against me and feel like you have something to prove in order to keep your temporary office. You think a sensational murder trial is the way to stir up publicity and keep your name in the headlines so you can win the next election. We both know I'm a pawn to your political aspirations."

Elizabeth might have chosen a more conciliatory approach. She didn't think antagonizing the woman was the best way to persuade her to a different point of view. But what did she know?

"You say I don't have evidence but an independent review of the case file by the state bureau of investigation says otherwise."

"They only looked at the skewed facts you fed them."

"You have to admit, those facts look damning, Mr. Hamilton. You can't deny the police were called on a domestic disturbance only a few days before your wife disappeared."

Oh. She had completely forgotten that day. Elizabeth cringed. Luke hadn't hurt her. She had been the one out of control that day, on a new medication that had bizarre and unwanted side effects. That was the day she had begged him to tell her he thought their family would be better off without her.

Luke had been patient when she cried and yelled and begged him to divorce her and find someone *healthy*. Unfortunately, some of this had happened on the front lawn, where some people who were house-sitting for neighbors had seen. They had ended up calling the police, which had sobered her enough, and she had slept for twelve hours straight.

Oh, she had been a hot mess. Why hadn't he filed for divorce?

"That was a misunderstanding, as I've explained to you and to the police. And to your predecessors numerous times over the past seven years. None of them found sufficient cause to arrest me, but the facts of the case don't appear to matter to you. You won't listen to your own law enforcement officers and you won't listen to me. The only way I can think to clear my name is for you to hear it from the horse's mouth."

She wasn't sure how she liked being a horse's mouth but she supposed it beat the other end.

"Christina Torres, I'd like you to meet my wife. Elizabeth Sinclair Hamilton."

Instead of looking impressed by this dramatic declaration, the district attorney merely raised an eyebrow.

"You really think I'm going to fall for that?"

"Fall for what?"

"You say this is your wife but she looks nothing like the

pictures I've seen of Elizabeth. You probably just hired some two-bit actress to pretend to be your wife. Do you have any idea how much trouble you could be in for this prank?"

"It's no prank," Elizabeth said. To her dismay, her voice wobbled. "I am...the woman he says I am. His...wife."

Not for long, but that was beside the point.

Christina Torres leaned forward and focused a laser-sharp gaze on her. "Exactly what I would expect a paid actress to say. Where's the proof?"

As Elizabeth Sinclair Hamilton, she had never had reason to be fingerprinted, so she couldn't offer that as proof. "My word is all I have now, but if you need further...evidence, you can test my DNA against my...children."

Luke appeared shocked at the suggestion, as if it had never occurred to him.

The DA looked intrigued at her suggestion, though Elizabeth suspected she still thought her a brazen opportunist.

"All right. That sounds like a reasonable idea. I'll play your game for now because I'm interested in seeing how far you can take it."

"Will you...test my DNA?"

"Oh, undoubtedly. Meanwhile, if you are indeed Elizabeth Sinclair, why did you leave, why did you change your appearance and where the hell have you been for seven years?"

She sighed. Here was the moment she had been dreading, if not for those entire seven years, then at least for the last few, once she was back in her right mind.

"That is...a very long story."

Christina Torres sat back in her chair, a pen in her hands. "I've blocked out a half hour. You've got that long to convince me you are Elizabeth Hamilton. Starting now."

The words tangled in her head, chasing each other around

and around. Her dysphasia of speech always hit worse when she was under stress and she could imagine few things more stressful than this moment in her life, when she had to confess everything.

Telling her story to this woman with the cold, appraising eyes was not nearly as difficult as having to tell her story to Luke.

"I don't...know where to start," she admitted, hating that her voice sounded so timid and weak.

"Why don't you start with the night Elizabeth Sinclair Hamilton disappeared."

"The night I...left, you mean."

Ms. Torres frowned. "All right. For the sake of argument, let's go with the assumption that you're Elizabeth. Tell me about that night. Why did you leave? Did your husband hurt you?"

"No," she declared firmly. "Never."

The woman's eyebrows rose. "Never? Explain to me, then, what that police report was all about. Neighbors said they heard shouting and officers showed up to find you bruised and bleeding?"

Shame burned inside her for the woman she had been, lost and hurting. It seemed another lifetime ago, that depression that left her feeling like she was alone in huge, deep waters, treading with all her might but still unable to keep her head from slipping below the surface.

"We...fought. Or rather, I yelled and he just stood there. That's...what the neighbors heard. Me yelling. I threw a plate and...cut myself." She hitched in a breath, hands folded tightly on her lap. Oh, this was so hard.

"Luke didn't hurt me. I...hurt myself. I was in a very dark place. It is hard to find the words to describe how...dark."

"The files indicate Elizabeth, er, you, had postpartum depression."

"And...clinical depression. Neither responded well to... drug therapy. I was...a mess. Suicidal. I was convinced my family would be better off without me. I tried to tell Luke to...divorce me."

And now that he was actually going to, she didn't know how she would bear it.

She couldn't look at him but could feel the tension radiating off of him. Oh, this was hard.

"That night, the night I left, I hit a...breaking point."

Christina Torres still looked skeptical. "What was different about that night that made you feel like you had to leave?"

Oh, she didn't want to talk about this. She gripped her hands together so tightly, she could feel her fingernails gouge into skin. "Have you ever felt...completely hopeless, Ms. Torres?"

The woman looked startled. "We're not talking about me."

"It's hard to explain...to someone who's never experienced how...debilitating a deep depression can be. It can lead you to think...horrible things. And to do them."

"What kind of things?"

"Things you would never think about in your...in your right mind."

She looked down at her hands, wishing she could stop now. But Luke needed his life back, the one she had taken from him, and she had to purge her conscience of this.

"I almost harmed my baby. Our sweet son. Bridger. I... He was teething and had a cold and was crying. Luke had been dealing with the children and...his business and...and everything for months and he crashed that night. I...I got up with the baby. I couldn't comfort him. He didn't want me. Why should he? I hadn't...bonded with him. He was almost a year old and I'd been...struggling that whole time with depression."

She had spotty memories of everything that had happened that night, impressions mostly, but she clearly remembered the terrible despair that had come over her as she tried to make Bridger stop crying.

She had stood at the window of his nursery watching the snow falling and thinking how easy it would be to walk into the night with him, to take him into the mountains where Luke couldn't find them. They would simply go to sleep, she and her child. It would be peaceful for both of them and would be far better off than living in this world that held so very much pain.

"I was...a threat to my own child. My sweet boy. I was out of my head but I kept thinking...the world would be better off without me and I didn't want my...my baby to have to grow up without a mother. I was...was going to carry him into the mountains and go to sleep with him in a...in a snow-bank somewhere."

Luke had grown rigid beside her. She could sense his shock and horror. Oh, how he must hate her.

She couldn't look at him, not ready to see it.

"Yet you didn't take the child when you fled," the attorney pointed out.

"No. I started to. I was...almost to the door when he... he made a little sound and fell asleep. I looked down at him and...something broke inside me." Her eyes felt hot, wet with the tears that dripped out despite her best efforts. "I... couldn't do it. I couldn't hurt him. Not my sweet little boy. But I knew how close I had come and that...that next time I might not stop."

The district attorney said nothing, her features inscrutable. "So you ran."

"Yes. I…managed to…to set him into his crib without waking him. Then I…I stumbled out of the house, intent only on getting away. I don't even know if I…thought about where to go. It was cold that night. So cold. I fell twice but managed to make it to the highway."

"That's five miles from here."

That walk was hazy, too. She only remembered feeling so ashamed and so afraid of her own actions. She had been a coward, even then, too afraid to walk into the mountains and let the elements take her.

"You expect me to believe you walked five miles in the dark, in the winter?"

"I'm only…telling you what happened. You can believe it or not. I…I managed to get a ride with a truck driver who was very kind to me. She was young, with dark hair and a tattoo of an…angel on her arm."

Her memory was so strange. She had remembered that angel, even when she didn't remember so many other things.

"I…I guess I fell asleep. When I woke up, we were in Oregon at a truck stop. I…I knew immediately I had made a terrible mistake. I wanted to go home. That was all I could think about. Home. My babies. Luke."

More tears leaked out and the district attorney finally handed her a tissue from a box on the credenza behind her.

"The truck driver let me out. I was…I was going to call Luke but I was…so ashamed. The waitress let me sit in a booth and even…even gave me coffee. I sat there for an hour trying to figure out what to do next. A…a man at the table next to me…noticed my distress."

This memory had come back later than many of the others, though it had been blurred around the edges, as if she had rubbed petroleum jelly around the window in her mind.

The only clear thing had been John Davis's kind smile and the pain in his eyes, though that might have been from the pictures of him she had seen later.

"He was heading to…Boise and offered a ride."

"Let me get this straight. You would rather take a ride with a stranger than call your husband, admit you'd made a mistake and ask him to come and get you?"

The doubt in Christina Torres's voice made her flinch. "I don't expect you to understand. I wasn't thinking…clearly. I suppose I was…too ashamed to face him. To tell him I was a threat to our son and maybe to Cassie, too."

She heard him hitch in a breath at that but still couldn't bring herself to look at him. Facing him now, seven years later, was harder than she'd ever thought it would be.

"If you thought you were a threat, why were you going back?"

"I…knew running off wasn't…the right way. Neither was ending it all. I needed help. A different med, a different therapist. Maybe an inpatient program. Something. I…I wanted my family back."

Christina Torres shifted in her chair. Had her features become less harsh or was Elizabeth imagining that?

"But you didn't go back. You disappeared for the next seven years."

"Yes."

"I'm still not saying I believe you're Elizabeth Sinclair, but if it's true, you apparently decided during that time to have extensive plastic surgery. What happened during those missing seven years, from that diner at a truck stop in Oregon and a man offering to give you a ride to this moment?"

So much. A dozen lifetimes.

Again, she didn't even know where to start.

"I...I don't remember this part well. Only bits and pieces and what I've been able to stitch together from what the... the doctors have told me."

"Doctors. What doctors?"

So many. Did this woman want an alphabetical list by surname or by specialty?

She released a long, unsteady breath and wiped at her eyes with the tissue so that the world wasn't so cloudy.

"You took a ride with a man you met at a truck stop," the attorney prompted.

Luke remained stubbornly silent, his features hard, closed.

Elizabeth nodded. "I do remember that part. He was... very nice. His name was...was John Davis. I remember sensing great pain in him."

He had been sweet and kind, genuinely concerned for her. She remembered that much from their brief acquaintance. He had also appeared to carry a heavy burden. Perhaps that was the reason why he had stopped at her table to try offering her some comfort.

That fateful moment and her decision to accept a ride with him had changed *everything* in her life.

She had often thought about the strange corkscrewing twists of life, how a single instant in time could dramatically alter a person's life. Waiting three more seconds at a red light, changing an airplane flight, deciding at the last minute to drive a different route home.

Or climbing into the vehicle with a stranger for what should have been an easy ride home.

"What happened?" Ms. Torres asked.

"About an...hour into our journey together, we encountered a storm. On a...lonely stretch of road, we hit a...patch of ice and the car rolled several times down a steep embankment. I found out later that John Davis was...was killed instantly. I was unconscious from a...head injury. No one saw the accident happen and...and no one found me for about eighteen hours."

She thought she heard a sharp intake of breath beside her but Luke's expression didn't seem to change.

Did he believe her? She couldn't tell. She supposed it didn't really matter. It was the truth, which was all she had.

"I was...badly injured. Unresponsive and stuck in my seat belt. Frostbitten. A snowplow operator finally spotted the wreckage."

That alone had been a miracle, as by then the car was close to being completely covered in snow.

"When rescuers found me, they thought I was dead, just like John, until...one felt a faint pulse. I had no...identification on me because I had left in such a hurry. They treated me as a Jane Doe at first, until...John's family arrived and assumed I was his wife, Sonia."

"His wife?" The attorney looked stunned. "Why would his own family immediately jump there?"

"I had...extensive facial injuries. My face was swollen, bruised, cut up. Unrecognizable."

"Still. Wouldn't his family know the difference?"

"She had only been married to him for a short time and his family didn't know her well. They met online and she had...come over from Russia to marry him."

"A mail-order bride?" the attorney asked, intrigued.

That assumption always made her feel sad for John Davis, whose letters and journals indicated he had genuinely loved his wife. She wasn't as certain about Sonia's feelings for him in return. The woman had left him after less than a year, ostensibly only for a visit to her family in her home country but it had stretched into several months by the time Elizabeth's path crossed with John's at that Oregon truck stop.

"I don't know. He didn't tell me, at least not that I... remember. Regardless, I was badly injured, in a coma with little...chance of survival. John's sister assumed I was his wife and doctors had no reason to...to doubt her."

That had been another twist of fate. What if everyone hadn't jumped so quickly into believing that she was Sonia, John's Russian bride? What if John had swallowed his shame and sadness and told his sister that his beloved wife had left him weeks earlier? Would authorities have made more of an effort to find out Elizabeth's true identity?

She had tortured herself over and over with what-ifs.

"I was the same height, approximate weight, with the same hair and eye color. My...facial shape and eyes were similar. They had no reason to think anything else."

"You're saying the doctors mistook you for another woman simply because you were in the car with her husband and didn't have any identification of your own?"

"Yes. It was an understandable mistake. I can't blame them. They thought I was her and for a...long time after I finally regained consciousness, I had no reason not to believe them."

"You also thought you were this Russian woman, Sonia. How do you explain that you didn't speak the language?"

The attorney looked intrigued, rather than skeptical. Was it possible she might actually believe her? Elizabeth was afraid to hope.

"I didn't speak *any* language. Not at first. I told you, I had a...severe brain injury."

Beside her, Luke made a sound that might have been doubt or might have been anguish. She couldn't be certain.

"I started coming out of the coma about a month after the...accident, but it took me several more weeks until I was...fully aware of what was going on around me. People were telling me I was...Sonia Davis. They were calling me that name. I answered, because they seemed to expect me to, but it never felt...right. The name never felt like my own."

"When did you remember us?" Luke's voice sounded rusty, gruff. Did *he* believe her? In the end, that was all that really mattered to her.

"Always," she said quietly. "Somewhere inside me, I remembered...I had another life. It was...just out of reach. I didn't know if it was a dream or a memory, but you...you and the children were there. Always."

"You said you were badly injured."

"I had to relearn everything. Walking, yes. But smaller things, too. How to...hold a pencil. Use a telephone. Talk. Speech was...hard. I still struggle to find the right words. It's called dysphasia of speech and isn't...uncommon in those with brain injuries."

"How long were you in therapy?" Christina Torres asked. She had gone from being openly hostile to interested.

"More than...a year. I went to live with John's sister about... eighteen months after the accident. She was...unfailingly kind. Like her brother had been. We became...dear friends. Sisters. While I was there, memories came to me a little at a time. A baby in my arms, laughing. Hiking in mountains so beautiful they took my breath away. A...a man."

Her voice caught and she swallowed, sneaking a look at Luke. He looked completely stunned, color drained from his features and his eyes a deep and murky green. "A man who...

who looked at me with love in his eyes. I had no idea who he was. Where he was. I only…I only knew we had…once been together."

And that she had loved him, with all her heart. She couldn't say that to this strange, intense woman she had only met a short time ago.

"It was a long and…difficult process. It took me another year before all the memories fully returned. Before I knew for certain…I was not Sonia Davis but Elizabeth Hamilton."

"All right. Let's do the math here. You're saying you knew approximately four years ago you are living another woman's life and you had a husband and children here who might be looking for you. *Four years!* Why didn't you come back then?"

At the question, Luke rose as if he couldn't remain seated any longer and paced to the window, where he looked down at the cars driving past.

Elizabeth wiped at the tears she could no longer control that were now falling freely down her cheeks. Oh, how she wished she had a better answer for this.

"I left because…I thought that was best for my family," she said, her voice small. "I stayed away for the same reason."

The district attorney leaned back in her chair, resting her chin on her steepled fingers as she studied Elizabeth. "This is a very far-fetched story, Mrs. Hamilton. Car accidents. Russian wives. Comas. Sounds like something out of a bad soap opera. How do you expect me to believe any shred of it is true, that you are indeed who you say you are?"

"In the end, does it matter whether you believe me or not? A simple DNA test can…prove I'm Elizabeth Hamilton."

"True enough. That's the only thing about this whole convoluted story I can verify."

"Not…the only thing. You can speak with… John's sister.

Alice Davis. Look at my...medical files. Speak with my... rehab physicians. To be...frank, ma'am, I don't care if you believe me or not. All I care about is that you clear my husband of any wrongdoing in connection with my disappearance and drop your...idea of charging him with...anything."

Luke turned around to look at her. The morning sun streaming in around him veiled his expression. What was he thinking?

"Let me be clear. No more...ambiguities. My husband did not have any idea I was...leaving. He did not contribute in any way to my...decision to leave. I left of my own... free will that night, thinking I was...protecting my children. After the accident, I...stayed away because I thought it was the right choice for my family. I have medical records dating back to the night I left. I have scars. You can...see those, if you'd like. I don't care. I just want you to...clear Luke of any wrongdoing."

"You've been living under an assumed name, using someone else's identity while a great deal of Lake Haven County resources have been wasted looking for you."

She had full permission from John's family to live under his wife's name, the wife who had left him and who Alice had discovered had been killed by her jealous lover, father of the child she had abandoned with her parents in Russia to pursue a new life overseas. Even knowing the truth, John's sister had given her all the proceeds from his life insurance for her medical costs, over Elizabeth's protests. Alice had claimed she deserved them, since his moment of inattention on the road had been responsible for the accident and for her life-changing injuries. At the time, she hadn't been sure if she would ever be able to work again, so she had grudgingly accepted.

Alice's husband was an attorney as well and had made sure the arrangement was legal and binding.

Still, she had taken on a name that was not her own, which had technically been illegal.

"Go ahead, then. Arrest me. Just leave…Luke out of it."

Luke returned to his chair beside her. He lifted a hand, almost as if he wanted to touch her, then dropped it back to his thigh.

"Why do I get the feeling you're surprised by this information?" the district attorney asked him. "You told me you knew your wife's whereabouts."

A muscle flexed in his jaw. "It doesn't matter how I feel. I hope this is the end of things. You're going to drop this misguided witch hunt to charge me in connection with her disappearance, right? You can't exactly put on trial for killing a woman who is very much alive."

"I find it interesting that you say you've known your wife's whereabouts for months, since Elliot Bailey uncovered them, but have chosen not to bring her forward until now. Why is that, Mr. Hamilton?"

"That is between my wife and me, Ms. Torres." He stood up. "Are we finished here?"

"I suppose there's nothing else to do at this time. You should know, Mrs. Hamilton, that a great deal of time and effort has been wasted. Hundreds, if not thousands, of law enforcement hours have been spent trying to find you over the past seven years."

"I am…sorry for that. More sorry than I can say. For the record, I wanted to come home almost from the…moment I left. I…I never expected to wind up in a coma and wake up with no clear memory of…who I was or…or all I had left behind."

This time, she did feel the warm brush of his fingers, gently touching the skin at the back of her hand where she gripped the armrest. It was only a fleeting touch but made her choke down a sob and fight the urge to collapse into his arms.

"Are we done here?" Luke demanded again.

The attorney sighed and threw her pen on the desk. "We're done. Goodbye, Mr. and Mrs. Hamilton. I hope I don't have to see you again."

Chapter Ten

As they left the district attorney's office and walked into the hallway of the courthouse, Luke felt as if he were the one who had just survived a terrible car accident.

Every muscle in his body ached from the impact of the last hour spent listening to the harrowing details of Elizabeth's story.

In all his wildest imaginings—that she had left him for another man, that she had been abducted and sold for sex trafficking, that she had walked into Lake Haven with rocks tied around her neck—he could not have guessed the truth about why she had never returned.

A car accident. A coma. Long, painful months of rehabilitation. Christina Torres was right. It sounded unbelievable—except the evidence had been staring him in the face since she opened the door and walked out onto the porch of that big house in Oregon where she had been living.

He had known something hard had happened to her. She

used a cane; her steps faltered; she stumbled over words. He had known life had not been kind to her since she left him. Some part of him had been selfishly, secretly glad of that. Now he was ashamed of himself. She had been trying to come back to face her unhappiness when fate had played the most cruel of tricks.

Luke had grieved for his wife for many long years, thinking she must have died or she would have come back to him and the children. When he had found out she was still alive, only living a different life away from him, that grief had shifted to hurt, betrayal, fury. It had clouded his judgment.

Now he simply did not know what to think.

The divorce papers rustled in his hand. He had forgotten all about them. Luke had intended to have her sign the papers here, where they easily could find a notary public. Then he planned to take them to his attorney to be filed.

He gripped the folder, hesitant to just thrust them at her after all she had been through.

He stood uncertainly for a moment, then noticed she looked pale, her features, so different yet oddly familiar, strained.

A couple of chairs had been set into an alcove overlooking the town's Main Street and the lake beyond. He led her there and she sank down, looking grateful for a momentary respite.

"Why didn't you tell me?" He had to ask.

She folded her hands together in her lap, fingers intertwined. "I tried when you first came to pick me up at… Brambleberry House. You…didn't want to hear it."

He had been so furious that day. Not that day. For months, since finding out she was still alive. He was tired of it, so very weary of the constant grinding pain in his chest.

What had she endured? It sounded like sheer hell, physically and emotionally, having to relearn everything. He hated knowing she had been alone during that time, facing all that pain and uncertainty without the support of her loving family. He and the children could have helped her through.

He cringed to think of his own rigidity, his unwillingness to listen to her explanations.

"I'm sorry." The words somehow forced their way past the lump in his throat. "I've been an ass. I should have let you explain when you tried to on the way here from Oregon."

Her hand fluttered out to touch his but she drew back quickly. "Don't apologize. Please. I could have...told you anyway. I should have. I should have found the courage to tell you...long ago."

"Why didn't you?" This was the point that still eluded him. "I know you've come back to Haven Point several times over the years. You could have said something. Did you think I wouldn't want to know? That I wouldn't care? I thought you were dead, Elizabeth. I grieved for you. You have no idea how I grieved."

She made a small sound of distress, that hand fluttering again. He wanted to take her fingers into his and warm them, protect them from any future harm.

"As soon as I could...safely travel by myself, I came to Lake Haven. I'm not sure what I intended. I just... I had to see you and the children. I missed you all so much."

"Why didn't you come to me and explain then? Were you...afraid of me for some reason?"

Luke had to ask the question he dreaded. What other conclusion could he reach? He'd tried to be a loving husband, not raising his voice or flying off the handle. But maybe there was more of his father in him than just the similarity of their appearance. Maybe he had done or said something that had convinced her he would hurt her if she stayed.

Her eyes widened in what appeared to be genuine shock. "No. Never! I wanted to see you. But the trip didn't...turn out the way I planned. I had a...seizure the first night, all alone in the hotel room. It...terrified me. I was lucky that I didn't hurt myself more than I did."

That *more* implied some level of injury during the episode. He suddenly couldn't seem to get the picture of her out of his head, trembling and afraid in an impersonal hotel room, while her husband who might have helped her was only a phone call away.

Why hadn't she told him?

"Did you go to the hospital?"

"I should have. But I didn't want the...questions here. I ended up flying back to Portland the next day and taking a taxi to the...hospital there. The next time, I came prepared with my...emergency seizure medication and...John's sister on speed dial so she could...call an ambulance if something went wrong."

All those contingency plans, when she could have simply dropped the subterfuge and told him who she was.

"You came back to see the children."

"Yes. I...came to the school's big Christmas program. It would have been...four years ago. Cassie would have been in...kindergarten. I...couldn't stop staring at all of you."

Had he seen her there? Been attracted to her? Wondered about her? He couldn't remember.

"I was...going to talk to you after the concert but then saw you were...with someone. A woman. You looked happy. Much happier than I had seen you those last hard months after

Bridger was born. I thought…maybe you had moved on. It had…been so long."

The divorce papers in his hand suddenly seemed heavier, somehow. "You misunderstood something you saw. Jumped to the wrong conclusion. I couldn't have been with anyone. I haven't dated at all."

Shock widened those blue eyes again. "No one?"

He made a face. "I'm not exactly prime dating material around town. When a guy is suspected of murdering his wife, most sane women tend to stay away."

He could not deny that a few women had the opposite re-action, considering him dangerous, unpredictable. The dark suspicions that swirled around him attracted a certain type of woman, those who wanted that walk on the wild side. A fling with one of them hadn't interested him and anything else was impossible.

"I'm a married man, under the eyes of the law. And a sus-pected murderer under the eyes of everyone else. Nice women don't want to have much to do with me."

"Oh. I must have…misunderstood what I saw. The woman was blonde and pretty and kissed you on the cheek after the show. That wasn't the…only time I saw you with her. She… seemed to have a kindergartner, too."

It took him another moment before he remembered sitting beside Pam Hartwell, whose son had been in Cassie's kin-dergarten class. She had been recently divorced around that time and they had hung out a few times, talking about some of the challenges of single parenting. It had purely been a friendship and she had started dating a guy in Shelter Springs not long after.

"You misunderstood," he said again. "I haven't dated anyone. It's been all I could do to raise the kids and keep the business going."

She was quiet. "I'm sorry. I can't say it enough. I should never have…left that night. But I had hit bottom and…and didn't want to drag you down, too. I didn't see…any other way."

All the years of grief and these last months of hate seemed such a waste of time and energy.

Could he have done something differently, helped her more than he had when she was struggling with depression? In retrospect, Luke knew he hadn't been the most supportive husband. He had been overwhelmed trying to care for a baby and a toddler by himself and work enough to support his family. He'd been short-tempered, tired, afraid and mostly filled with a deep yearning for the sweet, joy-filled wife he had married.

"Do you have…papers for me to sign?" Elizabeth asked, gesturing to the packet in his hand. "We can…file them while we're here."

Her voice faltered and he suddenly noticed she looked pale. Her hands were shaking and her mouth was pinched.

He couldn't imagine everything she had been through, the depth of the physical and emotional trauma she had endured. Trapped in a car for hours with a dead man, lost in a coma, then coming out helpless and alone.

His chest felt tight as he pictured her in a hospital, afraid, in pain, with no one to help her.

"You look like you're going to fall over." He avoided her question. "Did you eat breakfast this morning?"

She sent him a wary look. "I wasn't hungry. Too nervous, if you want the truth."

"Let's get something in your system," he said. He hadn't

been there to care for her when she had needed him but he could help her now.

"I'm still not hungry." She looked at the papers in his hand. "I know you want to…get this over with."

"You can sign the papers after we eat."

She seemed surprised but didn't argue as he rose and headed to the elevator. Neither of them spoke as they made their way out to his pickup truck. He had made her climb in alone, he remembered, and was ashamed all over again of his unfeeling attitude.

This time he lent an arm and helped boost her into the high vehicle. She offered him a tentative smile that made him feel even worse.

He climbed in to start his pickup. "Anywhere you would like to eat? If not, I was thinking I should just take you back home so you can rest."

"I can't…hide out in that house. If we're going to go to lunch, we should eat somewhere in Haven Point."

"Why?"

"We need to start repairing your…reputation. People can't accuse you of being involved in my…disappearance when they see us together. If I just leave…town, you'll be in the same position you are now. No one will believe you."

"I suppose there's some truth to that," he admitted slowly. He didn't want to trot around in public with Elizabeth simply to prove his innocence but didn't know any other way to quiet the gossip. "Where would you suggest we go? Anywhere you have been missing? You always liked Serrano's, if I remember correctly."

It had been their favorite place to eat when they were dating and after they were married, though they hadn't been able to afford it often.

"I still like it. I ate lunch there...by myself yesterday. It was as good as I...remember. And busy. Everyone eats lunch there."

"Sounds like a plan."

As he drove around the lake again, Luke's brain went into hyperdrive with all the questions he wanted to ask.

"Why Cannon Beach?" he asked.

It wasn't the most compelling among the many things he wanted to know, but he'd been wondering about what had led her there since he drove into the charming little beach town to find her.

"Oh. A friend of John's sister has a vacation house there. I was...staying in it for a time after...well, after my memory came back, when I just needed...time to think through everything. I liked it there and...found a part-time job at the local garden center."

"That doesn't surprise me. You always loved to have your hands in the dirt."

"It is soothing to me. Comforting. Also, I thought it would help me...regain some muscle tone. And I found I was...good at growing things. A client asked me to do some work at a... property she owned. Brambleberry House. Where you... picked me up. I ended up...falling in love with the place. An apartment opened up a few months later and she...asked if I wanted it at a discounted rate in exchange for...landscaping work. Of course I said...yes. That was...about three years ago. I've been there...ever since."

He had a feeling she had left many details out of her sanitized version of events.

"You said you have seizures. That's what happened that night in the hotel, isn't it? You said it was a bad dream but it didn't seem like a dream to me."

Her sigh was heavy. "Yes. A...small one. I haven't had one in a long time. They have been mostly controlled with medication, unless I find myself under great stress or overdo things."

He certainly had stressed her by showing up out of the blue and insisting she come back to Haven Point with him. He should have given her a little more warning.

He felt guilty for that but it warred with an unexpected lightness, something he hadn't known in a long time.

She had tried to come back.

The lake gleamed a vivid blue as he drove around it, brighter than he'd seen it in a long time.

He wasn't happy, exactly. Just relieved, he supposed. She had left him but she had been trying to make her way back.

She hadn't talked about everything that had happened to her, though, and Luke found he wanted to know more.

"What else are you dealing with from the accident, besides the seizures?"

"I told you they're mostly controlled."

"But not completely."

She sighed again. "I don't like...talking about the accident, Luke. Something hard happened to me, but I survived. It's part of me but doesn't...define me."

He was beginning to realize that. She was so much more than she'd been even a decade ago, when he'd fallen for her. "It was hard for you today, talking about it."

She nodded. "Even my best friends in Oregon don't know everything about...about the accident."

At least she hadn't been completely alone. She had John Davis's sister and the other tenants at Brambleberry House who had looked at him with such defiance.

"That woman I met the other day. Rosa. She seemed very protective of you."

"She's small but fierce. My other friend Melissa is much the same. They...watch out for me."

"So why haven't you told them your story?" he asked as he reached the Haven Point city boundaries. Almost without thinking, he turned away from downtown and headed toward his house along the lake.

"I suppose because I was too ashamed." She looked out the window, as if the passing scenery was the most fascinating thing she had ever seen.

"Ashamed? Why would you be ashamed? It was an accident. You weren't even driving."

"No. But I wouldn't have been there at all if I...hadn't run away that night. If I hadn't almost...hurt our son."

That part had been heartbreaking to hear, that she had felt desperate enough and so alone that she might have been willing to do something so terribly final.

"That wasn't you, Elizabeth."

"How can any decent mother even think...the kinds of things I did?"

He didn't pretend to understand everything she had been going through, but he had studied enough about mental health over the past seven years to understand a little about what had been going through her head.

"You stopped before you could hurt Bridger. You knew in your heart you couldn't do it, no matter what the chemical imbalance in your brain was urging you to do. You stopped, Elizabeth."

She turned to look at him and his heart ached at the tears in her eyes. "What if I hadn't?"

"Don't go there. You did. You fought off the demons and you left so you could protect our son. Do I wish you had turned to me instead of fleeing into the night? Yes. A thousand times, yes. But the fact that you made that choice doesn't mean you deserved what happened to you later."

She released a long breath, as if setting down a burden she had carried for a long time. "Thank you...for saying that. I still don't blame you for having...reservations about allowing me to see the children. I would, too, if I were in your place."

The kids. What was he going to tell the kids?

He had no idea, but he knew he couldn't keep her from them. Not now that he knew the truth.

"What if I'm beginning to have second thoughts about that?"

She stared, eyes wide, as if she was afraid to hope for such a possibility. "After everything I've told you, you would let me...talk to Cassie and Bridger?"

He really *had* been an ass.

"I don't think I have a choice. I never really did. They think you're dead or, worse, that you abandoned them."

She hitched in a breath and he longed to comfort her. He didn't quite know how to bridge the chasm between them made up of all those years without her.

"I wanted you to help me clear my name. In order to do that, we have to show people you're alive, which means the kids will have to know the story. I have to tell them something before word trickles back to them that you have shown up in Haven Point after all these years."

"I didn't think about that either. You're right. They should know first."

"Instead of Serrano's, I think we should just have something at the house so we can figure out our strategy before they get home from school."

When she met his gaze, the raw hope in her eyes broke his heart all over again. She loved their children, no matter what choices she had made since leaving town that night. He had no right to keep her from them.

"All right. Whatever you think best."

He didn't know what was best. Nor did he have any idea how his world had shifted so drastically in only a few hours.

Chapter Eleven

She might be able to see her children.

Elizabeth did not know how to contain the wild joy bubbling through her like the healing springs that surrounded Haven Point.

Was it possible Luke might find it in his heart to ever forgive her? She knew she didn't deserve it but she prayed he would be willing to overlook the terrible decisions she had made and let her into their children's lives, at least a little.

She felt giddy. Light-headed, even. She might have feared the onset of another seizure but suspected her shakiness could be attributed mostly to the stress of the morning and her foolishness in not eating something before she went to the courthouse with Luke.

"Here we are," Luke said a few moments later, pulling his pickup into the circular driveway of a large home perched on a bluff overlooking the lake.

Elizabeth couldn't seem to stop staring. "Oh, Luke. What a beautiful home."

The three-story structure of honey-colored logs should have been featured in a home show, with wide glass along the angled front, a steeply pitched roof, a porch that looked as if it wrapped around to overlook the lake and a large chimney of the same stones used on the porch pillars.

From the outside, the house looked warm and cheery against the wintry landscape.

She and Luke had purchased this property early in their marriage but couldn't afford to build on it. Their little starter home along the river had been enough for them at the time. Luke had been struggling to get his contractor business off the ground and she had been working at an insurance agency in Shelter Springs to help make ends meet.

Still, on the sweetly gorgeous summer evenings the people of Haven Point were lucky enough to enjoy, they used to meet here after work. They would set out lawn chairs right where the house sat and watch the sunset over the lake while they sketched out their dreams for the home that they would build together.

If she wasn't mistaken, the house in front of her bore striking similarities to the one they had imagined together.

He must have remembered those sketches. Oh, she knew he had not built the house for her. But if he had, it would have looked exactly like this one.

She always dreamed of having a house with a wide porch for entertaining, for watching the storms roll across the lake, for sitting out in the morning with a cup of coffee and a book.

She couldn't wait to go inside and see if the room layout and trims matched the perfection of the exterior.

"How long have you and the children lived here?"

"Since late October. I wanted to finish and be in by the end of the summer, but other projects had top priority, so it took me longer than I planned."

"I'm glad your business is doing well." She wanted to tell him he deserved to have everything he dreamed but couldn't find the right words.

"Well enough. I've been fortunate to stay busy with all the new development in the area from Caine Tech coming in. I do quite a lot in Shelter Springs but I've also finished some commercial remodeling to the buildings downtown after Aidan Caine bought several properties from Ben Kilpatrick."

Why wouldn't he be busy? Anyone would be stupid not to use him on their new build or remodel. Luke had always been a hard worker who specialized in high-end finishes and creative problem solving.

"It's really...lovely. You always did...beautiful work."

He looked surprised and, she thought, pleased at the praise. "Thanks."

As a contractor, he had always tried to keep prices reasonable while not sacrificing quality. He loved nothing more than building the perfect house for families.

She knew some of that desire to create beauty and peace for others stemmed from his own dysfunctional childhood, from having a father who had been vicious and abusive and made Luke's own home a living nightmare.

So much of his character had been shaped by his father. Other men might have become cold and angry themselves but Luke hadn't been like that. He worked doubly hard not to resemble his father in any way.

She wanted to think that when they were dating and first married, she had provided him a place of refuge and peace. Of course, all that had changed when she left.

"It will be nice when everything is finished," he said as he unlocked the heavy door inlaid with a glass panel that had horses etched into it. "It feels like we've been building it for the better part of four years."

"What do you have left?" she asked as they walked inside. She did her best not to gawk at the gorgeous soaring great room dominated by the fireplace the chimney outside had hinted at.

"The house itself is done. All I have left is mostly landscaping. That's our spring project but I haven't been able to wrap my head around it yet."

Landscaping had been her purview. He would plan the houses and she would spend hours designing the yards. Perhaps that was why she found such peace and calm working in the Brambleberry House gardens and at her part-time job at the garden center.

She looked out the window. Right now, snow covered everything, but she could tell the yard had possibilities, especially with that stunning view out the back.

With a craving so intense it took her breath away, she wanted to be the one designing that yard out there. She ached to be here in spring, picking out seedlings, bringing in topsoil, scouring local nurseries for exactly the right perennials and shrubs.

She wanted to create a beautiful garden for Luke and their children, somewhere they could escape the stress of life and find home.

She wouldn't be here, though. She would be back in Oregon, alone.

"It will be wonderful when you're finished," she said.

"I hope so."

A dog with floppy ears and curly yellow fur came racing

out of a back room. He growled a little at Elizabeth, then jumped for Luke to lift him.

"Who's this?"

"This is Finn."

"Hi, Finn." Elizabeth held out a hand, trying to look unthreatening. After a minute of scrutiny, the dog licked her hand and wagged his tail.

"Yeah, he's fierce. As you can see."

Still holding the dog, Luke led the way to the kitchen just off the great room, which featured gleaming professional-grade appliances and a huge island topped with textured, sand-colored marble.

"Is soup okay? Are you sick of minestrone?"

"Not at all. It sounds perfect. I can heat it, though."

"I've got it. Sit down. You're still looking pale."

She *was* feeling shaky still, but mostly she wanted to wander around the house to see if the rest of it matched her idea of perfection.

She obediently slid into one of the swivel bar stools attached to the island. Some instinct told her this was probably where their children liked to hang out best. Did they do their homework here or did they use the large table in the dining area and kitchen? Maybe they preferred to do homework in their rooms, without distractions.

What did she know? Her children were strangers to her in every way that mattered.

The reminder deflated her a little as Luke handed her a bowl of soup. She waited to eat until he heated one for himself, then sat down across from her, almost as if he was afraid to be too close.

"So," he said after a few spoonfuls of soup. "The kids. What do you think we should tell them?"

She set her spoon down next to her bowl, her stomach twisting with nerves. "I don't know. I...don't want to tell them anything."

"You can't just show up again without some kind of explanation, Elizabeth. We owe them some information."

She owed them. Luke shouldn't feel any responsibility in this.

"All of it?"

"I don't know if we need to get into all the nitty-gritty details."

She didn't know if she could bear telling Bridger and Cassie about the terrible darkness that had almost consumed her.

"We can stick to the truth," he went on. "I've told them before that you were sick and that you must have thought leaving for a while would help you get better. I told them something must have happened to you or you would have come back earlier."

"That was...uncannily accurate."

"It was a cop-out. I didn't want to tell them I suspected you might have hurt yourself."

She closed her eyes, hating that part of her history, hating everything she had put him through. "I'm sorry," she whispered.

He frowned. "You had severe depression. I should have figured out a way to put you into an inpatient program. I was in denial and we all paid the price for that. You, more than anyone."

"Nothing that happened was your fault."

He was always so good at taking responsibility for everything wrong in the world. It was part of his character, probably stemming back to childhood. He had always blamed himself for not being able to protect his mother or stepmother from Paul Hamilton's viciousness, despite the fact that he'd only been a boy at the time.

"I would say the same to you," he answered. "Look, neither of us asked for this situation but here we are. We have to deal with it in the smartest way possible."

"I don't want to upset the status quo."

He gave a rough-sounding laugh. "Our status quo is survival. Can both kids make it to the bus stop each morning before the bus pulls away? Can I remember to feed them breakfast and make sure they have a nutritious lunch packed? Will I be done at the job site after school in time to pick them up or do I need to call the babysitter? It's all a juggling act."

"As far as I can tell, you're doing it...well."

"Thanks." He studied her for a moment, long enough that she could feel herself blush, wondering what he saw.

"Thank you for lunch. I didn't...want to admit how much I needed to eat."

"I could tell."

Luke was a natural-born nurturer, always looking out for those he cared about. When she was pregnant with both of the children, he had been right there with her, running to the store to pick up anything she might have a craving for, handling as many of the household chores as he could while juggling his job, rubbing her feet when they were swollen and sore.

He had shown that same care and love to the kids when they came along. He was a wonderful father, so very different from his own example.

Elizabeth had lost the right to be counted among the lucky people Luke Hamilton loved. She tried not to let that realization break her heart.

"Could I...see the rest of the house?"

He looked at the large clock on the wall between the kitchen and great room. "Sure. The kids won't be home for another forty-five minutes. It will only take us a few minutes for the grand tour. But are you sure you don't need to rest a little longer? You still look pale."

She couldn't say she felt her strongest but she could certainly handle a trip through his house. "I'm not an invalid. Please don't think I am. My...my speech is slow and I don't move as quickly as I would like, but I am trying very hard not to let that stop me."

She would never win a marathon or be able to climb to the top of the Redemption Mountains, but she preferred to focus on the skills she had managed to regain instead of what had been forever lost.

After he took their bowls and rinsed them in the sink, he led the way through the house.

"I guess you saw the great room when we came in."

"Yes. It's beautiful. I especially love the...burled logs you used for the supports. They add character and...style."

He looked surprised that she had noticed. She remembered all those times they had looked through log home books together, studying methods and techniques. She'd always loved the way some builders focused on using burled logs, where diseases or other stress had caused the living tree to form an interesting outgrowth. They were imperfect, knotty and gnarled in appearance, but that was why she liked them.

"There's a master suite on this level but I made another one upstairs so I can hear the kids if they wake up in the night," he said.

Oh, he was an impossible man to resist. He always had been for her. Luke Hamilton might seem tough on the outside but inside he was as soft and gooey as hot caramel.

He showed her the large ground-floor suite, beautifully furnished with a huge four-poster bed and a seating area surrounding another rock fireplace with a gas insert that turned on with the flick of a switch. Large French doors led out to the deck that overlooked the lake and the mountains.

What a delicious retreat. She could imagine sinking into that sofa on a snowy afternoon with a book and a cup of tea.

If things had been different, this might have been the room she shared with Luke.

Her face grew hot at the idea, the seductive memories of being in his arms. They had never had trouble with intimacy. Luke had been an amazing lover, with that same attention to her needs that he showed in other aspects of his life.

She swallowed, trying not to remember how they had fit together so perfectly, how they couldn't get enough of each other in those early months of their marriage.

She had started every morning in his arms and gone to sleep the same way.

"This is lovely," she said. The words sounded strangled.

"It's one of my favorite rooms in the house. I use it for an office sometimes when I need a quiet place to work, though I have an actual office with a separate business entrance on the other side of the house."

"I wouldn't want to leave," she said when she trusted her voice again.

"When Bridger gets a little older, I'll probably move down here. He still has nightmares sometimes, though, so I like to stay close."

She didn't like knowing their son's sleep was troubled. Was it because he had lost his mother at such an early age? Did he have some subconscious memory of the night she had almost given in to the demons?

"Do you want to see more?"

"Of course."

"Can you make it upstairs?"

Yes. That was why she insisted on that second-floor apartment at Brambleberry House, so she could challenge herself each day to do hard things.

When she nodded, he led her up the winding staircase, with more burls and imperfections on the balustrade. He had paid attention to every aspect of the home, with his usual care. The house was a real showpiece, a clear demonstration of his abilities.

He showed her a guest room on that level as well as the room he used for his own, much smaller than the downstairs master bedroom but with an en suite bathroom and a lovely view of the lake.

It smelled like his soap, cedar and pine with a citrus undertone. She wanted to stand in the doorway and inhale, but by then he had moved to the children's rooms.

Seeing Bridger's and Cassie's personal spaces was both delightful and heartbreaking. She loved the little glimpses into their personalities. Bridger had a cowboy hat hanging on one bedpost and a baseball glove on the other. Cassie's room was decorated in lavender and brown but she had her own baseball glove on the bookshelf and posters of the latest pop heartthrob on the wall.

Elizabeth had tried to stay in the children's lives on the periphery, timing her visits around sporting events and school performances. The truth was, she didn't know her children. Not really.

"It's a beautiful home," she said as they headed back downstairs. "Perfect, down to the smallest detail."

"I tried. The basement is still mostly unfinished. Eventually that will be a hangout place where the kids can bring their friends. I'm planning a home theater as well as a game room with Ping-Pong and pool tables."

She couldn't quite imagine Bridger and Cassie as rambunctious teenagers but knew that that time was right around the corner. Cassie was almost ten. She would be dating before they knew it.

What would happen now between them all? Would Luke allow her to be part of the children's lives? She had already missed so much. She didn't want to continue on the periphery but the future seemed as murky as the gathering clouds outside.

She did notice one glaring exception to his penchant for detail as they returned to the great room.

"What about Christmas? Christmas Eve is a week away and you don't even have a Christmas tree."

He winced. "Yeah. Believe me, I'm aware. Both kids have been nagging me about that. Right after we moved in, I ordered a big tree that wouldn't be dwarfed by the two-story ceiling in the great room, but the company had shipping problems and it only arrived last week. We were planning to set it up and decorate it Sunday, but then I got the tip about Christina Torres planning to file charges and that took priority. Things were a little crazy last night, so it didn't happen, but we'll get to it."

He gave her a considering look. "Maybe you can help with that. You did a great job staging the other house."

"Me?" She stared at him, shocked at the suggestion.

"You don't have to. It was just an idea."

"No." She hurried to answer. "I would love to help. But I thought you wanted me to...leave town as soon as possible."

He leaned against the kitchen counter. "I've been thinking about that. About you leaving, I mean. You said you have an airplane ticket home on Christmas Eve. Maybe we should stick with those plans. You should stay at least until the program on Monday night."

She could hear her heart pounding in her chest, so loudly it seemed to echo in her ears. "You would let me...go to the program?"

"You're the one who said we still have work to do restoring my reputation. Christina Torres is only one person. You may have convinced her you're still alive and kicking. But what about the rest of the town? Bridger and Cass are most impacted by gossip at school passed down by kids who hear it at home from their parents."

"That's true."

"I was thinking maybe Megan might have some ideas of places where we could show up around town this week. The school program is one. Maybe the fund-raiser she and the other Helping Hands are throwing Sunday. She might have other suggestions."

Tuesday. She could stay until Christmas Eve. Was it possible he might let her stay through the holidays? She couldn't even imagine the joy. She had spent so many Christmases alone, aching for her children and the man she loved with all her heart.

The price she would have to pay would be steep, though. She would have to speak with people, despite her awkward, brain-injured speech. She might even have to confess why she had left.

Could she do it?

She had to. She owed it to Luke, after everything he had been through. This was the least she could do.

"Are you up for that?" he asked. "I don't want you to overdo."

He was watching out for her. The concern in his eyes made her want to cry. "I would love to spend this week with the children and you. I'll…gladly help you decorate and go to the school program and…anything else you want me to do. Anything, Luke."

She couldn't stop the tears from flowing down, and after another minute, he sighed and pulled her into his arms.

This was a much different embrace than their angry one the day before. This was tender, gentle. Healing. She cried for a moment longer, then became lost in the sheer wonder of being close to him.

She wanted to rest her cheek against his shirt and stay here forever, feeling his warmth and listening to his heartbeat. She'd thought she remembered how good he felt next to her, but her memories paled in comparison to the real thing.

This was heaven.

She nestled closer, wishing they could curl up together on the sofa and stay this way all day. Eventually, she knew she had to move. She lifted her face to meet his gaze. "Thank you. I'm…sorry I lost it like that."

"You've had a rough day," he said, his voice rough. "You have every right to be emotional."

She wanted to kiss him again. Not out of anger but from the sheer joy of being here in this beautiful house while a fire blazed in the hearth, from sheer relief that she had revealed the worst about herself and he was still willing to let her talk to their children.

"Thank you," she whispered again, then stood on tiptoe and pressed her mouth to the corner of his.

He didn't move for two seconds, maybe three. For one agonizing moment he stood frozen. Just before she thought he would push her away, he shifted his mouth with a desperate sound deep in his throat and kissed her.

Everything inside her seemed to sigh. Oh. This. She had missed his kiss so much. Missed the way his mouth fit hers perfectly, missed the slide of his tongue against hers, missed the soft, aching hunger rising up inside her.

This was her husband, the man she loved. The chance to be with him like this felt like a precious gift and she didn't want to waste an instant of it.

Chapter Twelve

This couldn't really be happening. Could it?

A few hours ago, he had been so furious at this woman in his arms. He hadn't wanted to look at her, forget about holding her like this, kissing her with this tender emotion swirling around him.

How had everything changed so quickly? In only a few hours, his perspective had completely shifted.

She hadn't left him and their kids. She had suffered a terrible accident and had had to relearn everything. That she wasn't dead, that she was here, warm and sweet in his arms, seemed like the most priceless of gifts.

Their kiss the day before had come from a place of anger and pain. This was far different. This was a reunion, a celebration of sorts. As he kissed her, tasted her, he was yanked back more than a decade, to those heady first months of their marriage when he couldn't get enough of the amazing woman who had miraculously fallen for him.

She didn't look the same now. Her cheekbones were different, her nose missing the little bump he had loved. But her mouth tasted the same and her eyes still seemed to see straight through him.

He had missed her every single day of the past seven years. She was here, right now, in his arms, and he felt as if he had been waiting for this moment forever.

They kissed for a long time, standing there by the fireplace in the great room. He kissed her until he couldn't think straight, until the initial tenderness gave way to hunger. He wanted to take her into the master bedroom off the kitchen, to explore every part of her he had missed so much.

He even moved in that direction, not really thinking it through but knowing he wanted to be closer to her. They had made it just to the door when Finn suddenly barked from his spot by the fire and the sound seemed to arrow straight through the haze of desire, especially when he heard what sounded like a key in the front door.

Cassie and Bridger were home from school.

He slid his mouth away, dazed and aching for more. Somehow he managed to pull his brain together long enough to step away from her an instant before the front door opened.

"Hey, Finn. Who's a good boy? Huh?" Bridger said. He could picture the boy petting the dog while he jumped all over him.

"Dad? Are you home?" Cassie called.

His eyes met Elizabeth's and the shocked arousal in them almost had him reaching for her again.

They had always been like this together, incinerating at the first touch.

"Wait here," he murmured to her, kind of nudging her

into the room, before he turned to face the children. "Grab a snack and I…we will be there in a moment."

"Who's we?" Bridger asked. "Is it Aunt Megan? I need to tell her about the new game we played at recess."

How was he supposed to break the news to the kids that their mother was alive and well and in their house? He had no idea how to find the right words for that kind of revelation.

"I'll be there in a minute," he called out again. "I have something I…need to tell you."

He couldn't see the children, but he could visualize their expressions. Bridger would be purely curious, his eyes eager to find out something fun and his dimples flashing as he grinned in anticipation.

Cassie, on the other hand, would be curious, too, but her expression would probably lean more toward apprehension. She didn't love surprises. She was a great kid but she had been through so very much—not only losing her mother, but dealing with the aftermath. The rumors and gossip and hurtful accusations.

Over the last few years, those rumors had begun to impact her more. She didn't say much about it but he knew she heard them and he knew they bothered her. He didn't need her to tell him that. He could tell by the way she seemed to shrink into herself.

Both his kids needed this to be resolved. It wasn't right that they had to live without their mom all these years and also had to be subject to gossip about their father.

When he walked into the master bedroom and closed the door behind him, he found Elizabeth standing in the middle of the room, arms wrapped around her chest. She had started to tremble, little shivers she probably wasn't even aware of making. Was it in response to his kiss or because she had heard the children?

Did he owe her an apology? He hadn't intended the kiss to spiral out of control like that. Another minute or two and he would have lowered her to the bed, just like old times.

"Elizabeth, I—"

"Don't," she said, her voice little more than a squeak. "It happened. The best thing is for both of us to…to forget about it now."

Forget about it? What kind of man did she think he was? In seven years, he hadn't forgotten one single detail about her: the taste or smell or silky smoothness of her skin. He remembered everything in vivid, painful detail.

"I don't see that happening," he said gruffly.

"Dad?" Bridger's voice sounded like it was coming right outside the room but was probably at the bottom of the stairs. "Can I have a bowl of cereal? I'm starving."

Right now he had more important things to think about than the stunning kiss he had just shared with his wife.

"Yes. Just give me a minute." It would take at least another minute or two to control his instant and shocking physical reaction to her closeness.

"Okay," Bridger called back.

"I'm sorry," Luke said to her. "I don't know what came over me."

"Please don't apologize," she said again. "I…missed kissing you."

Her words slid through him, filling a spot that had been empty too long.

"I missed kissing you, too."

Kissing and everything else. It had been so damn long since

he'd held a woman that it was taking all his strength to keep from wrapping his arms around her again.

They had other hurdles to overcome right now, though. He looked down at Elizabeth. "Are you ready to talk to the kids?"

"No. Not at all."

"I'll be right there with you."

He meant his words. He hadn't been with her after her accident or during her long recovery, but he could stand beside her when she faced their children.

"Thank you. That...means the world."

They walked into the kitchen with Elizabeth in front. She moved slowly but steadily. Luke's emotions were in an uproar and he didn't quite know what to do with them. He'd never been the best at handling strong emotions and the events of today were enough to challenge any man.

In the last four hours, he had gone from hate to shock to unwilling compassion to aching hunger and now to this growing respect.

When they walked into the kitchen, they found Cassie watching something on TV and Bridger eating a bowl of cereal at the counter.

"Hey, Dad." Bridge grinned around his spoon. "Before you ask, I don't have any math homework. I did it in class. I still have to read another twenty minutes, though."

"Good. Thanks for the info."

"I don't have homework either," Cassie said, her eyes still glued to the screen. "I did all mine in class, too."

"Great." At least they would have one less thing to stress about that evening.

He knew the moment they both noticed Elizabeth standing slightly behind him. Bridger set down his spoon, his cereal only half finished, while Cassie's jaw sagged so much, she almost spit out the piece of cheese stick she had just bitten off.

What was the matter? They'd never seen him with a strange woman before?

No. He answered his own question. When would they have, other than caregivers? He didn't date. He had a few good female friends, but they were all people the kids knew well and were usually married to one of his guy friends.

In general, his friends were a close-knit group who had stepped up to rally around him after Elizabeth disappeared. A few of them had dropped away, persuaded by the avalanche of doubt that sometimes threatened to suffocate him, but for the most part, he considered himself lucky in his friends.

The kids knew all of them, though. They didn't know this woman standing beside him.

"Kids. I need you to meet someone. Cassie, can you turn off the television? Bridger, are you done with your cereal? This is important, and I need your full attention."

"I'm done," Bridger said, pushing his bowl away as if to emphasize the point. Now both children looked apprehensive.

"What's going on?" Cassie asked.

He didn't know what to say. He really should have thought this through a little more, maybe warned them ahead of time before trotting out Elizabeth.

It was too late for any kind of warning. He simply had to plow through the situation, as he'd become fairly good at over the years.

"I have someone who would like to meet you. Well, to meet you again, anyway. Cassie, Bridger. This is your mother."

He held his breath, not sure what kind of reaction to expect from the children.

Both of them seemed frozen with shock, mouths open and eyes wide. Then Cassie shoved away from the table.

"No, she's not. Why would you tell such a terrible lie? Our mom is dead. You said so."

The distress in her voice ripped through him. He was an idiot. He really should have talked to them first by himself. He blamed the kiss that had left his thoughts scattered and had tossed his common sense out the window. He could have handled this so much better if he had made Elizabeth stay in the other room while he tried somehow to ready his children.

How could he possibly have prepared them for the sudden reappearance of their mother in their lives? No words of warning he might have uttered would have been adequate to explain away this sudden shocking turn of events.

He took Cassie's hands in his. They were trembling, much as her mother's were.

"For a long time, that's what I thought. That she was dead. I truly believed she was gone. Recently, though, Aunt Megan and Elliot found her. It took a lot of work and a lot of searching but I promise. This is your mother."

Cassie ripped her hands away. "You're wrong," she snapped. "This isn't her. It doesn't even look like her. I've seen the photographs. Plus, I remember her a little. I don't know who this lady is, but she's not my mom."

"You said our mom died." Bridger echoed his sister, looking baffled.

Luke grimaced. How the hell did he explain this complicated situation to his kids? He barely understood it himself.

"I thought she had died. I was sure of it. I never would have told you that if I didn't believe it myself. She was...sick and she left to get help, but when she was trying to come back, she had a bad accident."

He could see why she might feel guilty for her actions the night she left. Any mother should be horrified at the idea that she could even consider hurting her child. But as he'd told her, the important thing was, she *hadn't* done anything to Bridger or to herself. She had fought the demons and she had won.

"Did she get better from being sick?" Bridger asked. He cocked his head, studying Elizabeth as if wondering if she might have some obvious disorder like measles or leprosy.

"Eventually." Elizabeth answered his question, her voice low. "Not right away. As your dad said, I was in a terrible accident and I…I got lost for a few years, I guess you could say."

"Why is your face so different?" Bridger asked. "You're not like the lady in the picture Dad has by his bed."

Luke flushed, not sure he wanted Elizabeth knowing he kept a picture of her in his room. He didn't display it, though. That would have been too painful. It was in his bedside drawer. He looked at it every time he reached inside for his reading glasses or a tissue.

"In the accident, my face was…damaged. They had to… rebuild it with plastic surgery."

"Did it hurt?" Of course that would be the question his sweet, empathetic son would ask.

"Some of it did. I don't remember most of the first surgeries. I was in a…in a coma. Kind of like being in a deep sleep. But the…later ones did a little."

"I had to have stitches in my leg last summer when I fell riding my bike." He pulled up the leg of his jeans to show off the tiny scar that had only taken three stitches to close.

"Ouch."

"Do you have scars?"

Elizabeth nodded. "More on my…leg than my face. Under

179

my hair I do. You can still see some of them, if you look closely enough."

Bridger approached her and looked into her face without any sign of recognition. Luke wouldn't have expected any since their son had been less than a year when she left.

"I might look different, but I'm still...the same person."

Cassie didn't look at all convinced. "If you're really my mom, what song did you always sing when I was little?"

Confusion clouded Elizabeth's blue eyes. "I sang a lot of songs. I don't know which one—" Her voice broke off and comprehension slowly dawned. "Oh. The Cassiopeia song. I had...forgotten."

She began to sing a tune he remembered she had come up with herself, with lyrics about how much she loved Cassiopeia in the night sky, among the stars.

He had forgotten it, too. If he had remembered, he would have tried to sing it to his daughter himself, though his voice wasn't all that great.

How long had she been waiting for someone to sing it to her?

Tears trickled down his daughter's face as she listened to Elizabeth's soft voice.

"Why did you go?" she finally asked, her voice anguished, and Luke curled his hands into fists, wishing he could pull her into his arms for a hug. This wasn't about him right now. This was about a girl crying out for her mother.

Tears had begun dripping down Elizabeth's face, too. "Oh, honey. I don't...have a good answer for that. I was sick. Hurting. I...I left because I thought it was better for you."

"We thought our mom was dead. How would that be better for any kid?" She swiped angrily at her cheeks. Luke cursed himself. He shouldn't have just thrown this information at them without warning. He should have brought in some kind of professional, maybe the grief counselor he had finally taken Cassie to a few years earlier.

"Cassie, I'm so sorry."

"I don't want to hear how sorry you are," she cried. "Sorry isn't good enough."

"I know."

"You know what some of the kids at school say, like Rosie Sparks? They say Dad's a murderer. They say he killed you and hid your body somewhere. Dad doesn't even kill spiders. If he finds one, he catches it and puts it outside! But kids still call him a murderer. You should have come back before now so people wouldn't say that about him."

"What other people say doesn't matter. We knew the truth," Luke tried to tell her.

"But everybody else should have known you would never do something like that! I hate what some people say about you!"

"I was wrong to go," Elizabeth said, more tears trickling down. "So wrong."

Bridger looked as baffled and out of his depth with Cassie's outburst as Luke felt. He tried to hug his sister but she shrugged him away.

"You could have made it right and you didn't," she yelled at Elizabeth. "All this time, we thought you were dead and you let us! I don't care if you are my mom and you're back. We don't need you. We've been fine without you. I hate you. I wish you'd stayed away. You never should have come back."

She raced out of the kitchen and up the stairs, and a moment later they heard the slam of her bedroom door.

"Wow. Why is she so mad?" Bridger looked baffled.

"She has every reason to be mad," Elizabeth said, her voice shaking. "You do, too."

She looked defeated, heartsick. Luke longed to comfort her but knew nothing he said could make this right.

"I don't remember you much," Bridger said simply. "Cassie does."

Of all of them, Bridger seemed to be handling his mother's sudden reappearance in their lives with the most aplomb. Luke wouldn't have said his son was unfazed but he seemed more curious than anything, probably because he had been so young when she left.

"I should probably go talk to her." Luke was reluctant to leave Bridger alone with Elizabeth—for her sake as much as their son's—but if nothing else, he owed Cassie an apology for springing her mother on her that way without warning.

"Yes." Elizabeth looked devastated. "I...I hope she'll be all right. Do you want me to talk to her?"

"I'd better do it."

He headed for the stairs. As he did, he heard Bridger ask, "Why did they have to redo your whole face?"

"I broke...just about every bone in my face in the accident," he heard Elizabeth say.

"You really don't remember what they did?"

"No. I told you I was in a coma while my body was healing. When I woke up, I found a different person in the mirror."

Luke wanted to stay on the stairs and listen to more but his curiosity would have to wait. His daughter needed him right now.

He felt completely inadequate when it came to dealing with the mood swings that had hit Cassie over the last six months or so. Some days it was easier to just let Megan talk to her.

He was tempted to call his sister in for her preadolescent girl expertise but he knew that would be taking the easy way out.

He knocked on the door, pushing away his trepidation.

"Go away," Cassie snapped.

"That might work on TV but it doesn't in our house," Luke said calmly. "You don't get to tell me what to do."

"You tell *me* what to do all the time."

"That's because I'm your dad. It's my job. I'm pretty good at it, if I do say so myself."

The telling her what to do part, anyway. The rest of it, not so much.

After a moment, Cassie reluctantly opened the door. Her face was red and blotchy and she had several balled-up tissues in her hand.

"Is she gone? Did you tell her we don't need her? We're doing fine. We have Aunt Megan and Mrs. Mulvaney. She should have just stayed away."

He sighed, unable to admit to his daughter that he agreed with her to some extent, though an aunt and a housekeeper, no matter how beloved, weren't quite the same as a girl's mother.

"You should know I went to get her, Cassie. That's where I went when I had you stay with Megan. I brought her back to Haven Point."

Her outrage shifted to him. "Why? She didn't want us. She left us."

"Because I had to take care of a few things and I needed her here for that." He sat on her bed and put his arm around his beautiful, courageous daughter, who faced the world with her shoulders back and her chin out.

Would she have become so strong and resilient if she'd grown up with Elizabeth in her life?

"This is hard, grown-up stuff, kiddo. I wish things had been easier for you. I wish you and Bridger both had your mom here all these years to help you through hard times and be a friend and help you out with homework and teach you how to do hair. You know I stink at that."

She gave him a tiny smile but she still looked upset. "You really do."

He hugged her and she nestled against him, his sweet little girl. His children meant everything to him. Their uncomplicated love had healed many of the scarred and broken places inside him from his own childhood.

He felt a little ache inside for Elizabeth, who had missed so very much over the years.

"We can't change what happened. I know it's hard to understand. I still don't completely understand everything myself. I only know your mother was going through a really hard time when she left, and as she said, she didn't feel like she had any choice but to go."

"She *did* have a choice. She could have stayed and been our mom."

He kissed the top of Cassie's head. "I know. But she was sick and felt like she needed to go so she could get better."

As he said the words, he felt a sort of release, a lifting of his heart as a little more of the anger and hurt he had nursed over the years rose up like a weight had been cut from a hot air balloon.

"I can also tell you she never meant to stay away so long. She was trying to come back home to us when she was in the accident."

A few hours earlier, he never would have imagined he would be trying to defend Elizabeth to their daughter. His world had completely shifted and he still felt a little off-kilter from the reverberations.

Then again, some of his lingering disorientation could be from that emotional, intense kiss they had shared, he had to admit.

"We can be mad about what happened, that we didn't have the time with her we might have wanted. That's completely normal. It's been hard not having a mom. I know that."

She hugged him. "Not that hard when I have the best dad in the world."

Oh, that was far from the truth and they both knew it, but he appreciated her for saying it.

"It's fine to be mad about what happened. I would never tell you what you're feeling is wrong. But you do have to be polite. She is still your mother and she would like to stay in Haven Point long enough to see your school program next week. How do you feel about that?"

"I don't want her to. She's not my mom. Not really. I don't even know her and she doesn't know me."

"I know she's a stranger to you but will you give her a chance? You don't have to be best friends with her. But it's Christmas. We're supposed to open our hearts and be kind all year but especially during this season. Do you think you can do that? Politeness. That's all I'm asking."

She sighed and flopped back onto her bed. "I can try."

"Thanks, kiddo. I left her with Bridger and he's probably talking her ear off by now. I'd better go back down. She's been staying at the Riverbend Road house and I probably need to take her back."

"Do I have to go with you?"

Normally he would say yes. She was not quite ten, and while she was generally responsible and mature for her age and insisted she could handle herself, he didn't like leaving her alone yet.

In this case, he would only be gone a short time, long enough to drive Elizabeth to the little house and back. He sensed Cassie would benefit from a little time alone to come to terms with her jumbled feelings toward her mother.

"You can stay here. We won't be long."

"Thanks, Dad." She hugged him again. "I guess the best thing about her coming back is that at least people will see how wrong they've been about you."

"Yeah. There is that."

Over the years, he had tried not to let it bother him, but drip by drip, whisper by whisper, being the subject of speculation and gossip had worn him down.

He rose and headed for the door. "I'll work on dinner when I get back. I'll lock the doors downstairs and alarm the system. Keep your phone close."

"I'll be fine, Dad."

She was growing up. He couldn't stop time, as much as he might want to.

"We'll let you know when we're back."

She nodded and he headed back down the stairs to find his wife.

Chapter Thirteen

"I played soccer and baseball this year because I couldn't decide which one I liked more. But I think I like baseball more. I'm better at it, anyway. So I kind of think maybe I'll see if I can play more baseball. Maybe I'll skip soccer this year. That's what my friend Will does. He only plays baseball, not soccer. When I'm older, I could play on two baseball teams. I don't know. What do you think? Should I play soccer *and* baseball?"

Elizabeth had to fight back tears while listening to what was largely a monologue from Bridger. Her son—her *son*, whom she had never exchanged two words with except for when he was an infant—was asking her advice.

She couldn't seem to contain the joy washing over her like a summer rainstorm in the desert, cleansing the parched and thirsty landscape of her heart.

"I'm not sure what to tell you," she admitted. "It's…never a good idea to close your options off. You might end up changing your mind down the line about which…sport you prefer. Who knows? In a few years you might…like soccer better."

"Maybe. But I really, really, really like baseball," he said. "Really."

She smiled, wishing they had the kind of relationship where she could hug him or at least tousle his hair a little.

"This reminds me of when I was…younger and wanted to be a gymnast. It was…all I ever thought about. I was sure I would go to the…Olympics."

"Really? How old were you?"

"From about the time I was seven until maybe fifth grade. How old is that?"

"Cassie's in fourth grade and she's almost ten. So ten or eleven."

"Right. That's about right. I used to go every day after school to…train. Then in fifth grade, I broke my ankle…in gymnastics."

"Oh no! Did it hurt?"

Compared to everything else she had been through, that injury seemed minimal. "You know, I…barely remember it now. I'm sure it did hurt but it was so long ago, I don't…recall. The mind has a funny way of helping us deal with pain by allowing us to…forget a little."

Bridger took on a wise expression. "That's true. I told you I got stitches last summer when I crashed my bike. I know it hurt, but I can hardly remember how it felt."

She really hoped he might one day be able to get over the trauma of his mother walking away from him.

"The point is, I loved gymnastics more than anything else in the…world. After I broke my ankle, I couldn't do it anymore."

"Not even after you got the cast off?"

She shook her head. "My leg was never...as strong as it had been before. I knew I was going to have to find something else to love."

"Did you?"

"Yes. Many things. I tried out for a play at school and...really loved it. My best friend had horses and I fell in love with those, too. When I was old enough, I got a job at the garden center in Shelter Springs and discovered...how much I loved working with plants. If you love baseball and want to...only focus on that, fine. But don't close yourself off to other possibilities completely. You never know what might happen."

"Okay," he said cheerfully, then launched into a story about the game he and his best friends had invented at recess that largely sounded like a variation of the freeze tag she used to play with her friends, where a person could only be "unfrozen" if they yelled out the name of a favorite television show.

"It sounds like lots of...fun," she said.

"Oh, it is. Except when we run out of TV shows. Will wanted to use YouTube channels but we had to say that wasn't fair. There are, like, a million of them and some kids don't watch YouTube."

"I guess you have to draw the line...somewhere," she answered. She wouldn't mind spending all day here in this warm kitchen talking to her son, but Luke came down the stairs and joined them a few moments later.

Her heart kicked in her chest and her breath seemed to catch. Had she really kissed him only a short time earlier? She could still taste him on her lips, minty and delicious.

He was the only man she had ever slept with. The only one she had ever *wanted* to sleep with. She thought that part of her life was over with the accident but apparently not.

Desires that had been dormant for years were beginning to blossom to life.

He had kissed her twice, she reminded herself. Once in anger and once with a tenderness that stole her breath. That did not mean he ever intended for it to happen again. She might have to be content with her memories.

"Is Cassie...all right?" Elizabeth asked, in a voice that only wobbled a little.

"She will be, eventually. I'm afraid it will probably take some time."

Was it possible that she might have the chance someday to sit and talk with her daughter, as she had just done with her son? She was almost afraid to hope.

"She's angry and hurt right now. We have to give her that and let her work through it on her own time."

"Of course. It's a...lot to process." She didn't know what else she could say.

"Hey, Bridge. We need to take your mother back to the old house. Grab your coat and you can be my wingman."

"Sure!"

Their son jumped off his chair immediately, his features as delighted at the prospect of driving a few blocks as he might have been if his dad announced he was taking him to Disneyland.

"You're leaving...Cassie here by herself?" Elizabeth asked after Bridger headed into the mudroom for his coat.

"She's a pretty independent kid. She's almost ten and keeps telling me she's old enough to be on her own. We'll only be gone a few minutes. More than anything else, I think she needs her space right now."

He was a wonderful father. She had noticed it before in her clandestine visits to Haven Point. Even from a distance she could see how he always seemed to pay attention to the children, even when other adults tried to talk to him. They were his focus. How very grateful she was that he had stepped up to care for the children when she could not. She had not given him much choice, but Luke had taken the situation and made the best of it.

She was quiet as they drove back to the little house on the river, suddenly drained and exhausted from the emotional day. When she had waited for Luke to pick her up that morning, she had known the day would be tough, filled with the unveiling of difficult truths, but she had never expected her day to run as long as it had, into late afternoon.

She needed medication and also a rest. Everything inside her ached. She closed her eyes for a moment, breathing slowly to calm the chaos of her emotions. She must have fallen asleep for only a minute or two. She slowly became aware that the vehicle had stopped and Luke was calling her name.

"Elizabeth? Hello? Wake up."

"Oh. We're here already."

In the stretched-out afternoon light, the little house she had loved looked lonely and sad compared to the warm, gracious place Luke and their children called home now. It had been a place of love once, of promise. Now it was mostly a shell.

Someone would love it again, she reminded herself. That was why she was trying to make it as appealing as possible, so some young couple would buy it and make it into a home again.

"Thank you," she said, climbing out of the pickup.

Luke and Bridger both exited the pickup as well, coming around to her side.

"I'm a little hesitant to leave you here by yourself, especially after everything you've told me about your health problems," Luke said, worry creasing his forehead.

"I'll be fine. I live alone in Oregon," she pointed out.

"But you have friends in the same house there."

"Yes. But they're not always there. I'm often alone at Brambleberry House."

Melissa was a nurse and worked full-time at a clinic in Cannon Beach. She was also engaged and she and her daughter spent a great deal of time with her fiancé, Eli, as they prepared to merge their lives together. Rosa Galvez managed a gift shop in Cannon Beach for her aunt and also volunteered extensively in town, plus had a busy social life with many friends.

"Regardless. Maybe you should come stay at the new house with us."

"Yeah. That's a good idea," Bridger said. "Then I can show you my baseball trophies."

She would love nothing more than to spend as much time as possible with them while she had the chance. She wanted to know everything about her children, from how they liked their eggs to what stories they liked to hear to their favorite music.

Still, she couldn't shake the memory of Cassie's pain-filled eyes.

"I'm…not sure that's a good idea. You're the one who said you think Cassie…needs a little space from me right now."

He sighed. "You could be right. Maybe after a solid night's sleep, she'll see that having you back could turn out to be a good thing after all."

Did Luke think it was a good thing? She couldn't tell.

"I…hope so."

"You have a Christmas tree?" Bridger said in shock. "*We* don't even have a Christmas tree!"

"We have a tree," Luke said. "We just haven't put it up. We'll get to it, I promise."

"Tonight?"

"Maybe we can at least take it out of the box and set it in the stand."

She was torn, wanting to offer her help but also fully aware of her own limitations. She was already exhausted and knew she wouldn't have the strength to help deck his considerable halls. At least not tonight.

Luke seemed to sense it, too. "Try to get some rest. I'll call later to check on you."

"Thank you."

"Bye," Bridger said, then made a face. "I'm not sure what I should call you. I mean, you're my mom, but that doesn't seem quite right."

She had to earn that title back, she knew. Right now, she wasn't sure she ever would. "You can…start with Elizabeth."

"Okay. Bye, Elizabeth."

"Bye, son," she said.

"Try to get some rest," Luke said. "We'll figure things out in the morning."

"Thank you."

As she closed the door behind them, Elizabeth was quite certain that even as tired as she was, she wouldn't be sleeping for a long time.

"She's nice. I like her."

Luke spared a glance from the road heading back to the house to look over at his son. The words only confirmed his theory that Bridger was one of the most loving and kind people he'd ever had the pleasure of knowing—except when he resorted to punching kids at church in defense of his father.

"Do you?"

As far as Luke could tell, Bridger and his mother had exchanged about ten minutes of conversation while he had been upstairs talking to Cassie. Luke would have considered that too short a time to make a sound judgment call, but Bridger had an uncanny sense about people.

The boy looked thoughtful. "I don't love her, like you're supposed to love your mom. I don't even know her. But she seems nice. Did you know she used to do gymnastics and wanted to go to the Olympics?"

"I did know that. She was pretty good at it, too."

"Then she got hurt and had to find something else she liked."

She used to love a wide range of things, from crochet to watercolors to hiking. Every day had been a new discovery.

"Life is all about rolling with the punches, kid. We've talked about that before."

Even as he said it, Luke was aware that while the advice was nice in theory, in reality, he didn't know how to roll with the hard kick to the head he had sustained that day.

Elizabeth had been trying to return to them. She hadn't simply disappeared into the night without a backward glance. He still didn't know how to absorb the shock.

She had tried to come back to their family.

That thought seemed to ring through his head, over and over in a sweet, comforting refrain.

Chapter Fourteen

"Are you sure you're all right? We're all worried sick about you. Eli is about to call some of his army buddies in the area to do some reconnaissance and check out the situation."

Elizabeth set her paintbrush back in the drip tray, smiling a little at the overdramatic concern in Melissa's voice. "I'm fine," she said into her cell phone. "I told Rosa already. You two don't need to worry about me."

"Sorry, too late for that. We're worried. Wouldn't you be if you found one of your dearest friends had this whole life you knew nothing about?"

"I'm sorry I didn't tell you. I shouldn't have kept secrets from…my friends."

"No. You shouldn't have. We would have stood by you, you know. No matter what."

Grateful tears burned behind her eyes and she dashed them away with the sleeve of her paint shirt. She'd become such a crybaby since returning to Haven Point. "I know. When I come back, I promise, I will tell you everything you want to know."

"Be prepared. That is going to be a long conversation, honey. We want to know everything. I can't believe you kept a husband from us. And children!"

"It was...so complicated. I didn't know how to tell you."

"You must have been very desperate to leave and start a new life like you did," Melissa said, her voice gentle.

At the time, she had been desolate, but she didn't want to explain her reasons for leaving over the phone. "I was in a dark place and didn't feel I had many choices."

"You're sure you weren't being...hurt by anyone there?" her friend asked.

"Yes," she said firmly. "I promise, it wasn't like that. My husband is a good man who loved me and our children. He wasn't the reason I left."

"Is he treating you well? He seemed so angry that day."

That stunning kiss the day before flashed across her memory, leaving her a little light-headed. "Yes. Very well. We've... worked some things out."

Though they had many more things to sort through, she wanted to think they were heading in the right direction.

"Do you have any idea when you'll be back? Skye is still hoping you'll make it back before Christmas."

"I'm planning on it. I'll keep you posted if things change."

It would be difficult not to spend the holiday with her children, but she couldn't expect more than Luke was willing to give.

"Well, we miss you. The place isn't the same without you. Even the ghost seems restless."

She smiled a little at this. She and the other tenants of Brambleberry House were always comparing their woo-woo experiences in the house. The smell of freesia on the stairs. A feeling as if someone were watching out for them. Any paranormal activity—if indeed it existed and wasn't a figment of their shared imaginations—always felt benevolent. Protective, even.

Several times when she had been struggling with loneliness or pain, she had felt a warmth encircle her, as if someone's gentle presence had been there to push away the darkness.

She knew the others in the house had experienced similar things. She tended to believe the people who lived in a house left an imprint of themselves behind, and from all she had heard, the longtime owner of Brambleberry House had been a remarkable woman filled with love.

"I'm sorry," she said. "Tell Skye, Fiona and Abigail I'll be back as soon as I can."

They'd always referred to the ghost or echo or whatever it was as Abigail, the woman who had lived in the house for decades and left her indelible mark on it.

"I'll tell them. Just know you're missed by people and dogs on both sides of this earthly veil."

She smiled, then jumped a little when the doorbell to the house rang.

"Oh. Sounds like someone is here. I had better go."

"Okay, mystery woman," Melissa teased. "But I'm going to hold you to that night of true confessions when you get home. We'll make some kind of sinful chocolate dessert and stay up all night pulling out all your secrets."

"I…can't wait," she said, then severed the connection.

Of all the dark and difficult obstacles along her path over the last seven years, one thing had gone very, very right, when she had been lucky enough to find an open apartment at Brambleberry House. Rosa and Melissa had become dear friends to her, almost sisters. They had brought laughter and friendship back into her life.

It had been terribly unfair of her to keep so much of her history apart from them. They would have supported her. She knew that now. Yes, they probably would have encouraged her to move past her fear and return to Haven Point so she could reveal herself to her family. But maybe she had needed that.

Pushing away all the what-ifs, Elizabeth made her way to the door. Her leg ached but she did her best to ignore it. The bell rang a second time and her heartbeat quickened. It must be Luke. Who else would come calling?

She pulled open the door and had to swallow a gasp. It wasn't Luke. It was his sister.

"Hi," she said warily.

"Hello," Megan answered, then lapsed into silence.

It was snowing, Elizabeth saw, huge white flakes that floated down like feathers.

"May I come in?" the other woman asked after an awkward moment.

Elizabeth flushed and held the door open. "Of course. Sorry. I was just…surprised to see you here."

Megan sighed. "So am I."

She walked into the living room and pointed to Elizabeth's attire. "Did I come at a bad time? Are you painting something?"

Elizabeth looked down, suddenly aware of her paint-splattered clothes and the basic ponytail she'd pulled her hair into.

"Only the bedrooms. I'm trying to…freshen things up a little while I'm staying here to help Luke…get the house ready to sell."

Megan blinked, clearly astonished. "You're painting?"

"It's no big deal." She did not want to get into it. Her sister-in-law had clearly come here for some reason that had nothing to do with Elizabeth's spontaneous spruce-up project.

"Can I get you…something to drink? There are water bottles in the…refrigerator and some juice I made this morning."

"I'm fine. Thanks."

Megan shifted, her gaze flitting around the room. Anywhere but on Elizabeth. It might have been her imagination but she thought Megan didn't seem as hostile as she'd been the previous time Elizabeth had seen her, but it was hard to gauge what was going on in her head.

Elizabeth waited. Megan would tell her in her own time.

"So this morning I had a visit from my brother."

"Did you?"

"He told me the story you gave the district attorney yesterday."

She sat down on the sofa. "Did he…tell you everything?"

"Enough. He told me you left because you were afraid of hurting the children. And that you were trying to come back when you were in a car accident."

Elizabeth curled her hands together. She wasn't seeing condemnation in Megan's eyes, only confusion and wariness and perhaps even a hint of apology.

"He said you had a brain injury and reconstructive surgery and didn't remember who you were when you came out of a coma."

Sometimes she still wondered if she had *wanted* to forget, if she had been so horrified inside her psyche that she would even entertain the idea of ending her suffering and taking her beloved son with her that she had blocked out the memories.

Selective amnesia, Alice had called it.

"Yes," she said, not sure what Megan wanted her to say.

Megan sighed. "I've been so angry with you for seven

years. Now I don't know what to think. I wish Elliot were here to confirm some of the details."

Worry flitted across the other woman's features and Elizabeth felt an unexpected pang of sympathy. She really hoped Elliot was all right.

"You have...every right to be angry. I made a terrible mistake. I never should have left."

"It sounds as if you paid a heavy price for that decision. You were in a coma for weeks."

"Everyone paid a heavy price. Bridger and Cassie. You. Luke, most of all."

"Agreed. That's why I'm here. Obviously no further criminal investigation against Luke is warranted. Not when you're alive and well."

Was she well, though? That was a question she still hadn't figured out herself. She still carried such a load of guilt for the choices she had made and the suffering she had caused. She didn't know if she could ever absolve herself of that.

"I hope...that is the case."

"Giving your story to the district attorney is a good start but won't be enough to clear his name. You know that, right?"

"Yes."

"Rumor and innuendo have swirled around him for seven years. They're going to keep swirling, even when no charges are ever filed. The only way he's going to be able to truly move on is for you to show your face everywhere in town over the next few days while you're here. Make sure everyone who might be even a little tempted to accuse him of something terrible behind his back gets a good look at you."

Elizabeth couldn't imagine anything worse than having to be on display to everyone in Haven Point. "How do...you propose I do that?"

"You don't have to tell the whole story to everyone. About your postpartum depression or running away. That's none of their business. We only need to stick to the basic facts. You were in a terrible car accident, spent time in a coma and had amnesia when you came out of the coma. It's the truth, right?"

It sounded so unbelievable. If it hadn't happened to her, she would have found her own story ridiculous.

"Yes."

"We just have to tell people in town what happened so they can see how wrong they have been all this time about Luke."

"I want to clear his name. If I...if I had known what he was facing, I would have come back a long time ago."

"You're here now. That's the important thing. You came back, even if he had to drag you back to town. So we're agreed? Operation Redeem Luke Hamilton starts right now."

Elizabeth drew in a breath. She'd never expected to be teaming up with Megan, but it somehow felt right. "Where do we begin? I can take a DNA test and...make the results public."

"That's probably a good idea, but that will take time. Meanwhile, over the next few days while you're in town, you need to show up everywhere and be seen by everyone."

"I'm...going to the Christmas show at the school on Monday. Most of the town will be there."

"That's good but not enough. I'm giving a fund-raiser party Sunday night at the inn for the Haven Point Helping Hands. Couples. No kids. You and Luke need to show up."

"Your brother and I...aren't exactly a couple," she had to point out.

"I know that. But it's the perfect place for you to tell your story to as many people as possible."

She couldn't imagine anything worse, after all these years

of dealing with her issues on her own, than baring her mistakes to everyone in town.

For Luke and the children, she reminded herself. She could do it for them.

"All right. What else?"

"I'm sure Luke appreciates your efforts to spruce up the house a little, but you shouldn't be hiding away here by yourself. You would do far more good for the cause if you were seen out in public as much as possible, out talking to anyone you knew when you lived here before."

"I suppose I could do some…Christmas shopping."

"It won't take long before the word will get out, especially if you talk to the right people. The gossips in town are the same as they were seven years ago. Linda Fremont is a good place to start. Maybe you could buy something new to wear at the party."

"At Linda's boutique?" She couldn't keep the skepticism out of her voice.

Megan gave a surprised-sounding laugh. She cut it off abruptly, as if not quite willing to go so far in healing her relationship with Elizabeth. "The boutique isn't as bad as it used to be," she said. "Samantha has taken over a lot of the ordering now and she makes her own designs. You should check it out."

"All right," she said. She wasn't completely convinced but would take Megan's word for it.

"I also told Luke he should take you around town. The two of you and the kids need to be seen out and about together."

"We're not one big happy family. We're getting divorced."

The word still made her stomach hurt whenever she said it.

"I know, but you can pretend for a few days, can't you?"

She could for their sakes, even if it meant she was left with a broken heart.

★ ★ ★

"I don't want to go out to dinner with her." His obstinate daughter jutted out her chin. "I don't want to do *anything* with her. Why does she even have to be here? We don't need her."

Luke drew in a deep breath and prayed for patience. It seemed to be in short supply right now.

"I brought her to town to help me with some legal issues. And I invited her to dinner tonight. End of story. We're going. Now, I let you pick the location, and you chose Chinese food, which is fine. We'll go to Mandarin House."

It wouldn't have been his top choice, though they did have a good hot-and-sour soup. More important, it was a community favorite and usually did a brisk business on weeknights, when they discounted their family-style meals. As he was under strict orders from his sister to pick as public a place as possible to take Elizabeth, Mandarin House seemed a natural fit.

That didn't mean he was looking forward to it.

His daughter apparently wasn't either.

"I changed my mind. I don't want Chinese food. I would rather stay home than go to dinner with her." Cassie folded her arms across her chest. Bridger, who had been pretty casual about the whole thing and who had earlier that same afternoon seemed excited about seeing his mother again, folded his arms as well.

"I don't want to go either," he said, showing his usual solidarity to his sister. Somehow Cassie must have been hard at work persuading her brother to her side of things. Bridger tended to follow her lead in most things and this was apparently no different.

Luke didn't want to be the mean dad here but they weren't giving him a lot of options.

"Guys, this is important to me, okay? I need you to come to dinner with us and be polite."

"I don't want to be polite to her. I don't even want to talk to her," Cassie said. "She left us. Why do we have to be nice to her now?"

He sighed, hating this whole damn situation.

"You guys know the rules. You don't have to like everyone but you do have to be polite. You can make it through one hour of dinner."

Neither of them looked happy at the idea. How could he blame them? Luke wasn't sure he'd ever had such a mixed reaction toward a meal himself, both dread and this wary anticipation.

This was a dumb plan that wasn't going to work anyway. Megan seemed to think he only needed to show up in town with Elizabeth beside him and everyone would forget they had accused him of being a murderer. He could see so many flaws in that plan, he didn't know where to start listing them.

Like it or not, at least it was a plan.

He was still fretting about it as he loaded the kids up and headed toward the little house on the river.

"She's staying here? At our old house?" Cassie's outrage filled the pickup truck as he pulled into the driveway.

"I told you that last night. It was her house, too. We bought it together."

"And then she left," she retorted. "You shouldn't have let her stay here. This is our place."

He suspected that wherever Elizabeth had stayed, Cassie wouldn't have liked it. If she'd taken a room at the Inn on Haven Point or one of the guest cottages on Silver Beach, Cassie would have pitched a fit.

"Behave yourself tonight. I'm serious. You know how you

want to stay overnight at Evergreen Springs with Jasmyn over the Christmas break? Guess what won't happen if you can't be polite tonight?"

If anything, her outrage ramped up a notch. "You promised. Just like you promised we'd put up the Christmas tree and we haven't done that yet, have we?"

Luke sighed. It was *not* going to be a pleasant evening if things didn't improve.

"Tomorrow night, I promise."

"You said we'd do it last night."

"We set it up. It just took longer than we planned and we didn't have time to decorate it."

"Right. You said we'd do that tonight, and then the next thing I know, we're going to dinner."

What ever happened to his sweet, spunky daughter? She seemed to come and go. Right now in her place was this angry preteen who seemed to hate everything he did.

"It's up. It's lit. We'll decorate it as soon as we get a chance. Come on, Cassie. Christmas is next week. That's a good thing. And it's kind of a holiday miracle that we found your mom again. Can't you be happy about that?"

"I didn't want to find her. Things were fine the way they were."

Except they weren't and all of them knew it. There had been a huge hole in their lives that should have contained their mother.

He didn't know what the future would bring, if they could figure out some way to make this awkward situation work, but it suddenly seemed more important than ever that he do his best. His children needed their mother.

"Try to be nice," he said, then climbed out of the pickup truck and headed for the front door.

Elizabeth opened the door before he could even ring the doorbell. "Hi."

"Hi yourself."

She looked nervous, he realized. Her features were pale, her mouth set with determination. Out of nowhere, he felt a wave of protectiveness for her, the desire to hold her close and keep away anything bad that might threaten her.

"Are you ready for this?"

She gave a laugh that didn't quite sound genuine. "Not really. How about you?"

"I vote we go back to the new house for dinner. I've got some good steaks in the freezer I can grill."

Her smile was a little lopsided but was the most genuine amusement he had seen from her since he picked her up that day in Oregon.

"We can do this," she said, her words less faltering than he'd heard before, almost as if she'd been rehearsing them in her head all afternoon. "How hard will it be? I just have to… tell everyone in town that I ran away."

"You don't have to tell anyone anything. Once rumors spread about what went down yesterday at the district attorney's—and they've probably already started—neither of us should have to say anything. Everyone in town probably already knows you're back."

"I went dress…shopping today at Linda Fremont's store."

"How did that go?"

"I thought her jaw was going to hit the floor when I told her who I was."

"There you go. If Linda knows, everybody in town should, too. Maybe those steaks aren't such a bad idea after all."

She smiled again, though it didn't hide her nerves. "No.

Megan is right. This is Operation Redeem Luke Hamilton. I can do this. I just have to...grab my coat."

She reached around the door to the hook there, shrugged into it and picked up her purse. "Okay. I'm ready."

He glanced back at the pickup truck and the children watching them. "I have to warn you, Cassie is, uh, not super thrilled I'm making her spend time with you. Though Bridger seemed to have a different perspective before, somehow, she has persuaded her brother to her side. I hope she'll behave but dinner might be...difficult."

Her mouth pulled down briefly but she placed a hand on his arm. "She has a right to be upset, Luke. Please don't be hard on her. I left her. She has every right to hate me for that."

He wanted to tell her Cassie would come around eventually but he couldn't make such a promise. Both of their children had deep wounds. How could they not? Elizabeth's disappearance had left a void in all their lives. He had done his best to be a good parent to them and had received incredible help from Megan and good caregivers, but knew it wasn't the same as having their mother's presence.

"I've told them both that no matter what their feelings are, they have to be polite."

"Thank you." She suddenly seemed to realize her hand was still on his arm and dropped it abruptly.

He stopped himself just in time from telling her he didn't mind, that it had been a long time since a woman had touched him with affection.

The moment he helped her into the pickup truck and went around to his side, the tension started.

"You have a Christmas tree up," Cassie said, clear accusation in her voice. "Where did you get a Christmas tree?"

"I found one in the garage. The house seemed sad without

one. Oh." She looked suddenly guilty. "I hope it wasn't one you were planning to set up at the new house."

"We weren't. It's old," Luke answered. "You probably noticed half the lights don't work."

"I did see that. I found a string of lights in a box and put those on all the…branches where the pre-lit lights were out."

"I can't believe you have a Christmas tree here and we still haven't even decorated ours."

Luke sighed, feeling stuck between Cassie's anger and his sister's insistence that he make a public appearance with Elizabeth. Maybe he should have just canceled everything and stayed home to decorate the blasted tree so his daughter would get off his back about it.

He knew he'd been dragging his feet about Christmas. It was a bad habit he'd fallen into since Elizabeth left. The season had once been one of her favorites, filled with parties and music and delicious smells.

He did his best to create magical memories for his children, but without Elizabeth, everything had felt…empty. He usually had to dig and scrape to even pretend to find any hint of Christmas spirit in his heart.

"We have a tree," he reminded them. "And we'll decorate it as soon as we get the chance."

He looked across the width of the pickup truck. "Your mom is really good at decorating. She did a great job at the little house, even with a broken tree and only a few ornaments. I think she should help us with the big one at the new house."

"I'm happy to help," Elizabeth said.

"Yay," Bridger started to say, but his sister smacked him and he subsided into silence.

Luke sighed and backed out of the driveway. Yeah. Dinner was definitely going to be a treat.

Chapter Fifteen

Her children clearly did not want her here.

While not outright rude to her inside the restaurant as the hostess seated them at a prominent table, Bridger and Cassie talked mostly to each other and to their father.

She listened to their conversation, hesitant to interject her opinion or questions. She knew that introducing herself into their lives would be a process. She couldn't expect instant rapport with them. They needed to adapt to having her back first; then they might gradually come to accept her.

Luke did his best to turn the conversation in her direction.

"Do you have any pets in Oregon?" he asked after Bridger told his dad about a new trick he wanted to teach their cute dog, Finn.

"I don't," she answered. "My friend whose apartment is… upstairs from mine has an Irish setter and we've all kind of adopted her. Her name is Fiona."

"Whose name is Fiona? Your friend or your friend's dog?" Bridger asked, making her smile a little.

"The dog. My friend is named Rosa."

"Cassie has a friend named Rosie. Well, she's not really her friend. They're in the same grade but Rosie's kind of a jerk."

"Be quiet," Cassie ordered her brother on a hiss.

"What? You know she is. She's always saying bad stuff about our dad. Like that he did bad stuff and hurt..." His voice trailed off as he realized that he was speaking to the woman their dad had been suspected of hurting.

"She probably hears worse at home," Luke said quietly.

In how many homes throughout Haven Point had speculation about their relationship been a topic of conversation? She didn't even want to consider it.

People were certainly looking at them now, but she had to wonder how they would possibly know she was Elizabeth Hamilton when she did not look much like she had before. Maybe they all thought Luke was dating someone new.

Most of the people who came in were strangers to her, though many seemed to know Luke and the children. He greeted a few and introduced her, to startled looks and speculation.

Word would be everywhere in town before daybreak that she was back.

Shortly after they gave their order, Elizabeth finally noticed someone she knew. McKenzie Shaw Kilpatrick walked in with her husband, who was holding hands with a little toddler and gripping a baby carrier.

McKenzie gave her a friendly but casual wave, with no hint of their shared past. Elizabeth had tried to stop into McKenzie's store during her downtown visit, but McKenzie had not been working. As she hadn't known the salesclerk, she had bought a few gifts for the children and left quickly.

Elizabeth should talk to her here at the restaurant. If they were going to be all the buzz around Haven Point, the town mayor and her onetime friend ought to at least know what was going on.

"Excuse me, please." She rose from the table.

"Are you leaving?" Cassie asked hopefully.

"A…friend came in a moment ago. I'm…going to speak with her."

"Need me to go with you?" Luke asked.

His concern for her touched her deep inside. She shook her head. "I'll be fine. This shouldn't…take long."

She made her way across the crowded restaurant, aware of eyes on her as she moved. Were people staring at her because they knew who she was or because they thought she was simply a stranger in their midst? She had no idea.

At their table, McKenzie was busy pulling crayons out of a pencil bag for the toddler. She looked surprised but pleased when Elizabeth approached.

"Hi. Sonia, right?"

She could feel herself flush, caught out in her own deception. "Actually, no. I'm sorry I…told you that. I'm here with Luke and it's… I'm…" She faltered more than usual, the words slippery and elusive. "I'm actually…Elizabeth Sinclair Hamilton."

For several long seconds, the usual sounds in the restaurant of clinking dishes and chopsticks and diners seemed to fade away. McKenzie stared at her, mouth wide. Even her toddler had fallen silent.

"Really?" Ben asked.

At the word, McKenzie seemed to snap out of it. Her features grew angry, tight. "No, you're not. What kind of con are you running, ma'am? I knew Elizabeth. You don't look anything like her."

So she hadn't spoken with Linda or Samantha Fremont.

"On the...surface, I know I look different. If you look closer, you might see the...resemblance. I was in an accident and had...plastic surgery. It's me, though. You can...you can ask Luke. Or Megan."

"You said your name was Sonia."

"I know. I...shouldn't have."

"Why would you lie?" Ben asked. "If you're really Elizabeth, why not come clean the moment you came back to town?"

"It's not her," McKenzie insisted.

She knew how this must look. McKenzie had been a good friend. She didn't want to believe that she hadn't recognized Elizabeth the first moment she saw her.

"I am," she answered. "I'm sorry I...deceived you that first day. I...didn't know how to come out with the truth."

McKenzie still didn't seem convinced and Elizabeth sighed. "Do you...remember that time in high school when we borrowed my dad's...car and drove into Boise to look for prom dresses and ended up getting a flat tire on the way back? Those boys from Shelter Springs changed the tire for us and invited us to their prom, remember?"

"How do you know that?" The beginnings of doubt crossed her expression.

"Because I was there. They were...cute guys. I would have said yes, only you got all Haven Point proud and said you wouldn't be caught dead at their...lame prom."

McKenzie was kind of in love with their hometown, which Elizabeth supposed served her well in her job as mayor.

"Oh man. I'd completely forgotten about that until just this moment. I was such a dork."

"You're still a dork," Ben said, but with so much affection in his voice, a deep yearning seemed to catch in Elizabeth's chest.

"True enough." McKenzie stood and moved closer to her, eyes narrowed as she studied her closely. "I'm sorry but I still can't believe it's really you."

"It is. I promise. Ask Luke."

McKenzie looked at the other table where Luke and the children were watching their interaction. Luke gave a subtle nod and McKenzie turned back to her, eyes stunned.

"You look so different. How is this possible? I don't know what to say. You don't look the same. The eyes, maybe. And the cheekbones. I don't understand. This is unbelievable!"

"I know. But it's true. I was in an accident and ended up having to have...facial reconstruction. It's really me. I promise. I'm the same person who helped you run for...class president in seventh grade and took you skinny-dipping for the first time on your sixteenth birthday."

"You were so bad!"

She hadn't been. Not really. She had adored her parents too much to want to cause them a moment's grief. That wild summer night on an empty beach at the lake had been a fluke.

The reminders of their shared past seemed to have convinced the other woman Elizabeth was telling the truth.

"It's really you. It has to be, if you remember those things. And Luke wouldn't play a cruel trick like that. I don't know what to say. After all these years, it's really you! I don't quite know whether to call you Elizabeth or Sonia."

"Either one works."

McKenzie gazed at her, shaking her head in disbelief. Then, before Elizabeth could react, she reached out and folded her into a hug. The contact soaked through her, warming another frozen little corner of her heart.

"I don't know where you've been or why you were using another name. It doesn't really matter. I'm just so glad to have you back. I imagine Luke and the children are thrilled, too."

Elizabeth wouldn't go that far. "I'm here to prove to people... once and for all that Luke had absolutely nothing to do with my disappearance. I left of my own free...will and stayed away by my own...choice."

"That's going to be a hard sell around here to some people."

"I know. I would love it if you could...help me."

McKenzie looked thoughtful. "Are you planning to go to Megan's fund-raiser this weekend?"

Elizabeth tried not to break out in a cold sweat at the idea. "Yes."

"That will be the perfect place. Part business, part social. We can take you around to talk to everyone, those you might have known here before and those you don't."

She did not want to become the center of attention at Megan's event, though she could not deny it would be an efficient way to speak with many people in town who might want to hear her story. What better place to reach many of the movers and shakers around town? Everyone would want to hear her story and she couldn't deny it would be easier to do it all at once, rather than in steady drips for days, when the Haven Point grapevine was sure to spread the news with plenty of distortions.

"We can talk strategy later. I'm just so happy that you're here. I've missed you!"

McKenzie gave her another hug, which left her feeling guilty and weird.

Since her memories started to come back, she had spent so much time thinking about how very much she missed Luke and the children that she hadn't given enough room in her memories for everyone else who had once been important to her.

She had friends here. People who had cared about her, people she had loved, though she had pushed many of them away in the dark time after her parents died.

Her friends shouldn't have had to wonder what had happened to her all this time. She should have somehow found the courage to come back. The shame she felt at her own choices seemed a poor reason to put them through years of uncertainty.

She had no idea how she could make it up to everyone, especially Luke and their children.

"How did McKenzie take it?" Luke asked when she left the Kilpatricks and returned to her own family.

"Better than I...feared. She's not happy I didn't tell her the other day but she says she'll help me spread the word at the... fund-raiser on Sunday."

"She does love a project," he said as the server delivered their food.

She couldn't have said it was the most enjoyable dinner of her life. While the food was better than she remembered, she felt as if everyone was staring at her, wondering about her.

The children didn't make things easier. While Bridger seemed to warm up a little throughout the meal, Cassie basically ignored her. She quite deliberately offered tastes of her tiny spicy chicken to everyone except Elizabeth and seemed to find great delight in her fortune cookie message, *You should avoid untrustworthy strangers today.*

"That's good advice, isn't it? We should all follow it," she said to the table at large, with no subtlety whatsoever.

"Huh. Mine says, 'You will make a new friend in an unexpected place,'" Bridger said. Elizabeth sensed he was torn between supporting his sister and his natural inclination toward kindness and also a certain curiosity about the mother he didn't remember.

"What does yours say, Dad?" Cassie asked.

This was obviously a thing they did, comparing fortunes. Yet another tradition she hadn't shared with her family.

"Mine says, 'Be open to new opportunities.' That's a good one."

"Kind of boring, though," Cassie said. "I mean, why can't they ever be more specific in fortunes?"

"Sometimes they are," Bridger said. "Remember that time we got lottery numbers, only Dad wouldn't let us buy a ticket?"

"I guess they're vague because one fortune can mean a hundred different things depending on who opens it." Luke turned to her. "How about yours, Lizzie? What did you get?"

The familiar nickname seemed to send a flood of memories through her. When he kissed her for the first time, on a date when they'd gone hiking in the hills overlooking the lake. On their wedding day, when he had seemed to glow with joy. The day Cassie had been born, when he had laid their wriggling baby on her chest, tears streaming down his face.

She had loved every time he said her name with that low, sexy voice.

She pushed away the memories and the tangle of emotion. "I haven't opened it yet."

"Can I do it?" Bridger asked.

His features looked so eager, she couldn't resist passing the fortune cookie to him. "You can have it, if you want."

"Thanks. But even if I eat the cookie, the fortune is still yours. That's our rule."

He opened it and pulled out the little slip of paper. "It says, 'You are a product of your past mistakes but need not be a prisoner to them.' What the heck does that mean? It's not even a fortune."

"That's dumb," Cassie said as her brother popped the cookie in his mouth.

Luke cleared his throat. His gaze locked with Elizabeth's. "I disagree. I think it's pretty good advice for all of us."

"Yes," she managed, snatching up the fortune and holding it tightly between her fingers, as if she could absorb the message through her skin.

She had let herself become a prisoner, trapped inside this body that no longer worked the way she wanted and the face that wasn't her own. Was it possible that coming back here might help her break out?

"That was good," Bridger said with a satisfied sigh. "I'm glad we came here. We haven't had Chinese in forever."

"It was delicious," Elizabeth agreed.

"You hardly ate any," Luke answered with a look of concern.

It was a little difficult to use chopsticks when one felt like an animal in a zoo, with everyone in the restaurant watching to see what strange things she might do next.

She had signed up for this, Elizabeth reminded herself. If it restored Luke's reputation, all the discomfort would be worth it.

"I can take the leftovers home and have them for lunch tomorrow."

"Since we're done, can we leave now?" Cassie asked, not bothering to conceal her impatience. "I'm ready to go home."

She directed the question exclusively to her father, not even looking at Elizabeth at his side. She was not making much progress finding peace with her child.

"I'm finished, too." Bridger was quick to back up his sister, as if they had a pact.

"I'll call the server over."

After they had packed up the leftovers and settled the bill, they rose to leave. The area where patrons waited to be seated was packed with people. Luke had been right—Mandarin House was crowded on weeknights.

She thought she recognized a few people but was grateful he didn't stop to talk to anyone. Just before they reached the door, another couple came in and Elizabeth gave an internal groan as she recognized Billy Sparks.

The man had never liked Luke, in one of those completely ridiculous and one-sided feuds that went back to something that happened in high school. She didn't even know the details. She only knew Luke had beat him out for some position on a sports team and Billy had held a grudge all those years.

"New girlfriend, Hamilton?" He leered at her, making Elizabeth feel as if he could see beneath her clothing.

Too bad for him, he would get an eyeful of scars.

"No, actually. An old one. The one I made my wife. Elizabeth, you remember Billy Sparks."

"Yes." Unfortunately. "Hello."

"This is his wife, Tammy."

The woman looked tired, hardened by life. She nodded politely but Billy only stared at Elizabeth with the befuddled look that was becoming entirely too familiar.

"That's not Elizabeth. You're just trying to get some other bitch to pretend to be your wife. I heard rumors you're finally heading to the slammer, right where you belong."

Luke straightened, looking big and dangerous. "First, watch

your language around my family. Second, you heard wrong. The district attorney and I have come to an arrangement and no charges will be filed, ever. So you can cancel whatever party you might have been planning. Third, this is indeed Elizabeth."

"You're a damned liar."

Beside her, she could feel the tension radiating off of Bridger and Cassie. They didn't need to be here for this.

"Really, Billy?" Elizabeth's heart was pounding. She hated confrontations, but she hated bullies more, and she couldn't stand by and let this little rodent of a man malign her husband. "*He's* the liar? Luke isn't the one who told everyone at school they had three…scholarship offers to play football at… division one schools but turned them all down to stay here and work in his dad's…auto shop."

The words escaped in a rush, tripping over each other, but she got them all out anyway.

Billy glared at her. "I did have scholarships! Maybe I didn't want to go to any of those stupid schools."

"My point isn't about the…schools, Billy. I don't care whether you had a dozen football scholarships. But I was… here when you were telling everyone about them. Some woman Luke hired off the street to…pretend to be his wife wouldn't have known that, would she?"

"He could have told you."

"You're right. He also could have…told me about the time my dad hired you to mow the lawn at his office and you ended up breaking the…mower the first day, pocketing the money and never coming back."

Billy looked befuddled. She grew aware of others in the crowded waiting area paying careful attention to the conversation.

Elizabeth wanted to slip out the door and let it go at that. Her job here was to defend her husband against years of accusation and somehow she sensed Billy Sparks may have been one of those whispering loudest against Luke.

"It's me, Bill. I might not…look the same, but it's still me. Listen closely. I'll say it…slowly."

He didn't need to know that wasn't a dig against him, more necessity because the words weren't coming as eloquently as she wanted. Never had she regretted her fumbling speech more than she did in this moment, when she wanted to be smooth and precise and determined.

"I am…Elizabeth Hamilton. I left town on my own. People walk away from their…lives all the time. Luke had…nothing to do with it. He never hurt me, ever, and has been unfairly convicted by…small-minded people ever since. Any rumors or…or gossip to the contrary is dead wrong. Is that…clear?"

Billy's eyes widened. He opened his mouth as if to answer, but Elizabeth didn't want to hear anything he had to say. She made her way through the crowd, hoping Luke and the children were following her and that she could make it outside without tripping on her legs that suddenly felt weak and trembling.

Chapter Sixteen

As they walked outside Mandarin House into soft snow-fall, Luke's head was spinning.

She had been amazing.

His wife had just put Billy Sparks in his place with a few emphatic words.

It was about damned time. For seven years, the man had made Luke's life a misery and had passed that legacy on to his children, Jedediah and Rosie, who in turn had tormented Bridger and Cassie.

He hated bullies more than anything, no doubt because he had lived with one his entire childhood, until his father died.

"Thank you," he said gruffly when they reached his pickup truck.

She flushed under the lights in the parking lot and he fought the urge to wrap his arms around her and kiss that soft, sweet mouth, right here in front of the kids and anybody looking out the windows of the restaurant.

"I didn't do anything," she said. "I can't believe Billy is still such a…jerk."

"I guess some people never change."

That wasn't precisely true. Elizabeth had changed—on the outside, anyway. Inside, he was beginning to discover traces of that woman he had fallen in love with, who had always stood up to champion those in need.

With her generous heart and her unfailing love, she had healed so many of the scars left by his father. He knew that was why the years after her parents died had been so difficult, because he ached to know he hadn't been able to help her heal in return.

She said little as they drove through the night, back to the house on Riverbend Road. The kids didn't seem to be in very talkative moods either.

Luke was strangely reluctant for the evening to end, but it was a school night and he needed to take Bridger and Cassie home.

"I've got to work at a job site in Shelter Springs tomorrow. Will you be all right here? Have enough food?"

She held up the cartons of Chinese food. "Yes. No problem."

"Would you be willing to help us decorate the Christmas tree tomorrow evening? I could grill those steaks we talked about earlier."

"You want *her* to help us?"

Cassie looked obviously outraged at the very idea, but Luke cut her off. "Yes. Why not?"

"We don't want her there," Cassie said, her voice furious. "She's ruining everything! Why did she have to come back? We were doing fine without her."

They hadn't been, though. He'd barely been keeping his

head above water. His business was doing well, keeping him busy, but he knew he wasn't doing his best when it came to the children.

They pulled into the driveway of the little house on the river. "It's all right," she said softly. "I'm sure you can...handle the tree trimming without me."

Maybe, but he didn't want to.

"We need to clear the air here. Cassie, Elizabeth is your mother. I know you're angry that she hasn't been in your life all this time. That's completely understandable. Not having your mom here all those years hurt. But we talked about this. Some of those reasons she was gone weren't her fault. You can decide you don't want to forgive her. I won't argue with you about that or lecture you about the reasons I think you should. You have the right to your feelings. But you don't have the right to take your hurt and anger out on other people. Got it?"

She mumbled something in the back seat he didn't hear, crossed her arms and sank back.

With a sigh, he climbed out and walked around to open the door for Elizabeth and help her out. "I'll walk you up," he said.

"You don't have to. I'm...okay."

"It might be slick."

He lent her an arm and walked with her up to the front door.

Christmas lights from her tree and from the neighbors' houses twinkled merrily. It made a charming scene on this little street beside the river.

When she unlocked the door and opened it, cinnamon-scented warmth reached out and tugged at him, drawing him inside with her.

"I don't want to cause more...trouble with Cassie," she said, her features tight with worry. "She's struggling enough. I don't have to...make things worse."

"You're not causing trouble. I would like you to be there, helping with the tree. I think Bridger would, too."

"Cassie's feelings...matter. This is a hard situation. We can't expect her to just shove down her anger and pretend we're one big happy family."

"I'm not asking her to do that. I'm only asking her to be polite."

"She's a...child. She doesn't have your years of experience, learning to...conquer every strong emotion."

He snorted. "Conquer? Is that what you'd call it?"

"What else? You never crack and lose it like the rest of us, no matter how...upset you might be at a...situation."

She was so wrong. He had cracked apart in a thousand different pieces after she left.

"Controlling one's temper is a mark of inner strength." He sounded like a pompous ass but couldn't seem to help it.

"I agree. And...sometimes giving in to it is a mark of... humanity." She shrugged out of her coat. "We need to give Cassie time to come to terms with everything that's happened. I think if we...push her too hard, she's only going to retreat into herself and let her anger continue to boil."

She was probably right. He sighed. "All right. Maybe we'll hang a few ornaments by ourselves tomorrow night, just so they'll stop nagging me about it, and then you can help us finish it over the weekend."

"That sounds like a...good plan."

"Of course, that means we won't be able to hit the town again tomorrow. Do you mind?"

"I'm sure I'll manage to live with my...disappointment," she said dryly, which made him smile a little.

He liked Elizabeth. In the midst of his own anger and pain over the years, he'd forgotten how much. Yes, he had deeply loved his wife. But he had liked her, too. She was funny, kind, compassionate. All the things he knew he wasn't.

"Good night, then. I'll be in touch about where we go from here."

"Good night." She smiled that soft, sweet smile he loved so much. Though the children were still out in the car waiting for him, Luke couldn't resist leaning down and kissing the corner of her mouth.

It was supposed to be a tiny taste, just a polite kiss goodnight, but the moment he tasted her, he knew he needed more. He had been dreaming of kissing her since the afternoon before.

She wrapped her arms around his waist as she returned the kiss. They kissed for as long as he dared, with the kids waiting for him. Though he wanted more—so much more—he managed to ease away before things flared out of control.

"I'll be in touch," he repeated.

She nodded, eyes dazed, and he headed out the door. Only when he started to open the door to his pickup did he realize he was humming, happier than he'd been in a long time.

Two days later, Luke felt as if he were living in some kind of weird, distorted version of his dream life—like a pretty little snow globe that somebody had doodled on with permanent marker.

When he and Elizabeth had married, this was exactly the sort of Christmas scene he'd imagined: the two of them working together with their children to make cookies while snow gently fluttered down outside the window, holiday music played in the background and the smells of sugar and cinnamon encircled them.

That part was real enough. But he hadn't imagined the woman who was helping decorate the cookies would be a virtual stranger to him and would look so different than the woman he had married. Or that he would find himself just as attracted to her.

He had seen her every day since their Chinese dinner. The day before, he had managed to find time to take her to lunch while the kids were at school, choosing as public a venue as possible, Serrano's. He would have enjoyed a quiet meal with polite conversation, but that particular restaurant at lunch was the worst possible place for privacy. They spent the whole lunch hour speaking to other people who stopped by to say hello. Later he had taken her to Shelter Springs so she could do a little Christmas shopping for the children.

Somehow he had managed to keep his hands off of her, though it was becoming increasingly difficult.

His feelings for her were growing along with his desire and he didn't quite know what to do about either.

"Your Christmas tree looks beautiful," Elizabeth said.

"Thanks," Bridger said with a grin, before he aimed a guilty look at his sister and clamped his lips together. That had been the pattern for most of the day. Luke sensed that his son was desperate to make a connection with his mother yet was constrained because of loyalty to Cassie.

Luke had no idea how to bridge the chasm. All of Elizabeth's outreach efforts seemed to fall flat as Cassie grew increasingly withdrawn.

He sensed their daughter *wanted* to begin forging a relationship with her mother but didn't know how to let go of her anger and resentment. He had tried to talk to Cassie but subsided after she started to turn her anger onto *him*.

The therapist she had seen a few years ago didn't have any openings until after the holidays, so he had booked the earliest one available.

"All the Christmas trees around here look great," Elizabeth said to Bridger, admiring the cookies on the wax paper in front of him. "I really like the way you dusted powdered sugar on them to look like snow."

"Thanks. That was Cassie's idea."

"It was a great one. They look terrific. Maybe you should save a few to put out for Santa."

"We're too old for Santa," Cassie snapped. Luke frowned at her. *She* might be. Her brother, at not quite eight, was still holding on.

"You're never too old to believe in magic," Elizabeth said, her voice soft but firm. "For instance, never in my…wildest dreams would I have imagined a few weeks ago that I would be here with you guys, making…cookies. This is real-life magic."

He wanted to kiss her again, right there in the kitchen in front of the children.

Luke caught himself. He needed to cut it out. He had a long way to go, working through his own feelings about Elizabeth's reappearance in their lives. He wasn't ready to simply jump back into things with her.

He had been *destroyed* when she left. Heartbroken, angry, devastated. Yes, it healed a few of those scars to know she had been on her way back to them when she had suffered that terrible accident. Not all of them, though. He didn't know how to get past the hurt from knowing she hadn't turned to him when she found herself in such deep despair.

He had loved her and wanted nothing more than to help her through her dark times, but she hadn't let him inside. She had closed herself off. In effect, she'd done the same thing when she didn't come back to them the moment she started to regain her memory.

How could he trust that the next time something hard happened to her, Elizabeth wouldn't crawl back into that dark space and close the door behind her, shutting him out?

Some of his scars were so deeply etched, he didn't know how they could ever heal.

"Do you remember our first Christmas dinner together after we were married?" he had to ask.

For a moment, she looked confused. Then he saw the memories come flooding back. Her face turned pink in that adorable way she'd always had, and Luke had to focus on the really terrible job he was doing decorating an ornament-shaped cookie to keep from pulling her into his arms.

"One of the more…embarrassing moments of my life."

"What did you do?" Bridger asked.

She touched her hands to her cheeks as if she could cool them down, another mannerism he remembered vividly. "It was our first Christmas together and I wanted to make it perfect. I was a young newlywed very much in love with my husband."

Cassie made a snorty sound of disgust but he noticed she was listening. He decided to take that as a good sign.

"We were very poor," Elizabeth went on.

"So poor," Luke chimed in. They had to scrape together every penny for the down payment on the Riverbend Road house and there had been little left for anything else.

"I wanted to make Christmas Eve dinner amazing on a

limited budget and I managed to save a few dollars from each paycheck until I had a nice little nest egg."

"What were you going to have?" Bridger was always interested in food.

"Roast turkey."

"That's Dad's favorite," Bridger told her.

She glanced at Luke and smiled a little. "I...remember. I had never cooked a turkey before but figured it couldn't be that hard."

"Yeah. I thought the same thing when I tried to do the first one on my own," Luke said.

"Everything went fine, I thought. I thawed it for three days ahead of time. I brined it. I took out the giblets and the neck. I marinated it. Except I forgot that I had added some dish soap to clean the bowl before I mixed the marinade and never rinsed it out. So after all that hard work, money and days of planning, I ended up injecting marinade mixed with dish soap into my beautiful twenty-five-dollar turkey."

"Gross," Cassie exclaimed.

"It was."

"Did you puke?" Bridger asked.

It had been nasty, Luke remembered, but he hadn't wanted to hurt Elizabeth's feelings.

"He ate an entire piece without complaining," Elizabeth said. "He didn't say a word. I finally took a taste and realized what I had done and was so mad at myself, but we just laughed and laughed. I was *not* a cook."

"You got better," he said.

She gave him a soft smile that sent heat and memories tangling through him. She didn't tell them the rest, that after the disastrous dinner, still laughing, they had spent the rest of that Christmas Eve tucked together in bed, making love again and again and being deliriously happy together.

It had been his best Christmas ever. Not just because he had his wife in his arms, but because his heart had been so full of love and joy and *belonging*. He had felt like the luckiest man in Lake Haven County, to know that Elizabeth Sinclair wanted to be with him.

The next year, hugely pregnant with Cassie, she had done her best to put on another memorable Christmas dinner, but her grief over her parents' deaths that summer had sapped much of the joy from the holidays.

"I'm pretty sure I didn't add dish soap to the soup I'm making in the slow cooker," he said. "It should be ready anytime. We'd love to have you join us."

That was a bit of an exaggeration, at least on the part of his children, but it seemed the polite thing to say.

"It smells delicious. I'm sure it will be wonderful."

Was it possible they could begin to build new traditions this year? Maybe he just needed to be brave enough to try.

Elizabeth wanted to pinch herself. Could she really be here in the kitchen of Luke's beautiful new house, the home that they had designed in their heads together, making cookies and sharing memories?

It was the most magical of Christmas gifts, more precious because a few weeks ago, she never would have expected it.

"How many more cookies do we have to decorate?" Cassie asked in a put-upon tone. "I'm bored and I'm so tired of holding this knife."

If Elizabeth might have been a little tempted to think this was a perfect preholiday activity, Cassie's negative attitude would have quickly convinced her otherwise. It twisted around and between all of them like barbed wire.

Instead of easing, her daughter's hostility seemed to be amplifying, and Elizabeth had no idea how to make it better.

"We've got one more batch to decorate. Bridger and I can finish."

"Then can we take them to the neighbors?" her son asked.

"We have to shovel after lunch," Luke said firmly. "After that, we'll take the cookies. That storm has dropped about four new inches and we need to clear it away."

"Why do I have to? Can't you and Bridger do it? Maybe *she* can help." Cassie didn't look at Elizabeth, just said the feminine pronoun in a tone dripping with condescension.

"I'm happy to," Elizabeth said. She wasn't the strongest with the shovel, but had discovered that physical activity of any kind helped keep her joints lubricated and reduced pain.

"You're helping," Luke told Cassie in a tone that didn't invite argument. "What do we do in the Hamilton family?"

"We take care of business," the children dutifully recited, but Bridger spoke with enthusiasm while Cassie sounded like she was on the way to the principal's office.

After they ate Luke's delicious soup and had cookies for dessert, they put on their winter clothes and headed out into the snow.

"Do you...have a shovel for me?" Elizabeth asked as Luke headed for a snowblower in the garage.

"You really don't have to help us," Luke said. "The kids and I have a system. I use the blower or the four-wheeler plow on the driveway while they clear the walks with the shovels. We've got a couple of elderly neighbors who can't do their own, so we usually start there, then work our way back here."

"I don't mind helping, as long as you...have an extra shovel."

He frowned. "I don't want you to hurt yourself."

"I'm not an invalid, Luke. I'll be fine. I want to help."

With a sigh, he handed her another shovel. The children had already gone outside, and she followed them down the street to a plain house with a pretty fir wreath on the door.

"Where's a good place for me to start?" she asked.

"Cassie does the steps into the house and I do the sidewalk out front. You can help me there," Bridger said.

Other than Cassie grumbling about making cookies, the children didn't seem to mind work. It warmed Elizabeth's heart, another example of what a good father Luke was. He was showing them things they had talked about teaching their children together, how to work and how to serve others.

Elizabeth started by the mailbox and began clearing. She couldn't remember the last time she had shoveled snow but somehow the muscle memory was still there.

She had to stop to take frequent rests, but she didn't mind since it gave her the chance to admire her husband's broad shoulders.

They quickly finished that house and headed one more house down. Somehow she wasn't surprised that he helped his neighbors. He had always done that, cared about others. It was one of the things she had fallen hardest for after they first started dating. She still found it one of his most attractive qualities.

How had he managed to come out of his childhood with that compassion for others intact? She had no idea. Like so many other things, she gave much of the credit to Megan's mother, Sharon, his stepmother, who had been a kind, warm woman who made the unfortunate mistake of marrying Paul Hamilton.

When she and Luke first started dating, Elizabeth had no idea how difficult his home life was, the physical or emotional abuse he suffered at the hands of his father. She hadn't a clue, actually, as Luke never talked about it.

Megan was the one who had let a few of those details slip, only after Elizabeth had been dating him for several months, after she was already deeply in love and they were beginning to talk about marriage.

Luke hadn't wanted to tell her. As far as he was concerned, that was his past and had no bearing on what he did moving forward or the man he had become.

When she pressed, he had finally told her a few things. Even now she probably didn't have all the details, but what little she had learned about his childhood had only reinforced to her what an amazing man he was.

He was still an amazing man, a man she had never stopped loving.

Luke and the children were the first thing that popped into her head each morning and the last thing she thought about each night.

She loved being with them, she thought as they returned to the house and started on his driveway. She loved everything about it, even working in the cold to shovel snow and even with Cassie's belligerent attitude.

How would she ever be able to endure her solitary life at Brambleberry House, now that she had come to know her family again?

The question filled her with sorrow. Her life would be so much more lonely now that she had been given this tiny glimpse into how things could be.

She swallowed hard against emotions welling up in her throat. No. She wouldn't waste this precious time with them worrying about what would come when she left.

She started to lift another shovelful of snow when she suddenly felt the impact of something square in the middle of her back.

"Argh!" she exclaimed, turning to find Bridger standing some distance away, gloved hands folded behind him.

"What happened? What's wrong?" he asked, with an innocent expression that didn't fool her for a moment. No doubt his gloves would still contain icy remnants of the snowball he had just hurled at her.

She narrowed her gaze. "That was a sneak attack. No fair."

"Dad says all is fair in snowball fights," Cassie declared.

"Hey, leave me out of it." Luke gave a mock frown to his children.

"All is fair. Is that so?"

"Except rocks," Bridger answered. "We can't put rocks in the snowballs, because that's dangerous. My friend Carson did that once and broke a car's windshield."

"All right, then. No…rocks. Anything else?"

"Don't aim for the face. That's just mean," Bridger added.

"Got it. Let's do this, then."

While she had been talking, she had also been surreptitiously edging toward a deeper pile of snow, and now she scooped down, picked up a wad of snow and hurled it straight toward Luke.

"Hey!" he spluttered, snow dripping off his broad chest. "What did I do to deserve that?"

"You set the ground rules," she said over the children's hoots of laughter. "Apparently you are the one who said all is fair in snowball fights."

Luke's smile left her breathless. Where was the stern, hard, furious man who had come to her door only a week ago in Oregon?

"Okay. It's on."

"Each man for himself?" she asked.

He gave the kids a speculative look. "No. How about we split into teams? Boys against the girls."

"Perfect." She had been hoping he would say exactly that. Cassie, on the other hand, opened her mouth to argue, but Bridger had already cheered in agreement and raced toward his father.

After an awkward moment, Cassie hurried to Elizabeth's side. They ducked behind a conveniently placed landscaping boulder and started stockpiling weaponry.

"We've got this," Elizabeth said.

"You can't even walk in the snow without a cane," Cassie protested.

"My...arms are stronger than my legs," she assured her.

She *was* still weak in many ways but years of physical therapy had helped build muscles she probably hadn't had before the accident. In addition, her work at the garden center had built upper body strength that helped her even when her leg muscles didn't want to cooperate.

She wasn't sure if Luke let them win or if they simply got lucky—or if Bridger was too busy laughing to throw very straight or duck out of the way—but she and Cassie definitely seemed to have the advantage.

"Okay. I'm freezing," Luke said, just about the time she was starting to wear out. "Why don't we go in and have some hot cocoa?"

"Admit it," Cassie taunted as they headed inside. "We

kicked your butts. We hit you with probably twice as many snowballs as you hit us."

"Only because my teammate spent half the time rolling around in the snow, busting a gut."

"I couldn't help it," Bridger said. "You would have laughed, too, if you could have seen yourself. You looked like you had a snow beard. Like the abominable snowman or something."

Luke gave a mock growl, arms out like a menacing yeti, which sent Bridger into peals of laughter again.

Elizabeth soaked in every second, tucking it close to her heart.

"Good work," she said to her daughter, this child she barely knew. "I was honored to be on your team. You've got a great arm."

"I'm a pretty good pitcher," she said.

"Good?" Luke hugged her close. "She struck out thirteen batters in one game."

Elizabeth knew how good Cassie was. She had watched her from the stands in three games over the summer.

Would she be able to continue her trips back to Haven Point, now that her identity was out in the open? Would Luke want her here? Once they divorced, would she be able to have any relationship at all with them?

Would he allow her visitation? Maybe he would let the children come visit her in Oregon.

The idea should have thrilled her but it seemed impossible right now, with Cassie's hostility.

"How is the Christmas program coming?" she asked as they were sipping their cocoa. The elementary school always did a big program on the last day of school, which was the entire reason she had been planning to come to Haven Point this weekend. They filled the school auditorium with parents and charged admission in the form of a canned good donation to the local food bank.

"Fine. My group is awesome, anyway. We're doing a special musical number while the fourth and fifth grades change places on the stage."

"I can't wait. I'm so glad I get to see it."

Cassie looked torn for a moment, her gaze shifting between her and Luke as she fiddled with the candy cane she had used to stir her cocoa.

Finally she faced Elizabeth, eyes almost defiant. "Are you any good at hair?"

"Hair?" Elizabeth blinked, not expecting the question.

"You know. Using a curling iron and stuff. Dad tries but he's not that great, and I'm supposed to have an updo, like the other girls who are doing the song with me."

"I see." Elizabeth sipped at her hot cocoa for a moment to gather her composure. Her daughter was asking her for help with her hair. It might have seemed a simple request to most people, but not to her.

"If you can't, it's no big deal. I can ask Megan or my friend's mom Devin."

"No. I would love to help. I'll admit, I'm a little out of practice doing someone else's hair, but I used to spend hours fixing my doll's hair. I think I can remember."

"Okay. Good. Thanks. Can you do it after school on Monday? The show is at seven and I have to be ready by six."

"Yes. Of course." If she had to, she would walk through the snow to be here.

Elizabeth caught Luke's gaze. The warmth there almost made the emotions swirling through her bubble over.

Her daughter wanted her help. Something told her this was a huge step between them and suddenly Monday couldn't come soon enough.

Chapter Seventeen

It was completely ridiculous for him to feel like he was heading out on a date, but Luke was painfully aware of his sweaty palms and the nerves in his stomach as he pulled up to the little house on Riverbend Road.

He told himself he was edgy only because he had to go to a Christmas party with all the Haven Point Helping Hands, the most intimidating women in town. He knew that was a lie. Megan and her friends didn't make him nearly as nervous as the idea of spending more time with Elizabeth when he was finding it increasingly hard to resist her.

She would be leaving in only a few days, a reminder that seemed to cast a dark shadow on his thoughts whenever it popped in.

They still had so many things to work out between them. All the details with the children now. Visitation, custody.

He didn't want to think about any of it, not when his feelings for her had become more tangled than fishing line that had been left over the winter in the bottom of the tackle box.

That trip to Oregon a week before seemed like a lifetime ago. He had made it there in record time, fueled by coffee and anger and frustration.

She intended to return to Oregon on Christmas Eve. That gave him only tonight with her and one more day.

Could he persuade her to stay longer?

He didn't know but intended to try.

She was making progress with Cassie. Their daughter had not completely come around, but he could see the signs that she was softening. She had asked Elizabeth to do her hair for her program the next day, hadn't she? And she was making something in her room that he suspected might be a gift for her mother.

Elizabeth couldn't leave yet but he didn't know how to persuade her of that.

He would work on it throughout the party.

He climbed out of his pickup truck and walked through the clear night to the door. Like she had previously, she opened it before he could ring the bell, as if she had been watching for him.

Sweetly scented warmth poured out of the house, pine and cinnamon and vanilla, along with Elizabeth's flowery citrus soap.

Had it ever smelled so good when he and the children lived here? He seriously doubted that.

"Hi. I saw you pull up." She gave a smile that left him a little light-headed.

He leaned in and kissed her cheek, if only to inhale more of that delectable smell. "You look beautiful."

Pink dusted her skin. "Thanks. I had to scramble to find

something…appropriate for a party, since I never expected to be attending anything like this when I packed so quickly. Fortunately, a couple of the shops in town are within…walking distance. Linda Fremont's store has improved…considerably."

She wore a formfitting, glossy black long-sleeve dress along with a pashmina in maroon and silver. She had lost too much weight since she had been gone. He had a wild urge to feed her some ice cream.

"I hope this isn't too terrible for you, tonight at Megan's party. I know you don't like being the center of attention."

"Don't worry about me. I'll be…fine. I'm looking forward to seeing old…friends. I only hope this is enough to put the rumors to bed about my premature demise, once and for all."

"I hope so, too. Thank you for going through it."

"Of course. I'm just sorry we have to do this. That people ever…thought such terrible things."

He shrugged. "People will say what they want. Even after this week and all you've done to make sure everyone in town knows you're back and why you left, some people will still talk. There's nothing we can do about that."

"I suppose you're right. I'm still…planning on taking a DNA test when we can arrange it. I still wish there was… something more I could do to fix it all for you."

The regret in her voice prompted him to make a confession. "To be honest, the part I hated the most wasn't what people said about me. It was not knowing what had happened to you. I hated thinking you were out there somewhere. Thinking you were…dead."

To his dismay, his voice caught on the last word. He cleared his throat but it was too late. She caught the emotion and gave him a swift look.

"Luke," she said, her voice filled with regret and compassion and sorrow, and he couldn't resist the fierce impulse to wrap his arms around her and hold on tight.

"I missed you so much," he confessed gruffly. "Every morning for years, I woke up and looked over to your side of the bed, expecting to find you. Then I would remember and the world fell apart all over again."

"I'm sorry," she said, her arms trembling as she held him tightly. "So sorry. I don't know what to do except to…to tell you over and over how sorry I am."

Was it possible that they could work their way through this? For the first time, Luke began to feel the beginnings of hope, the first glimmer that after a long and difficult storm, the sun just might be coming out.

She cared about him. He had seen it in her eyes over the past few days as they had spent more time together and shared memories and laughter and time with their children.

Could they rekindle the love they'd once had? Something told him it would not be that hard. He had never really stopped caring about her. He missed her every day, even when he had hated her for leaving.

He was still hurt that she felt she had to leave, that she hadn't turned to him for help. He wasn't sure he could ever get past that. He *was* starting to understand her actions a little better. Desperate and afraid, she had felt she had no choices left.

He knew he wasn't without blame in the whole situation.

He had been supportive of her grief after her parents died, had tried to be encouraging and understanding when she struggled with postpartum depression after Cassie. She had been getting better, almost to her old self, when she insisted she wanted to try for another child. He never should have agreed, especially when he was not wholly confident that she had returned to full mental health.

Of course, that would have meant no Bridger and the world would have been without one amazing kid.

If only Luke hadn't fallen asleep that night or had chosen to stay on the inflatable mattress they kept in Bridger's room. She wouldn't have hit rock bottom and wouldn't have been tempted to hurt herself and their baby and subsequently wouldn't have felt she had to escape into the night.

They had all paid a price for that decision she had made when she felt desperate and cornered by her own demons, but he was beginning to see that Elizabeth had been the one to pay most dearly.

While he had known the joy of watching their children grow up and start to become their own people, she had been alone and in pain.

He leaned down to kiss her forehead, marveling again that her skin tasted the same, despite the years and her injuries and all the reconstructive surgery. She was still his sweet Elizabeth.

"I wish we could stay here all night, just like this," he said. It was nothing less than the truth. He found a peace in her arms that he had missed all this time, as if his crazy world could be still for a moment and take a calming breath.

"That would be...fine with me," she said with a sigh that sent delicious shivers rippling down his back. "Except I promised Megan and I would...hate to get on your sister's bad side."

He smiled at her dry tone. Both of them knew she had been on Megan's bad side since she left town. His sister was loyal to a fault.

"Good call. Neither one of us wants that. Where's your coat?"

He helped her into it and ushered them both out into the snow, which was about six inches deep now.

The inn was only about a half mile from the Riverbend Road house, halfway between there and his own house. He and Elizabeth were both quiet, both wrapped in their thoughts as he drove.

When they arrived, he could almost see her battle armor clicking into place. As he helped her from the vehicle, she lifted her chin, threw back her shoulders and walked toward the door with determination in her lopsided gait.

She did not want to be here any more than Luke did, but she was putting herself through the ordeal for *him*.

He was beginning to think his wife was one of the most courageous women he had ever known.

And he didn't know how he was going to live without that courage when she returned to Oregon and her stately home on the beach.

She couldn't remember when she had been so tired—and that was saying something, since she was always tired.

Fatigue seemed to weigh on her shoulders now like a heavy blanket, so heavy she wasn't sure how much longer her spine would be strong enough to keep her upright.

She had told her story at least a half dozen times. Everyone who had known her when she lived here before was curious about what had happened to her. She could tell some weren't sure what to believe.

How could she blame them? Her journey had been so convoluted and circuitous that she wasn't sure she would have believed it herself, if she hadn't lived through it.

She had a feeling most of these people never believed Luke guilty of any involvement in her disappearance. Megan wouldn't have kept them as her friends if they did. But she knew these were the influencers in town who would do their best to get the word out to everyone else.

She could endure any amount of scrutiny if it would make things easier for him here in town after she left.

"How are you doing?"

She looked over at Megan's question and found her sister-in-law holding out a charming little Christmas mug full of mulled wine.

"I've had more...enjoyable holiday parties. And I was...in a coma for one of them."

Megan's laugh seemed to take both of them by surprise.

"You probably forgot how intimidating folks in Haven Point can be."

"I did," she admitted. "But it's all...coming back now."

Megan's mouth pursed as if she wanted to say something else, but she seemed to give herself a little mental head shake.

"Thank you," her sister-in-law said, her voice stiff but without the animosity Elizabeth had heard there since returning to town. "I know this hasn't been easy for you."

"I want to help Luke however I can," Elizabeth answered.

"I know he appreciates it," Megan said. She looked around the room. "I know not everyone has been kind about you turning up out of the blue. People will come around."

Would Megan? Elizabeth wondered with deep sadness for the friendship she feared she had lost forever.

"I'm not here to win any...popularity contest, only to convince everyone that I left on my own and Luke had nothing to do with it."

"I have something for you," Megan said after a moment. "I was going to wait until after the party but I'm not sure when I'll have another chance. I would like to give it to you now."

Elizabeth blinked, not sure what to say. A gift from Megan

was something she never would have expected. Her sister-in-law still held deep anger at her for leaving town, abandoning her family and consigning Luke to be the victim of rumor and innuendo. Why would she be giving her a gift?

"Thank you."

"It's not much," Megan warned. "Come with me. It's in my office."

Her sister-in-law led the way. Elizabeth followed, not knowing what to expect when Megan handed her a blue-and-silver gift bag with snowflake tissue paper.

"You don't have to open it now if you don't want to. You can take it back to the house and look at it later."

"May I?" Elizabeth asked, intrigued.

Megan shrugged, her usual brash confidence nowhere in sight. If Elizabeth wasn't mistaken, she would have said her sister-in-law looked uncomfortable.

Elizabeth's hands were a little more unsteady than she would have liked, which she chalked up to the stress of the evening and the fact that she hadn't eaten much since breakfast except a few vegetable appetizers.

Growing more curious by the moment, she carefully opened the bag and withdrew another square present that was wrapped in more tissue paper and tied with a blue ribbon. Her hands were ridiculously shaky and she really hoped Megan didn't notice.

It was a book, she quickly realized, her heart pounding. She opened the cover and instantly felt tears begin to burn.

"Photographs. Oh, Megan."

Her sister-in-law had filled a photo album with photographs of the children at different stages of their lives. Hundreds of them. All the things Elizabeth had missed.

The first page was of Christmas, probably the first one after she had left. Bridger and Cassie looked to be about the ages she remembered, Bridger chubby and cute and Cassie with that bossy tilt to her head.

She quickly flipped through and saw their ages progress. She registered one of a toddler Bridger, arms outstretched as he tried to balance himself. Another of Cassie wearing a backpack and a gap-toothed smile and holding a sign that read First Day of Kindergarten. The two of them on a fishing trip in the mountains, both showing off strings of trout.

There were more. Pages of them. She wanted to grab the entire book and hold it close to her chest.

Heart pounding, unable to believe the magnitude of the gift, she lifted her gaze to her sister-in-law.

Megan shifted, her cheeks rosy. "It's not much."

"Not much." Elizabeth could hardly get the words out. "It's *everything*. I don't…I don't know how to thank you."

Megan was a brilliant photographer, had even displayed her work at an art gallery, Elizabeth had learned in her time back in Haven Point. In the few images she saw, Megan's skill showed through. None of them were elaborate or staged, only candid shots of the children going through their everyday lives, but they were perfect.

She wanted to sit in this office, lock the door behind her and spend hours staring at each picture.

"I made copies of as many candid photos as I could find. I have more but these are some of my favorites."

"Oh, Megan. This is a…a priceless gift. I…I can't thank you enough."

The tears she had tried to contain began to trickle down. Her makeup was going to run but she didn't care. No gift had ever meant as much.

"It was Luke's idea," her sister-in-law said briskly. "We

have home video as well, but I didn't want to bombard you with everything at once."

"No. This is…this is perfect. The best gift I've ever received."

"I'm glad you like it."

Megan's features seemed to soften a little. Was there some chance she could find peace with her sister-in-law?

She took a chance and approached the other woman.

"You didn't have to go to all this…work but I'm so very… happy you did."

She hugged Megan, and after an awkward moment, Luke's sister returned the hug, though she quickly stepped away.

"Feel free to hang out for a while in here and look at the book, if you want."

Oh, she did. More than anything. But she was here tonight for Luke, not to rediscover her children. "I want to look at it…later when I have time to pore over every…page."

"Your choice."

Megan turned to go back to the party. Elizabeth started to follow her, bag in hand, when the other woman stopped stock-still.

"Elliot," she breathed, her voice ragged. An instant later she was racing to a scruffy man standing some distance away.

This wild-looking man with the beard and longish hair was really the stuffy, buttoned-up Elliot Bailey? Elizabeth couldn't quite believe it but the sheer love on the man's face as he looked at Megan racing toward him confirmed it.

"Hey," he said, just before Megan leaped into his arms and started kissing him fiercely.

Oh. My.

She felt breathless, achy as she watched their joyful reunion. Luke once looked at her that way. She could remember it.

Even if they were apart for only a few hours, Luke always used to look so happy when he saw her, as if she was his salvation.

Could she ever get that back or would he always look at her with that sort of wary, watchful expression, as if afraid she would turn around and run off at any moment?

"I was afraid you wouldn't make it home for Christmas. Why didn't you tell me you were coming back?" Megan asked between kisses.

Elizabeth wanted to slip away and leave them to their reunion, but they stood blocking the hallway that led back to the party.

"I wasn't sure when the assignment would be done and I didn't want to give you false hope. We rounded everybody up and busted the whole ring this afternoon, and the minute I finished the paperwork, I hightailed it for home."

"I'm so glad." Megan didn't need to use the words. Her expression said everything.

"I'm sorry I didn't make it back for most of the party."

"You're here now. That's all that matters."

"I'm afraid I'm not really dressed to socialize. I didn't want to waste time going to the cottage to change. Not when I knew you were here."

"No one here will care about that. They'll just be so thrilled to see you, especially your mom and sisters."

Elizabeth never would have imagined Elliot would fall so hard. She used to tease him about being a workaholic, about being so focused on climbing the ladder at the FBI as quickly as possible that he was losing sight of his friends and family.

Somehow *Megan* must have helped mellow him, changing that focus a little.

She couldn't be happier for them.

A moment later, Elliot seemed to notice her. His eyes widened. "Elizabeth! You're here!"

"Yes. Luke found me in Oregon. Because of...you, I understand."

How he had found her, she still didn't entirely understand, but she was grateful. If not for Elliot, she wouldn't be here in Haven Point again, trying to rebuild a relationship with her children.

Elliot hadn't done it for Luke, she suddenly realized. All his efforts must have been for Megan, to help her clear her brother's name.

"We'll have to catch up," Elliot said.

"Yes. I'd like to hear how...you found me." Not now, when he and Megan couldn't seem to keep away from each other. "I should...return to the party. I would hate for people to think I've disappeared again."

Megan actually smiled a little at that.

"Thank you." Elizabeth held up the photo album. "Truly. This is the best...gift ever. I can't thank you enough. Not just for the photos of Bridger and Cassie but for...for loving them when I...couldn't."

Her voice broke a little on the words. She hoped they didn't notice as she forced a smile and hurried past them. She didn't want to return to the party with all those curious looks and probing questions. But Luke was there and she wanted to be wherever he was.

When she walked into the room, her gaze immediately found him. He was speaking to Ben Kilpatrick and Aidan Caine, a trio of very different but equally compelling men.

She wanted to cross the room to him, needing the reassurance she found from being close to him, but Wynona Bailey

Emmett caught her first and expressed her delight in having Elizabeth home.

"I feel like I owe you an apology," Wyn said.

"Why would you?"

Wyn sighed. "Our dad missed valuable evidence that might have led the investigation to you much earlier. The truck driver who gave you a ride actually called the police department a few months after you disappeared, but Dad didn't think she had credible information. Then he misfiled the report. I was sick when Elliot told me."

"That wasn't your father's fault," Elizabeth assured her quickly. She remembered John Bailey well. He had been a good police chief. A little old-school, maybe, but he had loved his town and the people he served. She had been saddened to learn during her first visit to Haven Point as Sonia Davis that he had been shot in the head during an altercation with a robbery suspect not many months after she left town.

"He should have investigated it further, though. I keep wondering what might have happened if Luke could have found you earlier."

Oh, she did, too. But it would have been impossible. He hadn't known the first place to look.

Her heart ached for all he had endured. How could she ever make it right?

A few minutes later, Luke broke away from the other men and made his way to her side. "Are you ready to go? We don't have to stick it out to the bitter end. You've been a trooper but I can see you're getting tired."

Right now, she wanted nothing more than to return to the little house, change out of her party clothes, slip under a quilt and spend all night looking through the photo album Megan had given her.

That wasn't her goal tonight, though. She was here for Operation Redeem Luke Hamilton.

"I don't mind...staying. I should mingle a little more, see if there's anyone...left who hasn't heard my...story."

"You've gone over it enough. If you keep talking, you won't have a voice for Christmas. I think it's time to go."

He didn't have to ask her twice. "All...right. I only need to grab my coat."

It took them several minutes to take their leave, by the time they said goodbye to friends. To her shock, many of the members of the Haven Point Helping Hands gave her hugs.

"You should come to another one of our Haven Point Helping Hands meetings," McKenzie said. "We would love to see you. Our next one will be after the holidays."

She started to tell McKenzie she was leaving town Christmas Eve but couldn't summon the energy for explanations.

"Thanks. I might do that," she lied. Then she and Luke walked out into the cold night toward home.

Elizabeth had been amazing.

Though he could tell the evening had been a struggle for her, she had spoken with nearly everyone at the party and told her story time after time.

The reaction to her explanation for leaving town seemed to be mixed, but many people had come up to him to tell him they were sorry for all his family had been through.

He had expected vindication to feel so much better. Yes, it was nice to have that burden off his shoulders and to know that he didn't have to face the possibility of an arrest. He would enjoy being able to attend the children's events without feeling the stares and hearing the whispers when he walked through a room.

She had paid a heavy cost for his new peace of mind.

When they reached the house they had fixed up together, he reached to take her arm but she held tightly to the gift bag she carried out of the inn.

Even after she unlocked the front door and walked inside, she didn't seem to want to set the bag down on the entry table, even to take off her coat.

"Who's giving you presents?" Curiosity finally made him ask.

"Megan. And it's the best present ever."

Megan? That was a surprise. His sister had made no secret of her animosity toward Elizabeth for leaving her children, though perhaps she was mellowing.

"Really? That was nice of her." He could only pray it wasn't a bottle of rat poison.

"You can see what she gave me, if you would like. It's re-markable, really."

She sat on the sofa he and the kids had left behind. After a moment, Luke sat on the other end and took the bag she handed him.

"It's a photo album," Elizabeth said before he could reach into the bag and see for himself. "But then, you know that. She said it was your idea."

Oh. After telling Megan about that first visit to the district attorney, Luke had suggested they find videos and pictures for Elizabeth to help her catch up a little on what the children had looked like at various stages of life.

It had been one of those random, off-the-cuff suggestions, but Megan had apparently run with it.

"Your dear sister made…copies of photos she's taken of the children over the…years and put them together in a book for me so that I could see some of the things I've…missed. I only had a moment to look through it but it's…amazing."

Her eyes were shiny, bright with unshed tears.

"If it's so amazing, why are you crying?"

"I missed so much. I knew it intellectually but the few pictures I looked at drove it home. Birthday parties and Halloweens and Easter egg hunts. And Christmas. I've missed all their Christmases. And now Cassie hates me and Bridger…Bridger doesn't even know me and…and I don't know how to fix it."

She burst into tears and buried her face in her hands. The ordeal of the evening had exhausted her, Luke realized. That was the source of this raw emotion, this self-recrimination. She needed to sleep.

"Hey, now," he said, feeling helpless. Not sure what else to do, he wrapped his arms around her and she came willingly with a little sigh that told him perhaps this was exactly what she needed. Just as he had drawn comfort from her embrace earlier in the evening, he hoped she could find comfort from his. "We can't change what happened, as much as we might wish we could."

"I know. I wish it so much."

He kissed the top of her head, soft tenderness soaking through him. "I know it does nothing to ease your pain but I hope you know the kids have been happy. I've had a lot of help over the years from good people who cared about them. Bridger and Cassie always knew they were loved by me and by Megan and all the caregivers they've had over the years."

She sobbed a little more, a tiny little whimpering sound. "How can I ever…make it up to them, especially when Cassie h-hates me?"

"We can't erase the pain of the past seven years. All we can do is try our best, moving forward."

She couldn't leave. He had to persuade her that the children needed her in their lives. A few random visits a year to see her in Oregon would not be enough.

"Do you think you can arrange your travel plans to stay in Haven Point through the holidays? At least through Christmas?" That was only a few days away. It wouldn't nearly be enough time with her but it would be a start.

"Christmas?"

"I know you had plane reservations and intended to stay only through Christmas Eve. How hard would it be to extend that a few days?"

"I would have to...check with the airline. But I'm sure I can."

"Let's start there."

"All right," she said after a moment. "I'll call them in the morning. I would...love to be here through Christmas."

"Perfect." While he was asking things of her, he decided to go for it. "And I think you should consider moving permanently back to Haven Point."

Her eyes widened. "Move back? Are you serious?"

He shrugged, feeling inordinately nervous, for reasons he couldn't have explained. "The kids are here. If you want to be part of their lives moving forward, you would be better off here. You can't forge a new relationship with them if you're eight hours away. There's email and messaging and video phone calls, but they're not the same as face-to-face contact."

Maybe the best thing would be to hold on to this house on the river. It was partly hers, anyway. She could live here and work on forging a new relationship with Cassie and Bridger.

"Is that...what you want?"

"It's not about what I want. It's what the kids need," he said bluntly. "That has been my driving force for almost ten years, since the moment I took Cassie in my arms in the hospital."

She looked stunned by the suggestion, and he quickly realized that springing this on her when she was already exhausted was wholly unfair. He should have thought things through a little better.

"You don't have to make any decision right now. We've still got the show tomorrow and Christmas to get through, especially now that you're staying a few extra days. Even after you go back to Oregon, we can work on figuring things out."

"Yes. I would need...time." Her voice sounded small and he could see the lines of fatigue feathering out from her eyes. Her hands were shaking slightly.

He wanted to tuck her into bed. Better, he wanted to tuck her back into his pickup truck and take her home, where he could watch over her.

His rapid shift in perspective still left his head spinning. Somehow he had moved from grief over the woman he thought was dead to anger and hurt when he found out she was living hours away under another name to this strange, tender protectiveness after he heard her story and learned all she had endured while she was gone.

"We don't have to make any decisions right now. I can see you're overwhelmed. Think about it and we can talk again later."

"Yes. All right."

Reluctantly, he rose from the sofa. "Get some rest. You wouldn't want to be worn out for the kids' big show."

"I...hope I'm not too much of a...distraction."

Tenderness welled up inside him, sweet, nourishing, beautiful. "You'll be great, as you were tonight. Good night, Elizabeth."

He kissed her forehead, then couldn't resist lowering his mouth to hers. One more quick taste. That was all he wanted. Even as he thought the words, he knew they were a lie. One more kiss would never be enough. He would always want more.

Her mouth was soft, tender. Eager. He could taste the need in it. She had missed him, too; he was certain of it. They kissed for a long time, until he was aching to lay her back on the uncomfortable sofa.

No, that wouldn't solve anything, especially with so many unresolved issues between them.

He wrenched his mouth away. "I need to go, or I won't be able to."

Her sigh was filled with regret and hunger. He wanted to throw caution to the wind, just pick her up and carry her to the bedroom, but things between them were complicated enough. Not to mention the fact that she was completely exhausted.

"Cassie wants you to do her hair tomorrow before the show, right?"

"Yes. Can you believe it?"

"Why don't I pick you up sometime after lunch? That way you can be at the house when the kids get off the bus."

"That works. I'll be ready."

Was he ready, though? It was one thing to have her in his life for a few days, maybe a week. It would be something else entirely if she moved back here permanently.

He wasn't sure he would be able to keep his hands off of her, at least judging by his track record that evening.

Chapter Eighteen

Elizabeth still couldn't quite believe her world had shifted so dramatically.

In her wildest imagination, she never would have expected that day that she would find herself sitting at the kitchen table of Luke's beautiful log home in Haven Point, brushing her daughter's hair while Bridger read a Christmas book aloud next to them.

She couldn't seem to stop smiling, sheer happiness like a thousand sparkling fairy lights glowing inside her.

She loved these children. Though she hadn't been with them in person for seven years, she had carried them in her heart, even when she didn't completely remember them.

"What do you...think?" she finally asked when she had arranged Cassie's hair in the style her daughter had said the other girls in her ensemble group had agreed upon.

Elizabeth did not consider herself an expert at hair, usually content with a quick braid or ponytail for herself. She had a photograph to go by, though, and thought she'd done a pretty good job.

Cassie held up the mirror and angled her hair from side to side. "It looks good. Wow. I look at least twelve or thirteen."

She made those advanced ages sound positively ancient and Elizabeth had to hide her smile. "You look very grown up. You're lovely." She paused, then added, "You resemble my... mother. She had your same smile."

"Really?" Cassie looked intrigued. "We go to the grave sometimes and take flowers to your mom and dad. One time Dad said he feels close to you there because you loved them so much."

"And he said since you weren't here to remember them, it was our job," Bridger added.

Her heart melted at the words. Luke had said that? How sweet of him, to show respect to her parents and to tell their children about them.

Oh, how her mother would have loved having grand-children. She would have spoiled them terribly.

The familiar sting of loss hit her but she refused to let it dim her happiness in this moment. Her parents would not want her grief over losing them so suddenly to cloud her joy in being with her children.

Her daughter studied herself in the mirror. "It looks great. So much better than Dad could have done. He tries hard but he can never figure out the curling iron. I think it's because his hands are so big."

Elizabeth loved those big hands. They worked hard but could be gentle, tender, loving.

She shivered and set the brush back on the table.

"He tries, though. A lot of fathers would just give up."

"He does. He's a really good dad."

"The best," Bridger piped up. "Except when he makes us do chores, which is every day."

"We are Hamiltons," Cassie said. "And Hamiltons take care of business."

"I just wish we didn't have to care of business all the time," Bridger said. "Plus, this summer we have to put a yard in, so we'll be working a lot more."

Elizabeth was filled with a deep ache, wishing she could be there with them to create a new yard at their home. She would love designing it from the start. Creating flower beds, bringing in soil, choosing plants. It was her very favorite thing.

She used to work in the garden with her mother. While they weeded and pruned and harvested, they would talk about life. School and friends, faith, boys. Whatever was on her mind. She had loved those chats in the sunshine while the bees buzzed across the blossoms and a breeze danced in the treetops.

Maybe that was why working the soil brought so much peace to her soul, because it was her way of carrying on and connecting to the parents she had loved.

"Are you putting in a…vegetable garden?"

"Yes," Bridger answered. "I want only peas and potatoes because that's all I like, but Dad said we have to plant more stuff, like tomatoes and carrots and maybe even broccoli. Yuck."

She smiled, both at her son's funny face and at the promise of spring. It seemed a long time away now, a few days before Christmas, but she knew the seed catalogs would be coming right after the holidays and soon she could start to page through them and imagine.

That was another reason she loved growing things. It taught patience, the peculiar joy of watching something you planted reach a little higher toward the sun until it fully reached its potential. A heavenly smelling rosebush, a plump, ripe tomato, a bright, cheerful sunflower. They were all miracles.

She supposed there was a metaphor there about parenting. You sowed the soil, tended religiously and kept your fingers crossed that what you were doing was enough and that your little miracles would grow up healthy and strong, able to withstand the inevitable hardships of life.

"What vegetables do you like, Cassie?"

Her daughter shrugged. "I like all of them, except asparagus."

How funny, especially since she had craved asparagus when she was pregnant with Cassie.

Before she could answer, the door from the garage opened, and their little dog, Finn, jumped up and headed in that direction.

"That must be Dad!" Bridger exclaimed, shoving his chair back and following after the dog.

It took all her self-control to keep from following after them. Oh, she had it bad for her husband.

She hadn't seen him since the party the night before. He had called her that morning to explain he was in the middle of trying to fix a problem at a job site and would be tied up all day. He had arranged for one of his workers to pick her up and take her to his house.

Of all the things she had lost in the accident, the ability to drive herself places was probably the most life-changing. She missed the days when she could hop in a car and take a drive for the sheer fun of it.

When he walked into the kitchen, his gaze immediately found her, his expression making her insides buzz as if a hundred honeybees had found a home there.

He looked dark, rugged, gorgeous in his work clothes. And dusty. He had obviously been working around lumber all day.

"How's the styling going?" he asked.

"She's really good at hair," Cassie said. "What do you think?"

She twirled around in front of her father, who gave her an admiring smile. "You look great. Wow. So that's how those curls are supposed to look. Did you tell Elizabeth thank you?"

"Thanks," Cassie said dutifully. "You did a great job."

To Elizabeth's shock, she approached her a little shyly and gave her a quick hug. It lasted only a moment before Cassie returned her arms to her sides, but it was enough to send thick emotions clogging Elizabeth's throat.

She cleared them away to smile at her child. "You're welcome. It was my pleasure."

Luke studied her carefully and she knew he had not missed her reaction.

"Do you need a…sandwich or something?" she asked him.

"We had PB and J after school. Mom makes really good PB and J sandwiches," Bridger said.

He had called her *Mom*. She didn't know how to contain all these emotions.

"I'm good for now but I'll be starving after the show. Right this minute, I need to take a quick shower," Luke said. "Do we have time for that?"

"I'm supposed to be there in a half hour, so it has to be *really* quick," Cassie said, tone bossy.

"Got it."

"I need…a few minutes, too," Elizabeth said.

"And I need to get in my dress for the show," Cassie said.

"Everybody meet back here in fifteen minutes, then," Luke said.

"I'm all ready, so I'll just sit here and eat all the Christmas cookies," Bridger said. Elizabeth smiled, her heart overflowing with love for him.

He had called her *Mom*!

She hurried to the guest room Luke had told her to use for the next few days, the beautiful master suite on the main floor.

She had been able to change her flight and had a new departure the day after Christmas. The idea of it filled her with dread. She didn't want to go back. But how could she stay?

She pushed away the worry as she quickly changed into a Christmas sweater, brushed her own hair and applied more mascara and lipstick.

Though she hadn't wasted a moment, when she returned to the kitchen, she found Cassie ahead of her, dressed in a beautiful burgundy dress edged with white fake fur.

"Wow. Gorgeous dress!"

"My friend's mom made them for all of us." Cassie twirled around.

"You still have fifteen seconds," Bridger told Elizabeth with a grin.

She smiled back, loving this boy with his funny sense of humor and his unique way of looking at the world.

"In that case, maybe I'll go...read a book. *A Christmas Carol* or something."

He giggled. "Too bad. Time's up now. Where's Dad?"

"Right here." Luke hurried in, hair still wet. He was wearing a blue oxford shirt and a sport coat along with jeans and cowboy boots.

Her insides whirled and danced and she wanted to kiss the hard curve of that freshly shaved jaw.

Something of her wayward thoughts must have reflected

in her expression. Luke's eyes darkened and he almost took a step toward her but Cassie spoke first.

"We better go or we'll be late," she said.

"Let's do this, then," Luke said with a smile. "On with the show."

Luke always enjoyed the holiday extravaganza put on by the school.

It was a fun little small-town tradition, like the Lights on the Lake Festival and the summer boat show and Lake Haven Festival. He had been in the show when *he* was in elementary school and so had Megan.

His dad hadn't ever come, he remembered now. Paul Hamilton would never have been caught dead at something like this. Good thing, too. Luke would have hated having to perform in front of his father.

This one seemed special, somehow. Anticipation zinged through him as he settled into the uncomfortable chairs that were made for elementary-school-size rear ends and not adult men.

Part of that was because of Cassie's part, the special musical number she had prepared with her friends.

The rest had more to do with the woman beside him. Elizabeth's eyes were bright, her color high, and he knew she couldn't wait for the performance.

She loved their children.

And he was beginning to realize he loved her.

He let out a sigh. What the hell was he going to do? He wasn't ready to jump back into things with her. Was he?

She had left him. When trouble hit, as it no doubt would again, she had turned away from him instead of *to* him. How could he open his heart completely to her when some part of him would always be afraid she might run away again?

"Thank you," she said softly.

"For what?"

"For being...open enough to let me come tonight with you. While I was fixing Cassie's hair, I was thinking that this all...seems like the most wonderful dream. I have been looking forward to this program for weeks but thought I would be sitting in the back, as I've done before. This is... so much better."

"I'm glad."

He wanted to reach for her hand but the moment didn't feel right. That would be a declaration he wasn't quite ready to make yet.

"I... It means the world that you would...be willing to let me spend time with them. They are wonderful children. You've...you've done an amazing job of raising them."

"I don't know if I had much to do with it. They came out pretty amazing."

"You did. Trust me. You're a wonderful father, Luke. I always knew you would be."

How could she have known that, when his own father had been such a piece of work? He hadn't wanted kids when they first started dating. In fact, they'd almost broken up over it, he suddenly remembered.

She had finally told him that he had every right not to want children, that people made that choice every day, often for very sound reasons. But she said he had to make that choice for himself, not out of fear because of the poor example his own father had been.

"You're the exact opposite of your father in every other

way. You work hard to prove that. What makes you think fatherhood will be any different?" she had said.

What if he hadn't taken her words to heart? What if he had let fear control him and had pushed away the possibility of having children? His life would have been very different.

Cassie and Bridger were the joy of his life. Everything he did was for them.

He was in danger of repeating that pattern with Elizabeth—allowing fear to keep him from the possibility of joy with her. He still loved his wife, had never stopped. Did he have the courage to let her into his heart completely?

"We need to talk about where we go from here," Luke said.

He hadn't meant to blurt that out so abruptly but it was out there now.

"Did you…want to go somewhere for dinner?" she asked, misunderstanding him.

"I didn't mean after the show. I meant what happens between us after Christmas."

"Oh." Her cheeks suddenly turned rosy. "I don't…"

Whatever she was going to say was cut off by a commotion in the aisle. With reluctance, he shifted his gaze and found Megan and Elliot heading toward them at the very moment the lights in the school auditorium began to dim.

"Just in time," he said.

Megan winced. "I know. Sorry."

"Blame your sister. She was working on a photo and you know how she can lose track of time," Elliot whispered, looking much more clean-cut than he had the night before.

They settled into the seats Luke had saved them, on the other side of Elizabeth, just as the principal of the elementary school came up to announce the program.

He would worry about the future later. Right now, he intended to enjoy this fleeting, magical moment in time.

She thought her happiness jar was full to the brim earlier, when she had been spending time with her children at Luke's house. But being here with him while they watched the performance showed her she had an endless capacity for joy.

It was a delightful variety show featuring each grade at the elementary school, focused on the true spirit of kindness during the holidays. There were Christmas songs, Hanukkah dances, a Kwanzaa skit.

Cassie and her small group of girlfriends did a lovely a cappella rendition of "Away in a Manger" that had Elizabeth and more than a few around her in tears.

Anyone who didn't feel the warm spirit of community, no matter what holiday they celebrated or if they observed none at all, had to be coldhearted and small.

When they finished, she rose along with the crowd and clapped enthusiastically for all the children. She swayed a little, the beginnings of a headache pressing in. Oh. She had been so busy doing Cassie's hair, she hadn't taken one of her anti-seizure pills on schedule, she suddenly realized.

She did *not* want to have one here, in front of the whole town. "Excuse me," she said abruptly to Luke, grabbing her purse with her emergency pill supply. "I, um, I need to use the restroom."

"Now? The kids will be coming out."

"I'll find you…in a moment."

She found a drinking fountain and had taken the necessary medication when the crowd started filing out of the auditorium.

Needing a moment to gather her composure, she turned

her face to the wall, pretending to look at a spelling bee trophy case. She heard people behind her but didn't see their faces.

"Did you see that woman sitting beside Luke Hamilton?" one woman said. Elizabeth froze, keeping her face averted.

"Yes. She was pretty. I hope he's finally dating again."

"You haven't heard? That's his wife, Elizabeth."

"His wife? I thought she was dead!" the second woman exclaimed.

"Everybody did. But apparently she ran off with another man, became addicted to plastic surgery, completely altered her appearance and changed her name, too."

"Wow! I always liked Elizabeth. That's hard to believe."

"I heard she might have even worked as a stripper for a while."

A stripper? That was a new one.

"What's she doing here? I hope he's not thinking of taking her back. He'd be a damn fool to do that."

The women moved back into the crowd, still talking, but Elizabeth had heard enough.

Luke had been living with the same sort of whispers for seven years, gossip and hearsay he could do nothing to combat.

Most people in Haven Point were kind, good-hearted people, but there were the few outliers. They must have made life hell for him.

The women were right, though. Luke would be a fool if he took her back. Why would he want her now? She didn't struggle with depression anymore. Funny, how a brain injury could have one bright spot. But in its place were a hundred other medical problems with far more complicated side effects.

Luke and the children came out of the auditorium. He

scanned the crowd in the foyer and she saw relief on his features when he found her.

Did he think she might have escaped again into the night?

That worry would always be there between them, she realized grimly.

The noise in the foyer became deafening as excited children and parents talked about the performance. It was a very good thing today had been the last day of school until after the New Year because none of the children in Haven Point would be able to focus on schoolwork right now.

"Did you like it?" Bridger asked her.

"You were fantastic," she told him. "I couldn't stop laughing at the motions you did to your song."

Cassie didn't ask her opinion, but she could tell her daughter wanted to know what she thought. "And your song was beautiful," Elizabeth said softly. "It made me cry."

"Really?"

"I was so proud of you both."

They beamed at her and Elizabeth was deeply grateful she had been here to see them. No matter what happened, she wouldn't have missed this for anything.

We need to talk about where we're going.

Luke's words echoed in her head. She knew where she had to go. Back to Oregon. She would visit again and try to maintain a relationship with the children long-distance but that was the best place for her.

Luke had done a wonderful job raising the children without her. None of them needed the complications she brought along, a wife and mother who couldn't drive herself to the store, who fumbled with her words, who couldn't walk long distances without the aid of a cane.

It wasn't the future she wanted but she didn't see any other choice.

Chapter Nineteen

"What was your favorite part?"

Despite her lingering sadness, Elizabeth had to hide a smile at her son's question. She had answered the same thing from him at least a half dozen times. "I have two favorite... parts. One was your class song, of course, and the other one was Cassie's...special musical number. No comparison. They were the...the very best parts of the entire show."

"You really think so?"

"She wouldn't have said it if she didn't mean it," Luke said, giving Bridger an exasperated look. "Give it a rest now, kid."

"Can I have another piece of pizza?"

"One more, then I'm cutting you off. If you have more than that, you're going to be sick."

Luke had the great idea to pick up pizza for them on the way home from the school program but apparently everyone else in town had the same idea. It had taken him nearly an hour to get their order while Elizabeth waited in the pickup truck with Bridger and Cassie.

The wait had been worth every minute, she had to admit. Serrano's still had the most delicious crust she'd ever enjoyed.

"I thought the show this year was much better than last year. Didn't you, Dad?" Cassie asked. She had changed out of her lovely dress so she didn't drip tomato sauce on it and was wearing red-striped leggings and an oversize sweater that made her look like an elf.

"Every year seems better than the one before." Luke diplomatically took a sip of his beer.

"I don't know how they can possibly make it any better next year," Cassie said.

"Those teachers are pretty good. I'm sure they're already thinking about it."

Elizabeth had attended the annual event for the past few years, and as far as she was concerned, this had been the best one ever. She had loved being able to sit with Luke, to feel part of the family instead of being relegated to the back row.

"All right, kids. It's bedtime," Luke said when the pizza was mostly gone. "It's been a long day."

"It's Christmas Eve tomorrow!" Bridger exclaimed, as if suddenly remembering. "That means today is Christmas Eve Eve."

"That's right. And our schedule is packed full of fun tomorrow."

"Can we go sledding?" Bridger asked.

"It's on the list."

"And we need to give out our friend gifts," his sister said.

"Planning on it."

"And our award for best Christmas decorations!"

"Oh yeah. I completely forgot about that," Cassie said.

"I didn't," Luke said. "I bought the prize the other day when I was shopping in Shelter Springs. It's under the tree."

"What prize?" Elizabeth had to ask.

"Every year, the kids vote on their favorite holiday display in someone's yard around town. I buy a little prize and we deliver it on Christmas Eve."

"Last year it was my friend Sarah's house," Cassie said.

"The year before that, it was Mr. and Mrs. Leclair," Bridger added.

"What a...fun idea."

"Hey, you can help us award the winner this year," Bridger said with delight. "Maybe you can be the tiebreaker."

"I don't know if I'm...ready for that kind of responsibility," Elizabeth said gravely.

"It's not hard. It's just for fun," Bridger answered, tone serious.

"Oh, whew."

"Go put on your pajamas and brush your teeth and I'll be up to read to you shortly," Luke said.

"I want to read to myself," Cassie said. "I'm rereading my favorite series since I hope I get the latest book for Christmas. I only have fifty pages to go."

"You probably will get some kind of book. That's what Aunt Megan always gives us." Bridger's disgusted tone made her smile.

"Books are the very best gifts," Elizabeth said. "You know my...favorite quote about that? Books are the...best gifts because you can open them...again and again."

"Ha ha. I get it. Not open the present, open the book," Bridger said with delight.

Oh, how she adored him. Bridger was funny and smart and creative. When she thought of how she almost hurt this innocent child that terrible night, she became physically ill.

"Will you read to me tonight?" he asked her now.

She looked at Luke, who shrugged. "Go ahead. I don't mind."

"Yay!"

"What book are you going to read?" Luke asked.

"I don't know. Something good out of the Christmas basket. Do you want to pick?" Bridger asked her.

"What...Christmas basket?"

"We keep all our holiday-themed storybooks in a basket by the Christmas tree. It helps to keep them organized. The kids like to pick a new one every night. Well, Bridger, usually."

"You pick one for tonight while I go get my pajamas on," her son ordered.

"Deal," she answered. While the two children raced up the stairs, she went into the great room and found a basket overflowing with storybooks. For some reason, the sight of them touched her, bringing tears to her eyes.

It took work to create a collection this big. She pictured Luke going through school book orders or letting the kids make a choice at a book fair. Megan probably helped add to the collection, at least according to Bridger, and they may have received some as gifts from teachers.

This collection represented all the Christmases she had missed with her children. All the stories she hadn't read to them, all the moments that had slipped past her, never to be recaptured.

She stood for a moment, hands on the spines of the books.

"Are you okay?"

She turned, not realizing Luke had followed her. "Yes. Of course. Why?"

"You've been sitting there looking through the books for ten minutes. I can tell you, it doesn't really matter which one you pick. Bridger likes whatever you read to him. He's easy that way."

She grabbed a random book from the back of the collection and made her slow, awkward way up the stairs.

"I'm ready," Bridger told her when she knocked on his bedroom door. He was already in his bed, covers up and playing with a couple of superhero action figures.

"Did you...brush your teeth?" There. That was a motherly thing to say.

In answer, he widened his mouth in a rictus sort of grin. "See? Sparkly."

She smiled. "How...does this work?"

"Dad usually sits on the chair or on the other bed." He pointed to the twin bed next to his that must be for friend sleepovers. "Only when he does that, sometimes he falls asleep there, right in the middle of the story. When he does, I put a blanket on him and let him stay there."

She sat down where Bridger indicated, touched by the picture her imagination conjured of Luke stretched out at the end of a long day of trying to be a mother *and* a father.

The book she selected turned out to be a good one, a funny, charming tale about a mouse trying to make it home to his family for Christmas and encountering obstacle after obstacle. Reading someone else's words was so much easier than trying to come up with her own. She didn't stumble over them, didn't struggle to find the right one. If only someone would write a script she could follow in all other aspects of her life.

Though the story line hit a little too close to home, she made it through the book without becoming too emotional.

"Thanks, Mom," Bridger said sleepily when she finished. "Will you still be here tomorrow?"

The innocent question seemed to suck the air out of the room. He had lived most of his life without his mother. It was only normal for him to worry she might leave again without warning.

"I'll be here. Don't worry. I'm not going back to Oregon until the day after Christmas. We have more time together."

"Good." He smiled. "I like having you here."

She heard a sound by the door and looked over to see Luke leaning against the jamb. The expression in his eyes left her suddenly breathless.

"Thank you, son," she said. The word felt foreign on her tongue but so perfect, she had to fight tears again.

She didn't need Christmas presents. She only needed this precious moment with her child to fill her heart to over-flowing. She leaned forward and kissed his forehead. "Good night, sweetheart."

"Good night, Mom."

On legs that suddenly shook, she rose and headed out into the hall. Luke turned the light off in Bridger's room. "Good night," he said.

"Merry Christmas Eve Eve," their son said.

"Same to you," Luke answered before closing the door behind him.

Cassie's light was still on, so Luke knocked on the door.

"Come in," she called.

He opened her door. "You can read another half hour, then lights out. Even if you're not finished with the book."

"I should be done by then. Good night, Dad. I love you."

"Love you, too, bug."

She looked past him toward Elizabeth, standing in the hallway. "Night."

Of course her daughter would not say the same words of

affection to her. Elizabeth had not earned Cassie's love. Not by a long shot. At least Cassie seemed to be tolerating her much better now than she had a few days earlier.

After Luke closed their daughter's door, the two of them stood rather awkwardly in the hall for a moment.

"I, uh, should put the leftover pizza away and clean up the kitchen."

"I can help."

"That's not necessary."

"It is to me."

Gripping the banister, she made her way slowly down the stairs. Going down was always so much more difficult than making her way up, probably because gravity added more strain to her bad leg. Tonight she felt weaker than normal, her balance unsteady. Was it because Luke was there behind her, watching her slow progress?

She was breathing hard by the time they reached the bottom, tired and sad that the simple act of tucking her children into bed could turn into such an ordeal.

At least the kitchen cleanup was easy, only wrapping the leftover slices and stowing them in the refrigerator, throwing away the pizza box and loading their plates into the dishwasher.

They worked together, finishing the job in only a few moments.

"Okay. That's done," Luke said, leaning back against the edge of the table and giving her a careful look. "Now can you tell me what's wrong?"

She glanced up from the sink, where she was wringing out the dishcloth she had used to wipe down the counters.

"What do you mean?"

"You've been quiet since the show at the school ended. Something is obviously bothering you. Are you feeling okay?"

She didn't want to tell him about the conversation she had overheard or how it had forced her to face the grim reality that she couldn't continue spinning ridiculous fantasies about building a life again with him and their children.

She forced a smile. "Just tired. I took my...seizure medicine later than normal and it...kind of wiped me out."

He blinked a little, as if he had forgotten about her seizures. "Oh. Never mind, then. I was going to ask if you would mind helping me wrap some last-minute presents for the kids, but I can handle it."

"Of course," she said quickly. "Wrapping gifts doesn't take much effort. I would be glad to help you."

At least that was something she could still do.

"We should probably wait a few more minutes to make sure they're asleep and don't walk in on us."

They both seemed to realize what else his words could represent. Memories of her body entangled with his, of the heat and wonder they always found together, soaked through her, and Elizabeth had to catch her breath. Luke's eyes darkened and somehow she knew he was remembering those same moments.

Tension seemed to swirl around them, sweet and heady and impossible.

"Wrapping presents, I meant. I don't want them to walk in on us wrapping presents," he said gruffly.

"I knew...what you meant."

She couldn't manage to say anything else, filled with a longing so intense it made her ache.

"If you're too tired, don't worry about it. I've done most

of them already and it won't take me long to finish wrapping the rest."

The children. She needed to focus on the children now. "I want to do it. I need to make a phone call to my...friend Melissa in Oregon and then I can help. Where are the gifts?"

"Christmas Central is my office right now. It has a walk-in closet I can lock from curious little snoopers, so I've stored everything there."

She nodded. She could imagine Bridger and Cassie scouring the house for their Christmas gifts. Something told her that if they set their minds to it, a locked closet door wouldn't be enough to keep them out.

"I'll go...make my phone call and...meet you in a few minutes."

In the large master bedroom, she took a moment to collapse onto the bed, holding her hands against her flaming cheeks. She had to quit letting her imagination run away with her. She missed the physical connection she had once shared with her husband so fiercely it kept her awake at night. That didn't mean she should make a stupid mistake that would make leaving even more difficult.

After splashing a little water on her face, she pulled out her cell phone and punched in Melissa's number. She had promised Skye she would be home in time for Christmas and owed the girl an apology for breaking that promise.

Melissa answered on the first ring. "There you are! We've been so worried about you."

"I told Rosa I was staying through Christmas. She said she would tell you."

"She passed on the message but we still worry. All of us. How are things there?"

"Good. I should be home in a few days."

"And how's that gorgeous husband of yours?"

Still gorgeous. And still completely out of her reach.

"He's...fine. May I speak with...Skye? Has she gone to bed yet?"

"Not yet. She's right here."

A moment later, Melissa handed the phone to her daughter. "Hi, Sonia."

That name seemed completely unfamiliar now, after a week as Elizabeth. How would she go back?

"Hi, sweetheart. I need to tell you I'm not going to make it back tomorrow to see you on Christmas Eve like I promised. I'm staying here a few more days."

"Mom told me," Skye said, disappointment clear in her voice.

"I'm sorry."

"It's okay. Mom said you're with your family. That's the most important thing."

"Thanks for...understanding."

"You'll be here for my mom and Eli's wedding, right?"

"I wouldn't miss it. Merry Christmas and...I'll see you soon."

"Bye, Sonia. Merry Christmas."

Skye handed the phone back to her mother, and Elizabeth and Melissa talked wedding details and holiday plans for a few moments before wrapping up the call.

When she ended the connection, Elizabeth sat for a moment, grateful she had good friends in Oregon. Something told her she was going to need them more than ever in the coming days.

Chapter Twenty

When she made her way to the other wing of the house and the room Luke was using for an office, she found him setting up a small folding table, along with a couple of chairs.

"Hey. Everything okay in Oregon?"

"Yes. I...promised my friend's daughter I would see her at Christmas. I needed to...apologize for not making it...back when I said I would." She felt stupid for even mentioning it. "I suppose that must seem...ridiculous compared to all the time I've missed with Bridger and Cassie over the...years."

"Not at all. I'm glad you have people there who care about you."

She looked around at the tubes of wrapping paper he had laid out on the bed.

"Do you wrap each of the children's presents every year?"

Luke looked embarrassed. "Megan helps me sometimes. And I'll confess, there have been times I've taken the easy way and used gift bags as much as possible. When he was younger, Bridger had a big thing about opening presents. He loved that even more than whatever was inside. If he had the chance, he would rip open everybody's presents. He won't admit it but he still likes opening gifts, so I always feel like *not* wrapping them deprives him of a little extra joy."

He was a remarkable father. The contrast between Luke and all she had heard about his own father was stunning.

"With all that practice, you'd think I'd be better at it, but my gifts still always look like they were wrapped by a monkey wearing mittens."

She smiled a little. "Where do you need me...to start?"

"Everything's wrapped except a few things I ordered online that came later than I expected. All I have left are the things on the table."

There were a few board games, some books, new earrings for Cassie, as well as new soccer balls for both kids.

She picked out wrapping paper, tape and ribbon and went to work.

"Wow. That took you half the time it would have me," Luke said when she tied the last bow with a flourish. "They look great."

"Thanks. Is that everything?"

"I think so. I can't believe it but I think that means Christmas is ready. Thanks for your help."

"I didn't do very much but I'm glad I could contribute at least a little."

He was quiet. "The kids loved having you there tonight."

"I'm glad."

"So did I," he added.

His low, gruff words seemed to hover between them. She was suddenly breathless.

"Have you thought more about my suggestion last night that you move back permanently?"

Had she thought about anything else? "Yes," she said slowly.

"Think about how wonderful it would be for the kids. They're hungry to have you back in their lives."

"Maybe...Bridger. I'm not sure about Cassie."

"Things are better with her, though, right? She doesn't seem as angry. It will just take time. We've got an appointment with the child and family therapist after the New Year."

"That will help." Elizabeth certainly knew the value of a good mental health professional.

"This is me speaking and not the therapist, but it makes all the sense in the world that she would adjust more quickly if she has you as a regular part of her life, not only as a long-distance mom."

Elizabeth wanted that, too, so very much. Seeing them every day would be a dream come true.

"Think how great it would be if you could attend all their games and school events, not only a couple times a year when you can arrange trips back here," he pressed.

Images crowded through her head. Helping them with homework. Going to the library. Teaching Cassie how to bake the prized apple pie Elizabeth's mom used to make.

"You could live in the other house. For now, anyway."

"For...now." She sounded like a stupid parrot. She couldn't seem to make her brain cooperate, the words more slippery than normal.

He sighed and took her hand in his. Could he feel how her fingers were trembling? "I still have feelings for you, Elizabeth. I would like to see if maybe we could try again."

"You want to...stay married?"

He appeared to choose his words carefully. "I think we

should give it another shot, anyway. If you moved back to the other house, we could maybe test the waters. Spend more time with each other and the kids. Get to know each other again. Be a family for real, after all this time."

The image he painted was exactly what she yearned for, as if he had reached into her head and plucked it out. She loved her husband, her children. She wanted to build a future with them.

It was impossible, though.

She couldn't lie to herself.

She had already taken so much from him. She loved him too much, which was why she couldn't rob him of his chance at a real marriage, with a wife capable of standing beside him in all things. Someone healthier, stronger, *more* than she could ever be now.

His life and the children's would be better if she returned to Oregon.

Yes, she was fully aware of the irony. The entire reason she had left seven years ago was because she had been certain they would be better off without her.

At the time, she hadn't been thinking straight, lost in the dark, thick fog of depression. Now in the cold, clear light of reality, she knew exactly what choice she had to make.

Her family *was* better off without her. Oh, she would continue to stay in contact with them. She would message, call, visit when she could. That would have to be enough.

"I'm afraid…that's impossible."

He blinked, looking stunned. "Impossible? Why?"

She looked away, unable to face his heated gaze. She didn't want to lie to him. But what choice did she have?

"I…I have a life in Oregon. Friends. A job. I can't just pick up and leave everything behind to come here…permanently."

"Why not? Do you have a loving family there? Children who need you?"

She let out a shaky breath. "You know I don't."

"Do you have a community of friends where everyone wants to help you?"

"I...have several good ones there."

He was silent so long she finally lifted her gaze to his. He had moved closer, until she could feel the heat radiating off him and the movement of each breath.

"Do you have a husband who loved you with all his heart once and would like to see if he still can?"

"Luke."

Whatever she intended to say was lost as he lowered his mouth and kissed her with a hunger that matched her own.

The kiss was emotional, intense, filled with a longing that made her ache. He held her close and it was as if her muscles had memory where he was concerned, too.

She sighed and gave herself to the kiss for long, heady moments. How tempting it was to surrender everything to him, to let him take her to her bedroom with the fireplace and the big, luxurious king-size bed and let him persuade her that she belonged nowhere else but here with him, in his arms.

She couldn't. Fear stopped her from taking his hand and dragging him down the hall. If they made love again, she would never be able to leave.

Somewhere deep inside she found the strength to slide her mouth from his and step away on legs that trembled.

"No. This isn't what I...what I want, Luke. I'm sorry. We had something once but that was a...a long time ago. We don't know each other anymore. I'm grateful to you for...letting me back into the children's lives, but I think...I'll be a better mother to them from a...from a distance."

"You don't really believe that."

"I do. I'm sorry. I wish…I wish things could be different."

She wanted to make a quick exit but she did nothing quickly these days. She limped out of the room toward the other side of the house, her heart aching more with every slow step.

Luke watched her go, his thoughts in turmoil.

He couldn't believe she had rejected him. He had put his heart on the line, had found the courage to tell her how he was feeling and ask if she would stay, and she had turned him down flat.

He hadn't expected it, especially not after the eager way she returned his kisses or the softness he saw in her eyes when she looked at the children. He thought she *wanted* to stay, to be part of their lives again.

She had seemed to love attending the holiday show that evening and had been enjoying herself until she left to use the restroom.

Had something happened after she left him and walked out of the auditorium? Had someone said something malicious or unkind?

It didn't matter. Whatever had happened, she had withdrawn from him, retreating into a place he couldn't reach.

How could he have misjudged the situation so completely?

More important, what the hell was he supposed to do now?

They still had Christmas Eve and Christmas to make it through. For the children's sake, he would do his best to give them a memorable holiday, filled with all the joy of the season.

He had been doing the same thing for seven years, pretending everything was okay for their sake when inside he was dying. Why should this year be any different?

Chapter Twenty-One

"**A**re you guys about ready to wrap it up?" Luke asked Bridger and Cassie after about twenty trips up and down the good-size hill at Pine Tree Park, with its beautiful view of the lake and the Redemption Mountains in the distance.

"I am," Cassie said. "My feet are freezing and I think my nose is going to fall off."

Despite his lingering sadness and the tension that sizzled between him and Elizabeth, the day had been a good one so far. He didn't think the kids noticed anything wrong as they did chores and worked to get everything ready for Christmas.

Sledding down the hill at Pine Tree Park had become a tradition for them. Luke knew if he didn't take them, he would hear about it.

"That was super fun, Dad," Bridger said as they loaded up the sleds into the back of his pickup truck. "It's too bad Mom couldn't come with us."

Luke tensed at the reference to Elizabeth but forced himself to relax. "She's waiting back home, keeping Finn company."

"I know," Bridger said, pulling off his beanie to reveal crazy hat hair. "But it still would have been fun to have her there."

"She can't walk very well," Cassie pointed out. "Do you think she would really be able to make it up the hill, over and over again?"

Bridger looked stricken. "Oh. I didn't think about that. I guess you're right. Maybe we could have pulled her up on the sled."

Luke tended to forget about the things Elizabeth couldn't do. She didn't complain about her physical limitations; she just plowed through with everything, whether that was climbing the stairs at his house or shoveling snow outside with him and the kids.

She didn't seem to let anything stop her—except when it came to letting him back into her life.

Why was she putting barriers between them?

When they walked inside the house, Luke was startled to find the delicious scent of roasting poultry filling the air.

Bridger gave an exaggerated sniff. "Wow! What smells so good?"

Elizabeth smiled, though she looked a little nervous. "I know we talked about grilling steaks again. That would have been...delicious and we can still do that, if you...if you want. But I thought a traditional turkey might be good today and we can save the steaks for dinner tomorrow."

"Where did you get a turkey?" Luke was fairly certain he didn't have one in the house, but maybe Megan had dropped one off when he wasn't looking.

"The grocery store...in Shelter Springs delivers. It costs

a little extra, especially for a fresh one, but it's worth it for the...convenience."

His mouth watered. "It really does smell delicious."

"I know how much you like turkey and thought you might...enjoy it."

"I just hope you didn't put dish soap in the marinade this time," Cassie said.

"I tried very hard...not to," Elizabeth assured her with a smile. "I'm afraid dinner won't be ready for a few more hours."

"Perfect. That will give us time to take a few gifts around to the kids' friends."

"Don't forget," Bridger said. "We still have to give our grand prize for the best decorations."

"Except we can't do that until dark," Cassie reminded her brother.

"Would you like to come with us to deliver the gifts?" he asked Elizabeth.

He saw uncertainty cross her lovely features, but then she glanced at the children before nodding. "Yes. I would love to. Let me grab my coat."

She seemed as determined as he was to give the children a memorable holiday.

Even if they couldn't be together beyond this season, at least they could share that.

Except for her aching heart, this was everything she dreamed Christmas Eve should be.

After the children delivered their gifts to friends, they returned to the house and worked together on the remaining side dishes to go with the turkey. While holiday music played through speakers in the house and the fire blazed merrily in the great room, she and Cassie peeled potatoes to be boiled and mashed while Luke and Bridger worked on making a salad and setting the table.

They played silly word games throughout dinner, and by the time they ate the apple pie she had baked, everyone was laughing.

After dinner, they changed into church-appropriate clothing, then again loaded into Luke's big pickup.

"We're a little early for church services," he said. "That should be just enough time to drive around one last time and look at Christmas lights."

"Yes!" both children said in unison.

"Do you have our grand prize?" Cassie asked.

"Right here."

He presented a small wrapped rectangular box bearing the label of the hand-dipped chocolate factory in Shelter Springs.

She and her parents used to drive around looking at Christmas lights, too. They had never awarded prizewinners, but she still found a sweet sense of continuity in carrying on the tradition with her own children.

While a light snow fluttered down, dusting everything in sight, they drove through Haven Point to admire the different decorations people had used to adorn their houses. In the end, it came down to two choices. An elaborate flashing light show set to Christmas carols on a newer house near the lake or a small clapboard house in one of the poorer areas of town where the owners had formed a huge star out of light strings on the roof of a dilapidated barn and had strung white lights radiating down from it to land on a rather primitive manger scene.

She fully expected the children to go for the light show. It was flashy and fun and obviously popular, judging by the cars lined up to enjoy the show. Instead, they unanimously chose the manger scene.

"Are you sure this is the one you want to award first prize to?" Luke looked doubtful.

"Yeah," Bridger said. "I really like that star and I bet it wasn't easy to hang."

"It's sweet," Cassie said.

"What do you think?" Luke asked Elizabeth.

"I'll vote with the majority. I like the manger and the star."

"Okay. If that's what you want."

Luke drove back across town and pulled up in front of the house. It looked even more modest now that Elizabeth looked closer.

"Do you want to come with us to give the prize?" Luke asked.

"You don't just drop it off?"

"Sometimes. The last few years, we've been stopping in person to say thanks."

"We carol, too," Cassie said. "That was my idea. Dad and Bridger only do it because I make them."

"We may want to skip the caroling this year," Luke said. He looked a little wary, though Elizabeth couldn't figure out why.

"I don't want to skip it. That's my favorite part!" Cassie said. "What song should we sing?"

The boys didn't say anything, both looking reluctant. Finally Elizabeth spoke. "How about...'Joy to the World'?"

"That's a good one," Cassie said. "Okay. We'll ring the door, and while we wait for them to answer, we start singing."

"If you're sure," Luke said.

Something was going on here. Something Elizabeth didn't quite understand.

"I am," Cassie said firmly. "Okay, Bridger. Ring the bell."

He obeyed his sister, pressing hard and long. The minute he lifted his hand, Cassie started singing. It was a little higher key than Elizabeth felt comfortable in but she did her best. Luke pitched his voice to a lower octave and sang along.

They had just finished the chorus when the door opened. All their voices seemed to die off at once when they found Billy Sparks and his two kids peering through the doorway, all dressed in Sunday clothes, too.

"Rosie!" Cassie exclaimed.

"Jed!" Bridger said at almost the exact moment.

These were the children who had tormented hers, calling their father a murderer. Elizabeth wanted to sweep her family away from this house, but then she looked at Luke.

He knew. He had to have known exactly who owned the house where they were delivering the grand prize. Haven Point was too small for him not to know where Billy Sparks lived.

Billy had treated him horribly but Luke was reaching out anyway. Love for him, fierce and powerful, soaked through her and she had to fight tears.

If her children were startled, she saw the Sparks family was even more so.

"Hamilton. What are you doing here?" Billy asked after an awkward moment.

Cassie was finally the one to speak. "Every year our family picks one house that we think has the best decorations in town. Bridger really liked your star this year." She paused, then continued as if honesty compelled her, "And I did, too."

"I bet it took a lot of work to get it up that high," Bridger said.

"I helped." The boy about his age spoke up.

"You did a really good job," Bridger mumbled.

Luke smiled down at his son, pride in his eyes.

"Here's your prize." Bridger thrust out the wrapped box of chocolates.

"Merry Christmas," Luke said.

Billy blinked, clear astonishment on his blunt features. "Uh. Merry Christmas to you, too."

"Bye. See you at school next year," Bridger said to the boy, who giggled.

"Bye, Rosie," Cassie said to the girl, who acknowledged her with a nod.

They were all silent as they walked back to the pickup truck.

"I didn't know that's where Rosie lives," Cassie said when they were all buckled in again.

"I'm glad we gave them the prize," Bridger said. "Jedediah was kind of a jerk to me but I shouldn't have punched him at church."

Elizabeth smiled at him in the back seat. "I guess that's what Christmas is about. Forgiveness. Second chances. Being kind to those who sometimes make it hard."

"It's easy to be nice to people who are nice to you back," Cassie said. "It's harder when they say mean things about you and don't treat you like the Golden Rule says they should. Rosie can be a jerk sometimes, but I guess I'm still glad we gave them the prize."

"I am, too," Luke said gruffly.

More than anything, Elizabeth wanted to take his hand, to thank him again for raising such amazing children. A tear dripped out as he drove the short distance to church, and she wiped it away, hoping he didn't notice.

The church service was tender and touching, with lovely

music and heartfelt prayers. The entire evening was absolutely perfect, she thought as they drove home through the snow toward Luke's house.

"What's…next?" she asked when they walked inside.

"Usually we get in our jammies and have popcorn. Then we stay up late playing games or watching a Christmas movie," Cassie said.

"Not *too* late or Santa can't come," Bridger said. Though he might be turning eight in a few months, she sensed Christmas Eve was a time when he still wanted to believe in the magic.

She didn't blame him. She did, too.

"Sounds…perfect. I'll go get into my jammies, then."

She was glad she'd packed a fairly decent pair that was comfy and not too threadbare. It was adorned with candy canes, so perfect for the evening.

When she came out of her room, she found the children in the kitchen helping Luke pop the corn. He hadn't changed into pajamas but had taken off his sport coat and changed into jeans and a more casual shirt than he'd worn to church.

"It's kind of weird not to have Aunt Megan here this year," Cassie was saying when Elizabeth joined them.

"We'll see her tomorrow. She was going to a big family party with Elliot's family at Katrina's house," Luke explained to Elizabeth.

"Oh?"

"We were invited, but I thought it might be fun to have Christmas here since it's our first year in the new house, especially since you're here to enjoy it with us."

"This is…nice."

Her words were a vast understatement. It was better than nice. The whole day had been perfect. She didn't want it to end. She tried to console herself that at least she would have wonderful memories when she returned to Oregon, but the thought was bittersweet.

The children opted for board games instead of a movie. Elizabeth didn't mind. Luke brought out the same folding table she had wrapped presents on the night before and set it in front of the fireplace. While the Christmas tree sparkled behind them and the fire blazed in the hearth, they played the children's favorite strategy game.

In the end, she and Cassie emerged victorious.

"I guess we are the undisputed…champions this year," she said to Cassie after the scores were totaled.

"We'll beat you next year," Bridger said. His words made her heart ache. How could they ever recapture this magical season?

"Look at the time," Luke said suddenly. "You guys need to get to bed or you-know-who won't be able to come."

Cassie rolled her eyes but played along for her brother's sake.

"We need a story first," Bridger said.

Luke glanced at Elizabeth. "How about we read down here tonight? Then you can say good-night to your mother and I'll tuck you in."

"Can we each pick a story tonight?"

"Of course," he answered.

"Then you can each read us one," Bridger said.

Cassie picked *The Night Before Christmas* and gave it to Elizabeth to read. Bridger insisted he wanted to hear the Christmas story from the Bible, so Luke read the familiar story about shepherds and mangers and angels saying *fear not*.

"Okay. That's it. Now you really do need to get to bed," Luke said.

"Can Finn sleep with me?" Bridger asked. "I don't want him to scare away Santa if he's down here."

That was highly unlikely since Finn had probably never scared anything in his life but Luke agreed. "Tonight only," he said.

To Elizabeth's joy, both children gave her hugs, though Cassie's was a little awkward. Then they finally climbed the stairs with one last "Merry Christmas" and she and Luke were alone.

Chapter Twenty-Two

Luke didn't want to be alone with his wife, not with this wild riot of emotions in his chest.

He couldn't seem to control them. Every time he thought he had a handle on how he was feeling, another wave of sadness would crash over him.

She didn't want to be with him. That was a tough pill to swallow, especially because these last few days had felt magical to him. He had loved spending time with her and could have sworn she felt the same. There were times he would look over at her and she would be watching him and the children with an expression of sheer joy on her face.

He wasn't a guy who handled excess emotion well. He had learned early to hide what he was feeling so he didn't give his father one more weapon against him.

Right now, that was proving more difficult than he'd ever expected.

"I need to give the kids an hour or so to fall asleep before

I can bring out the presents and fill their stockings. You don't have to stay up. You can go to bed, if you want."

"Do you want me to go to bed?"

No. He wanted her to change her mind and decide she wanted to move back to Haven Point to give them a chance.

"Your decision," he answered.

"I would...like to stay, if you don't mind."

"Okay. Can I get you anything? Eggnog? Something stronger?"

"I was thinking of...cocoa. Would you like some?"

"Sure," he answered. As long as he could add a healthy shot of Baileys to it.

In the kitchen, she went to work making the hot cocoa the old-fashioned way, heating milk on the stove and adding sugar and cocoa. Soon the kitchen was filled with the delicious aroma. She ladled some into a Christmas mug, topped it with a dollop of whipped cream and slid it to him. After the first sip, Luke decided it was delicious enough he could forgo the Baileys for now.

As if by tacit agreement, they made their way back to the great room, to the fire in the hearth and the tall, gleaming Christmas tree he and the children had decorated.

She sat on the sofa where she had the perfect view of both, as well as the snow softly falling outside the window. He knew it probably wasn't wise, but he wanted the same view, so he sat beside her on the sofa.

He almost reconsidered the Baileys when he felt the heat of her scrutiny on him, her gaze intense and her features unreadable. "I need to ask you something."

He sipped at his cocoa, suddenly wary. "Go ahead."

She glanced at the tree, then back at him. "You knew that was the Sparkses' house tonight, didn't you? We drove past it on purpose. It wasn't on a main road. You wanted the kids to choose Billy's house for their grand prize."

Heat inched over his cheeks and he knew he couldn't blame either the fire or the cocoa.

"Yeah. I knew," he admitted. "I thought it wouldn't hurt the kids to see that everything is not always black-and-white."

"He has been such a...a *jerk* to you. And by the sound of it, his kids weren't any better to Bridger and Cassie."

He wouldn't have used the word *jerk*. A few more colorful words came to mind, but yeah. Sparks had definitely made things tougher for him here in town, spreading rumors and keeping Elizabeth's disappearance on everyone's mind. And his kids had carried on doing the same thing to Cassie and Bridger.

"Billy and his kids didn't deserve a box of fine chocolates, after the way they have treated you all," she said vehemently. "They deserved a box of...of rotten eggs."

Her passionate defense of their family made him smile, which quickly turned to an ache. Why wouldn't she stay?

"I figured there has to be something good in that family. It's tough to see on the outside but it must be there."

"What makes you think that?"

"They went to all that trouble to decorate for Christmas. That has to mean something, right? When you decorate the inside of your house, that's a personal thing for you and your family. When you climb to the top of a ramshackle barn and hang a star forty feet up in the air, that's to bring a little light and joy and holiday spirit to others."

"I...suppose that's true."

"I wanted to teach the kids to dig a little deeper. To find the good. If they can do that, they might be able to get along a little better at school with Rosie and Jedediah."

She set down her cocoa mug on the coffee table and gazed at him, eyes shining. "You're a wonderful man, Luke Hamilton."

Oh, how he wanted to be the kind of man who could inspire that sort of admiration in a woman's eyes. He had worked his entire adult life for it. Only now did he realize it had all been for this particular woman, Elizabeth Sinclair Hamilton, whether she had been here to see it or not.

As their gazes locked, he thought he saw something in her eyes beyond the admiration he knew he didn't deserve. Something...raw and wild and unrestrained.

The emotions there left him breathless. Suddenly he could feel each beat of his heart, each pulse of blood.

The two of them were alone here in this warm, sweet-smelling room, and Luke didn't want to be anywhere else.

"All right. I answered your question," he said, his voice low. "Now I would like to ask you one in return. I want the truth, straight up. I think I deserve that. Don't you?"

"I'll...I'll try," she whispered, her features suddenly nervous.

"When I asked if you wanted to move back to Haven Point and try again, what's the real reason you said no to me?"

She stared at him, eyes wide.

"You gave me all these excuses about your friends and your job and your life there. Now that I've had time to think about it, I don't buy any of it."

She hitched in a little breath and swallowed hard. "You... don't?"

"You might have all those things in Oregon. I hope so. But here in Haven Point, you have two children who want the chance to love you. Two children who need you in their life every single day, not only once or twice a year.'"

"I love them. Please don't doubt that."

How could he? Everything she did seven years ago had been to protect them, whether or not she was ready to accept and understand that yet.

"You have our kids. You have friends here who want to help you."

He paused, drawing in a deep breath before plowing forward. "And you also have a husband who loved you once with all his heart and...who still does."

At his words, she jerked involuntarily, almost spilling her cocoa.

The silence stretched out, uncomfortably long, before she finally spoke.

"How can you...love me after I *left* you?"

Her voice quavered but it wasn't like her usual slow, measured speech. This sounded completely stunned.

Taking a chance, he reached out and gripped her hands. They were cool, slender, fragile. Trembling.

"You want to know how? I'll tell you. I love you because you're kind and compassionate. Because your courage has no limit. Because with you I can *feel* again, after seven long years in what felt like an endless emotional winter. I love you, Elizabeth. I never stopped loving you. I want to give us a chance again and I'd like to know why you don't."

Her eyes were huge in her face, the edge of the irises dark. Her fingers trembled against his.

"Tell me the truth," he pressed. "I think you want to stay. So why are you insisting you have to go?"

His words seemed to reach right into her chest and yank out her heart.

She had to tell him. She couldn't continue lying to Luke, pretending she didn't love him.

She wanted the amazing gift he was offering. Oh, how she wanted it. With everything inside her, she ached to be here with him in this beautiful house he had built beside the lake. She wanted to plant a garden here in the spring, to nurture it over the summer, to spend every possible moment with the family she loved so dearly.

Tears began to burn behind her eyes and she could feel the heat of one breaking free to trickle down the face that was no longer her own.

"Look at me," she said softly. "What kind of wife can I be to you now?"

He frowned. "A wonderful one, judging by the past few days."

"I can't drive anymore. I can't…speak without these stupid pauses while I gather my thoughts. I can't walk much…better. I have seizures. You haven't really seen one but they're…horrible. I have seizures and I have scars. I'm a…I'm a mess."

With each word, his features seemed to tighten more, until he appeared carved out of granite. His hands were rigid around hers.

"Do you think I care about *any* of those things? Do you really believe I'm the kind of man who would love you less because you have scars, because you have physical limitations from an accident that wasn't your fault? We took vows, Elizabeth. In sickness, in health. I meant every word of them."

She slid her hands away. "All I have given you in this marriage is the sickness part! From the time I was…pregnant with Cassie, you have had to bear the burden of caring for me. This is the rest of my…my life. There is no cure for brain injury, Luke. This is…what you get."

She had to make him understand. She had to help him see

the road they would face would be entirely too difficult. She couldn't ask him to travel it.

"Yes, you face physical challenges now," he growled. "They're hard and unfair and make my heart hurt for you. But do you know what I see when I look at you?"

She could imagine. He probably saw what she did when she looked in the mirror. She saw a stranger who had lost everything she loved because of one fateful night.

He took her hands again and she couldn't pull them away. Not when his fingers were so very warm and when she seemed to draw strength from that contact of skin against skin.

"I see a loving mother who made a choice to protect her children seven years ago and who has paid a terrible price for that choice. I think you have more courage and strength than any woman I've ever known. I think you're so full of love, you can't hold it all in. You're all I want. All I will ever want. It's been that way since the day we met."

Her face felt hot again and she realized more tears were trickling down. He reached a thumb out and brushed one away, and the sheer sweetness of the gesture made her weep more.

He framed her face with his hands, his thumb pressing against each tear. "You're beautiful to me, no matter what you look like. I love you. I spent seven years afraid you were dead. The fact that you're here right now with me is a straight-up miracle. And that's coming from a man who had long since given up believing in them. I want you in my life, no matter what challenges you face. I *need* you in my life and so do our kids."

She had to try one last time to convince him. Though it was the hardest thing she had done in a long time, she jerked away from him and with effort lifted her leg onto the coffee table, then pulled up her pajamas above her knee so he could see the network of scars there, the red, angry skin, the mangled tissue.

"Like…this?"

To her dismay, he reached a hand out and traced the scars, his features raw with emotion. She felt each stroke of his fingers straight through to her core.

"When you met me," he said softly, "I was scarred on the inside. You knew that and you married me anyway. With that courageous heart of yours, you took on my damaged spirit, the boy inside me who was broken and bruised, and you healed me. I wish you could trust me now to do the same in return."

She heard a small, soft sob and realized it was coming from her own tight throat.

How could she possibly withstand his words? How could any woman? How could she continue pushing him away when everything inside her cried out to embrace this chance he was offering her?

He called her courageous but she wasn't. Far from it. Fear was consuming her like that blaze in the fireplace ate through logs. She had put him and her children through so much pain, she couldn't bear it. She didn't deserve another chance.

But she wanted it. Oh, how she wanted it.

She gazed at him there in the glow from the fire and the sparkling Christmas tree.

He was the miracle, this man who saw all her flaws and all her mistakes and all her challenges and somehow loved her anyway.

She let out another sob. Then, drawing every ounce of courage that had carried her through the past seven years, she reached out as he had done and framed his face in her hands.

He watched her intently, his eyes filled with emotion, and she tried to show him everything inside her heart. "I love you, Luke. I never stopped either. You and the children were...all that kept me going when life seemed so dark and lonely. I don't...deserve you. I know that. But I want you. I want this. With all my heart, I want to stay if you...if that is still what you want."

In answer, he turned his head slightly, just enough that he could press his mouth to one trembling hand and then the other before he slid his arms around her, pulled her close and kissed her with fierce, breathtaking tenderness.

A long time later, he lifted his head. They were stretched out on the sofa now and she was wrapped in his arms, exactly where she wanted to be.

"I have something for you," he said.

"A gift? I can wait...until tomorrow."

"I want to give you this now, before the kids wake up. While it's just the two of us."

She could imagine other things she would like him to give her while they were alone, things she had missed desperately for seven years, but she decided those things could wait. A little while, anyway. Maybe until after they filled the children's stockings.

"All right."

She sat up, readjusting her candy cane pajamas.

He knelt by the Christmas tree and sorted through the gifts there until he found one about the size of a coffee table book, wrapped in red paper with a silver bow.

"Here you go," he said with an odd, intense look on his face.

Curious and a little apprehensive, she tore apart the wrapping slowly, not sure she really wanted to see what was inside.

It was papers, she realized. Legal documents.

"Our...divorce papers."

"I've been trying to figure out the best time to give them to you. Earlier, I thought this was what you wanted. Now I'm giving them to you so you know that whatever you decide is completely your choice. You know how I feel. I want you back. And not in the little house on Riverbend Road either. I want you here, in our lives, in my arms."

That was all she wanted, too. She looked down at the papers, knowing they represented the choice between giving in to her fear and finding the strength and courage to take this chance with him.

It wasn't any choice. Not now. She rose, and with her gaze locked with the man she loved, she headed to the fire and threw them in, page after page.

When she was done and the divorce papers had all burned away to nothing, like the last of her fears, she returned to the man she loved and kissed him with all the love in her heart.

Epilogue

One year later

"Bridger. Turn off the video games. It's time to set the table."

"But I almost beat the monster on this level!"

"It's Christmas Eve," Luke answered firmly. "Give the poor monster a break and go set the table. It's your turn. You can always conquer him tomorrow, after we open presents. Or maybe you can talk Uncle Elliot into playing with you after dinner. He's pretty good with weaponry, I understand."

With a grumble and sigh, his son saved his progress and turned off the television and the gaming system and followed Luke back to the great room, where delicious smells emanated through the house.

In the kitchen, he could hear Elizabeth humming a Christmas carol as she worked, and the sound arrowed straight to his heart. After a year of having her back in their lives, every day still seemed like a priceless gift.

"Can we open a present tonight? My friend Ty says he gets to open one thing on Christmas Eve."

"You'll have to talk to your mom about that," Luke started to say but was interrupted by the doorbell.

"Hey! Maybe that's Aunt Megan and Uncle Elliot." Before Luke could move, Bridger raced to the front door and pulled it open.

To Luke's shock, it wasn't his sister and her husband. It was someone completely unexpected—Billy Sparks, along with his wife and kids.

His former nemesis stood on the porch, a red-and-green plaid tin in his hands. "Hey," he said, looking uncomfortable.

"Hey, Billy. Arlene. Kids. Come in."

Bridger immediately headed straight to Jedediah and launched into a play-by-play description of the video game he'd been playing and the skills he'd used to almost conquer the monster.

Luke wasn't sure how it had happened, but somehow over the past year, Jedediah and Bridger had become best friends and often hung out together after school, their onetime fist-fight completely forgotten.

Luke couldn't say he would ever be best friends with Billy, but the two families had come to tolerate each other over the past year.

"Uh, merry Christmas. Arlene fixed some gingerbread and it's real good. She, uh…we wanted you to have some."

Luke blinked at the unexpected holiday offering. "That's very kind of you. Thank you."

"We loved the candle and the cookies your wife brought over the other day. Billy ate half of them by himself," Arlene said, which was probably the longest consecutive string of words he'd ever heard from the quiet, rather meek woman.

"Good to hear."

"I'll be glad when Christmas is over and I can stop being tempted by all these goodies, am I right?" Billy said with a forced-sounding laugh.

Luke smiled and nodded, though he didn't necessarily agree. He had loved everything about the season this year, from the treats to the music to the holiday parties. Everything seemed more rich and nuanced when he had Elizabeth by his side.

"Thank you for this. I'm sure they're delicious. Would you like to come in?"

"No. We better run. We've got more deliveries to make. Plus, we're giving out our own award for best holiday decorations. My kids were so tickled last year when you gave us the award, we decided to pass it on and do the same thing for someone else."

"That's great. Thanks for the gingerbread and merry Christmas."

"Give our best to your wife."

"I'll do that."

Bridger and Jedediah were reluctant to be separated, too busy talking about when they could get together over the holidays, until eventually Billy grabbed his son's hand and ushered him out the door.

After closing the door behind the Sparks family, Bridger hurried ahead of him to grab plates and silverware while Luke added the tin of gingerbread to the little collection of neighbor gifts on the counter by the family computer.

Elizabeth, turkey baster in hand, looked up from the oven, where she was doing something to the roasting pan containing a golden-skinned turkey that made his mouth water.

"Sorry I couldn't come to the…door. I have my hands full at the moment. Who was…that?"

"Billy and Arlene Sparks and their kids. They brought us some homemade gingerbread."

"Oh, how nice." She apparently didn't find anything unusual in that turn of events, which was completely typical. Elizabeth saw the good in everyone, even Billy Sparks.

He was so happy to have her here after so many Christmases alone that his heart seemed to overflow with happiness. Unable to resist, he wrapped his arms around her and kissed the soft, warm skin at her neck.

She leaned back against him for a moment with a little shiver, then gave a flustered laugh. "Your turkey still needs to be basted."

"That's one way to phrase it, I guess." He couldn't resist, mostly because he knew it would make her laugh.

She rolled her eyes, cheeks rosy. "You're terrible, Luke Hamilton."

"That's not what you said this morning," he murmured.

She rolled her eyes again and slid the roasting pan back into the oven. Once she had closed the door, she wrapped her arms around his waist and lifted her mouth to his. Even after a year, he couldn't get enough of her.

"Ew. Must we?"

Luke lifted his gaze from the very enjoyable pastime of kissing his wife in time to see Cassie, nearly eleven and full of attitude, walk into the kitchen with a look of disgust.

"Yes. We absolutely must," he answered, giving Elizabeth another loud smack on the mouth that made her smile and made Cassie groan.

"Can you put your phone away for a few minutes, honey?"

Elizabeth said. "I could use your...help with the salad. Our guests will...be here in an hour."

Cassie sighed but shoved her phone in her back pocket. "What do you need?" she asked.

Over the past year, his wife and their daughter had reached a peace of sorts. Their relationship wasn't quite the easy, uncomplicated one that Elizabeth had with Bridger, and Luke wasn't sure it ever would be, but Cassie was gradually learning to trust that her mother wasn't going to disappear from their lives again.

Now, a year later, they were like many other families. They had squabbles; they made up; they laughed and worked and loved each other.

"What can I do?" Luke asked.

"You're on the...support crew tonight. You can either help Cassie with the...salad or give Bridger a hand setting the table."

He would rather stand in this warm kitchen and kiss his wife again but figured that wasn't one of his options.

"I don't need help with the table," Bridger said. "I'm almost done. Then can I go back and beat the monster?"

"Sure," he said. "Because nothing says holiday spirit like smashing a monster to bits."

Bridger giggled and hurried through his chore while Luke went to work with his daughter chopping green onions for the pasta salad.

While they worked, Elizabeth and Cassie sang along to the Christmas music playing through the whole-house speakers he had installed when he built the place, and Luke couldn't help thinking about how all their lives had changed over the past year.

Not everything had been perfect. Elizabeth had needed

surgery on her leg in the springtime that had led to a painful and difficult recovery and left her forced to mostly supervise the landscaping of the house, which had broken her heart. Just as she was getting back to herself, she'd suffered a bad seizure in August that had terrified all of them.

Despite the challenges, he wouldn't trade any of it. Having her here, sharing the experience of raising their children and building a life together in this house beside the lake, still seemed like the very best miracle.

"What are you smiling about?" Cassie asked him.

"I'm happy. That's all. It's Christmas, I'm with my favorite people in my world, and we're about to enjoy a great meal with family we love. What's not to smile about?"

"You're so goofy," his daughter said, though he was pretty sure she was working hard to hide her own smile.

He glanced over at Elizabeth, his wife, his miracle. She was smiling, too, her eyes soft as she watched them, and Luke was quite certain his heart couldn't contain any more joy.

★ ★ ★ ★ ★

Chapter One

"This is totally lame. Why do we have to stay here and wait for you? We can walk home in, like, ten minutes."

Daniela Capelli drew in a deep breath and prayed for patience, something she seemed to be doing with increasing frequency these days when it came to her thirteen-year-old daughter. "It's starting to snow and already almost dark."

Silver rolled her eyes, something *she* did with increasing frequency these days. "So what? A little snow won't kill us. I would hardly even call that snow. We had way bigger storms than this back in Boston. Remember that big blizzard a few years ago, when school was closed for, like, a week?"

"I remember," her younger daughter, Mia, said, looking up from her coloring book at Dani's desk at the Haven Point Veterinary Clinic. "I stayed home from preschool and I watched Anna and Elsa a thousand times, until you said your eardrums would explode if I played it one more time."

Dani could hear a bark from the front office that likely

signaled the arrival of her next client and knew she didn't have time to stand here arguing with an obstinate teenager.

"Mia can't walk as fast as you can. You'll end up frustrated with her and you'll both be freezing before you make it home," she pointed out.

"So she can stay here and wait for you while I walk home. I just told Chelsea we could FaceTime about the new dress she bought for the Christmas dance there and she can only do it for another hour before her dad comes to pick her up for his visitation."

"Why can't you FaceTime here? I only have two more patients to see. I'll be done in less than an hour. Then we can all go home together. You can hang out in the waiting room with Mia, where the Wi-Fi signal is better."

Silver gave a huge put-upon sigh but picked up her backpack and stalked out of Dani's office toward the waiting room.

"Can I turn on the TV out there?" Mia asked as she gathered her papers and crayons. "I like the dog shows."

The veterinary clinic showed calming clips of animals on a big flat-screen TV set low to the ground for their clientele.

"After Silver's done with her phone call, okay?"

"She'll take *forever*," Mia predicted with a gloomy look. "She always does when she's talking to Chelsea."

Dani fought to hide a smile. "Thanks for your patience, sweetie, with her and with me. Finish your math worksheet while you're here. Then when we get home, you can watch what you want."

Both the Haven Point elementary and middle schools were within walking distance of the clinic, and it had become a habit for Silver to walk to the elementary school and then walk with Mia here to the clinic to spend a few hours until they could all go home together.

Of late, Silver had started to complain that she didn't want to pick her sister up at the elementary school every day, that she would rather they both just took their respective school buses home, where Silver could watch her sister without having to hang out at the boring veterinary clinic.

But then, Silver complained about nearly everything these days.

It was probably a good idea, but Dani wasn't quite ready to pull the trigger on having the girls alone every day after school. Maybe they would try it out after Christmas vacation.

This working professional/single mother gig was *hard*, she thought as she ushered Mia to the waiting room. Then again, in most ways it was much easier than the veterinary student/single mother gig had been.

When they entered the comfortable waiting room—with its bright colors, pet-friendly benches and big fish tank—Mia faltered for a moment, then sidestepped behind Dani's back.

She saw instantly what had caused her daughter's nervous reaction. Funny. Dani felt the same way. She wanted to hide behind somebody, too.

The receptionist had given her the files with the dogs' names that were coming in for a checkup but hadn't mentioned their human was Ruben Morales. Her gorgeous next-door neighbor.

Dani's palms instantly itched and her stomach felt as if she'd accidentally swallowed a flock of butterflies.

"Deputy Morales," she said, then paused, hating the slightly breathless note in her voice.

What *was* it about the man that always made her so freaking nervous?

He was big, yes, at least six feet tall, with wide shoulders, tough muscles and a firm, don't-mess-with-me jawline.

It wasn't just that. Even without his uniform, the man exuded authority and power, which instantly raised her hackles and left her uneasy, something she found both frustrating and annoying about herself.

No matter how far she had come, how hard she had worked to make a life for her and her girls, she still sometimes felt like the troublesome foster kid from Queens, always on the defensive.

She had done her best to avoid him in the months they had been in Haven Point, but that was next to impossible when they lived so close to each other—and when she was the intern in his father's veterinary practice, with the hope that she might be able to purchase it at the end of the year.

"Hey, Doc," he said, flashing her an easy smile she didn't trust for a moment. It never quite reached his dark, long-lashed eyes, at least where she was concerned.

While she might be uncomfortable around Ruben Morales, his dogs were another story.

He held the leashes of both of them, a big, muscular Belgian shepherd and an incongruously paired little Chi-poo, and she reached down to pet both of them. They sniffed her and wagged happily, the big dog's tail nearly knocking over his small friend.

That was the thing she loved most about dogs. They were uncomplicated and generous with their affection, for the most part. They never looked at people with that subtle hint of suspicion, as if trying to uncover all their secrets.

"I wasn't expecting you," she admitted.

"Oh? I made an appointment. The boys both need checkups. Yukon needs his regular hip and eye check and Ollie is due for his shots."

She gave the dogs one more pat before she straightened

and faced him, hoping his sharp cop eyes couldn't notice evidence of her accelerated pulse.

"Your father is still here every Monday and Friday afternoons. Maybe you should reschedule with him," she suggested. It was a faint hope, but a girl had to try.

"Why would I do that?"

"Maybe because he's your father and knows your dogs?"

"Dad is an excellent veterinarian. Agreed. But he's also semiretired and wants to be fully retired this time next year. As long as you plan to stick around in Haven Point, we will have to switch vets and start seeing you eventually. I figured we might as well start now."

He was checking her out. Not *her* her, but her skills as a veterinarian.

The implication was clear. She had been here three months, and it had become obvious during that time in their few interactions that Ruben Morales was extremely protective of his family. He had been polite enough when they had met previously, but always with a certain guardedness, as if he was afraid she planned to take the good name his hardworking father had built up over the years for the Haven Point Veterinary Clinic and drag it through the sludge at the bottom of Lake Haven.

Dani pushed away her instinctive prickly defensiveness, bred out of all those years in foster care when she felt as if she had no one else to count on—compounded by the difficult years after she married Tommy and had Silver, when she *really* had no one else in her corner.

She couldn't afford to offend Ruben. She didn't need his protective wariness to turn into full-on suspicion. With a little digging, Ruben could uncover things about her and her past that would ruin everything for her and her girls here.

She forced a professional smile. "It doesn't matter. Let's go back to a room and take a look at these guys. Girls, I'll be done shortly. Silver, keep an eye on your sister."

Her oldest nodded without looking up from her phone, and with an inward sigh, Dani led the way to the largest of the exam rooms.

She stood at the door as he entered the room with the two dogs, then joined him inside and closed it behind her.

The large room seemed to shrink unnaturally and she paused inside for a moment, flustered and wishing she could escape. Dani gave herself a mental shake. She was a doctor of veterinary medicine, not a teenage girl. She could handle being in the same room with the one man in Haven Point who left her breathless and unsteady.

All she had to do was focus on the reason he was here in the first place. His dogs.

She knelt to their level. "Hey there, guys. Who wants to go first?"

The Malinois—often confused for a German shepherd but smaller and with a shorter coat—wagged his tail again while his smaller counterpoint sniffed around her shoes, probably picking up the scents of all the other dogs she had seen that day.

"Ollie, I guess you're the winner today."

He yipped, his big ears that stuck straight out from his face quivering with excitement.

He was the funniest-looking dog, quirky and unique, with wisps of fur in odd places, spindly legs and a narrow Chihuahua face. She found him unbearably cute. With that face, she wouldn't ever be able to say no to him if he were hers.

"Can I give him a treat?" She always tried to ask permission first from her clients' humans.

"Only if you want him to be your best friend for life," Ruben said.

Despite her nerves, his deadpan voice sparked a smile, which widened when she gave the little dog one of the treats she always carried in the pocket of her lab coat and he slurped it up in one bite, then sat with a resigned sort of patience during the examination.

She was aware of Ruben watching her as she carefully examined the dog, but Dani did her best not to let his scrutiny fluster her.

She knew what she was doing, she reminded herself. She had worked so hard to be here, sacrificing all her time, energy and resources of the last decade to nothing else but her girls and her studies.

"Everything looks good," she said after checking out the dog and finding nothing unusual. "He seems like a healthy little guy. It says here he's about six or seven. So you haven't had him from birth?"

"No. Only about two years. He was a stray I picked up off the side of the road between here and Shelter Springs when I was on patrol one day. He was in a bad way, half-starved, fur matted. I think he'd been on his own for a while. As small as he is, it's a wonder he wasn't picked off by a coyote or even one of the bigger hawks. He just needed a little TLC."

"You couldn't find his owner?"

"We ran ads and Dad checked with all his contacts at shelters and veterinary clinics from here to Boise, with no luck. I had been fostering him while we looked, and to be honest, I kind of lost my heart to the little guy, and by then Yukon adored him, so we decided to keep him."

She was such a sucker for animal lovers, especially those who rescued the vulnerable and lost ones.

And, no. She didn't need counseling to point out the parallels to her own life.

Regardless, she couldn't let herself be drawn to Ruben and risk doing something foolish. She had too much to lose here in Haven Point.

"What about Yukon here?" She knelt down to examine the bigger dog. Though he wasn't huge and Ruben could probably lift him easily to the table, she decided it was easier to kneel to his level. In her experience, sometimes bigger dogs didn't like to be lifted, and she wasn't sure if the beautiful Malinois fell into that category.

Ruben shrugged as he scooped Ollie onto his lap to keep the little Chi-poo from swooping in and stealing the treat she held out for the bigger dog. "You could say he was a rescue, too."

"Oh?"

"He was a K-9 officer down in Mountain Home. After his handler was killed in the line of duty, I guess he kind of went into a canine version of depression and wouldn't work with anyone else. I know that probably sounds crazy."

She scratched the dog's ears, touched by the bond that could build between handler and dog. "Not at all," she said briskly. "I've seen many dogs go into decline when their owner dies. It's not uncommon."

"For a year or so, they tried to match him up with other officers, but things never quite gelled, for one reason or another. Then his eyes started going. His previous handler who died was a good buddy of mine from the academy and I couldn't let him go just anywhere."

"Retired police dogs don't always do well in civilian life. They can be aggressive with other dogs and sometimes people. Have you had any problems with that?"

"Not with Yukon. He's friendly. Aren't you, buddy? You're a good boy."

Dani could swear the dog grinned at his owner, his tongue lolling out.

Yukon was patient while she looked him over, especially as she maintained a steady supply of treats.

When she finished, she gave the dog a pat and stood. "Can I take a look at Ollie's ears one more time?"

"Sure. Help yourself."

He held the dog out and she reached for Ollie. As she did, the dog wriggled a little and Dani's hands ended up brushing Ruben's chest. She froze at the accidental contact, a shiver rippling down her spine. She pinned her reaction on the undeniable fact that it had been entirely too long since she had touched a man, even accidentally.

She had to cut out this *fascination* or whatever it was immediately. Clean-cut, muscular cops were *not* her type, and the sooner she remembered that the better.

She focused on checking the ears of the little dog, gave him one more scratch and handed him back to Ruben. "That should do it. A clean bill of health. They seem to be two happy, well-adjusted dogs. You obviously take good care of them."

He patted both dogs with an affectionate smile that did nothing to ease her nerves.

"My dad taught me well. I spent most of my youth helping out here at the clinic—cleaning cages, brushing coats, walking the occasional overnight boarder. Whatever grunt work he needed. He made all of us help."

"I can think of worse ways to earn a dime," she said.

The chance to work with animals would have been a dream opportunity for her, back when she had few bright spots in her world. Besides that, she considered his father was one of the sweetest people she had ever met.

"So can I. I always loved animals."

She had to wonder why he didn't follow in his father's footsteps and become a vet. None of his three siblings had made that choice, either. If any of them had, she probably wouldn't be here right now, as Frank Morales probably would have handed down his thriving practice to his own progeny.

Not that it was any of her business. Ruben certainly could follow any career path he wanted—as long as that path took him far away from her.

"Give me a moment to grab those medications and I'll be right back."

"No rush."

Out in the hall, she closed the door behind her and drew in a deep breath.

Get a grip, she chided herself. *He's just a hot-looking dude. Heaven knows, you've had more than enough experience with those to last a lifetime.*

She went to the well-stocked medication dispensary, found what she needed and returned to the exam room.

Outside the door, she paused for only a moment to gather her composure before pushing it open. "Here are the pills for Ollie's nerves and a refill for Yukon's eye drops," she said briskly. "Let me know if you have any questions—though if you do, you can certainly ask your father."

"Thanks." As he took them from her, his hands brushed hers again and sent a little spark of awareness shivering through her.

Oh, come on. This was ridiculous.

She was probably imagining the way his gaze sharpened, as if he had felt something odd, too.

"I can show you out. We're shorthanded today since the veterinary tech and the receptionist both needed to leave early."

"No problem. That's what I get for scheduling the last appointment of the day—though, again, I spent most of my youth here. I think we can find our way."

"It's fine. I'll show you out." She stood outside the door while he gathered the dogs' leashes, then led the way toward the front office.

After three months, Ruben still couldn't get a bead on Dr. Daniela Capelli.

His next-door neighbor still seemed a complete enigma to him. By all reports from his father, she was a dedicated, earnest new veterinarian with a knack for solving difficult medical mysteries and a willingness to work hard. She seemed like a warm and loving mother, at least from the few times he had seen her interactions with her two girls, the uniquely named teenager Silver—who had, paradoxically, purple hair—and the sweet-as-Christmas-toffee Mia, who was probably about six.

He also couldn't deny she was beautiful, with slender features, striking green eyes, dark, glossy hair and a dusky skin tone that proclaimed her Italian heritage—as if her name didn't do the trick first.

He actually liked the trace of New York accent that slipped into her speech at times. It fit her somehow, in a way he couldn't explain. Despite that, he couldn't deny that the few times he had interacted with more than a wave in passing, she was brusque, prickly and sometimes downright distant.

He had certainly had easier neighbors.

His father adored her and wouldn't listen to a negative thing about her.

She hasn't had an easy time of things but she's a fighter. Hardworking and eager to learn, Frank had said the other night when Ruben asked how things were working out, now that Dani and her girls had been in town a few months. *You just have to get to know her.*

Frank apparently didn't see how diligently Dani Capelli worked to keep anyone else from doing just that.

She wasn't unfriendly, only distant. She kept herself to herself. It was a phrase his mother might use, though Myra Morales seemed instantly fond of Dani and her girls.

Did Dani have any idea how fascinated the people of Haven Point were with these new arrivals in their midst?

Or maybe that was just him.

As he followed her down the hall in her white lab coat, his dogs behaving themselves for once, Ruben told himself to forget about his stupid attraction to her.

Sure, he might be ready to settle down and would like to have someone in his life, but he wasn't at all sure if he had the time or energy for that someone to be a woman with so many secrets in her eyes, one who seemed to face the world with her chin up and her fists out, ready to take on any threats.

When they walked into the clinic waiting room, they found her two girls there. The older one was texting on her phone while her sister did somersaults around the room.

Dani stopped in the doorway and seemed to swallow an exasperated sound. "Mia, honey, you're going to have dog hair all over you."

"I'm a snowball rolling down the hill," the girl said. "Can't you see me getting bigger and bigger and bigger."

"You're such a dorkupine," her sister said, barely looking up from her phone.

"I'm a dorkupine snowball," Mia retorted.

"You're a snowball who is going to be covered in dog hair," Dani said. "Come on, honey. Get up."

He could tell the moment the little girl spotted him and his dogs coming into the area behind her mother. She went still and then slowly rose to her feet, features shifting from gleeful to nervous.

Why was she so afraid of him?

"You make a very good snowball," he said, pitching his voice low and calm as his father had taught him to do with all skittish creatures. "I haven't seen anybody somersault that well in a long time."

She moved to her mother's side and buried her face in Dani's white coat—though he didn't miss the way she reached down to pet Ollie on her way.

"Hey again, Silver."

He knew the older girl from the middle school, where he served as the resource officer a few hours a week. He made it a point to learn all the students' names and tried to talk to them individually when he had the chance, in hopes that if they had a problem at home or knew of something potentially troublesome for the school, they would feel comfortable coming to him.

He had the impression that Silver was like her mother in many ways. Reserved, wary, slow to trust. It made him wonder just who had hurt them.

"How are things?" he asked her now.

For just an instant, he thought he saw sadness flicker in her gaze before she turned back to her phone with a shrug. "Fine, I guess."

"Are you guys ready for Christmas? It's your first one here in Idaho. A little different from New York, isn't it?"

"How should we know? We haven't lived in the city for, like, four years."

Dani sent her daughter a look at her tone, which seemed to border on disrespect. "I've been in vet school in Boston the last four years," she explained.

"Boston. Then you're used to snow and cold. We're known for our beautiful winters around here. The lake is simply stunning in wintertime."

Mia tugged on her mother's coat, and when Dani bent down, she whispered something to her.

"You can ask him," Dani said calmly, gesturing to Ruben.

Mia shook her head and buried her face again, and after a moment, Dani sighed. "She wonders if it's possible to ice-skate on Lake Haven. We watched the most recent Olympics and she became a little obsessed."

"You could say that," Silver said. "She skated around the house in her stocking feet all day long for *weeks*. A dorkupine on ice."

"You can't skate on the lake, I'm afraid," Ruben answered. "Because of the underground hot springs that feed into it at various points, Lake Haven rarely freezes, except sometimes along the edges, when it's really cold. It's not really safe for ice-skating. But the city creates a skating rink on the tennis courts at Lake View Park every year. The volunteer fire department sprays it down for a few weeks once temperatures get really cold. I saw them out there the other night, so it shouldn't be long before it's open. Maybe a few more weeks."

Mia seemed to lose a little of her shyness at that prospect. She gave him a sideways look from under her mother's arm and aimed a fleeting smile full of such sweetness that he was instantly smitten.

"There's also a great place for sledding up behind the high school. You can't miss that, either. Oh, and in a few weeks we have the Lights on the Lake Festival. You've heard about that, right?"

They all gave him matching blank stares, making him wonder what was wrong with the Haven Point Helping Hands that they hadn't immediately dragged Dani into their circle. He would have to talk to Andie Bailey or his sister Angela about it. They always seemed to know what was going on in town.

"I think some kids at school were talking about that at lunch the other day," Silver said. "They were sitting at the next table, so I didn't hear the whole thing, though."

"Haven Point hosts an annual celebration a week or so before Christmas where all the local boat owners deck out their watercraft from here to Shelter Springs to welcome in the holidays and float between the two towns. There's music, food and crafts for sale. It's kind of a big deal around here. I'm surprised you haven't heard about it."

"I'm very busy, with the practice and the girls, Deputy Morales. I don't have a lot of time for socializing." Though Dani tried for a lofty look, he thought he caught a hint of vulnerability there.

She seemed…lonely. That didn't make a lick of sense. The women in this town could be almost annoying in their efforts to include newcomers in community events. They didn't give people much of an option, dragging them kicking and screaming into the social scene around town, like it or not.

"Well, now you know. You really can't miss the festival. It's great fun for the whole family."

"Thank you for the information. It's next week, you say?"

"That's right. Not this weekend but the one after. The whole thing starts out with the boat parade on Saturday evening, around six."

"We'll put it on our social calendar."

"What's a social calendar?" Mia whispered to her sister, just loud enough for Ruben to hear.

"It's a place where you keep track of all your invitations to parties and sleepovers and stuff."

"Oh. Why do we need one of those?"

"Good question."

Silver looked glum for just a moment but Dani hugged her, then faced Ruben with a polite, distant smile.

"Thank you for bringing in Ollie and Yukon. Have a good evening, Deputy Morales."

It was a clear dismissal, one he couldn't ignore. Ruben gathered his dogs' leashes and headed for the door. "Thank you. See you around. And by around, I mean next door. We kind of can't miss each other."

As he hoped, this made Mia smile a little. Even Silver's dour expression eased into what almost looked like a smile.

As he loaded the dogs into the king cab of his pickup truck, Ruben could see Dani turning off lights and straightening up the clinic.

What was her story? Why had she chosen to come straight from vet school in Boston to set up shop all the way across the country in a small Idaho town?

He loved his hometown, sure, and fully acknowledged it was a beautiful place to live. It still seemed a jarring cultural and geographic shift from living back east to this little town where the biggest news of the month was a rather corny light parade that people froze their asses off to watch.

And why did he get the impression the family wasn't socializing much? One of the reasons most people he knew moved to small towns was a yearning for the kind of connectedness and community a place like Haven Point had in spades. What was the point in moving to a small town if you were going to keep yourself separate from everybody?

He thought he had seen them at a few things when they first came to Haven Point, but since then, she seemed to be keeping her little family mostly to themselves. That must be by choice. It was the only explanation that made sense. He couldn't imagine McKenzie Kilpatrick or Andie Bailey or any of the other Helping Hands excluding her on purpose.

What was she so nervous about?

He added another facet to the enigma of his next-door neighbor. He had hoped that he might be able to get a better perspective of her by bringing the dogs in to her for their routine exams. While he had confirmed his father's belief that she appeared to be an excellent veterinarian, he now had more questions about the woman and her daughters to add to his growing list.

Don't miss Season of Wonder
by RaeAnne Thayne,
available wherever
HQN books and ebooks are sold!